# OFF THE RECORD

## ANTI-BELLE BOOK TWO

### SKYE MCDONALD

Anti-Belle Books

*For you.*

# 1

## NICK

"Oh, Nick, you're *amazing.*"

Those words made me grin every time I heard them. "Thanks. I'm glad it's what you wanted."

"What I wanted? I never imagined it would be that good." The girl fixed wide, excited eyes on me. She wet her lips and held out her hand.

I set the square plastic case on her palm and gestured to the monitor by my sound board. "It's a strong demo. I hope it gets picked up."

She gazed at the CD with her name printed on it. "It means a lot that you'd say that. I'm hoping one of the local labels will give me a shot." She glanced up. "Could I—well, I mean, maybe I could buy you a drink to say thanks for all your work?"

The regretful smile I flashed was meant to tell her my answer before I spoke. "I'd love to, but I better not. Got another project starting tomorrow I need to focus on."

"Oh, no, of course." Her cheeks flushed as her words fumbled. "Uh, maybe you could call me if you're ever free?"

I straightened my glasses and looked her over. "Yeah, maybe so. Good luck."

She shook my hand and hurried out of the studio. Alone, I dropped into my chair and leaned back. Already her songs were fading in my mind, blurring into the long litany of indie albums from aspiring Nashville ingénues I'd engineered a demo for recently. What started as my niche here at InSight Studios had somehow become my entire clientele. It was safe to say I'd fallen into a rut.

My mouth twisted in a wry smile. *Yeah, but all that's about to change in a few minutes. For better or for worse.*

"Field!"

"Yeah, boss?" I didn't need to look up to know who was shouting.

Rick Alvin appeared in the control room. "Showtime. Follow me." He jerked his thumb behind him toward the commotion echoing down the hall.

The lobby was so packed we had to squeeze through a wall of shoulders to join the fray. Every employee of InSight Studio ringed the room's perimeter. I took my place and looked around at my colleagues. Their faces wore various states of awe at the dozen-plus reporters popping flashes and shouting questions to the men in the center of it all.

Well, to one of the men. The guy in the suit was irrelevant; the guy in the black harem sweatpants, long white tunic, and aviator sunglasses was the man of the moment.

"Jesse, how does it feel to be home?"

"Incredible."

"Jesse! Jesse, what's your first single titled?"

"'Would You Mind.'" I mouthed that answer along with him.

"Jesse, when does the album drop?"

"When we get it done," was the laughed answer, but I

rolled my eyes. *Labor Day or bust.* It might not matter to him, but the "or bust" was my ass on the line.

"Jesse, is your girlfriend happy to be home, too?"

"Jesse, are the rumors true that you lied about your age to get on *American Pop*?"

"That's enough," the man in the suit—his manager—announced abruptly.

"My lady is thrilled. I've never lied a day in my life," Jesse Storms shouted with a cheeky grin before turning his back on the reporters to meet Rick.

Jesse's manager squared his shoulders and helped the press make a quick exit. Meanwhile, my colleagues tightened the circle around our boss and newest, flashiest, most famous client.

Six weeks ago, Jesse Storms won *American Pop*, the most popular of the reality/talent TV competitions. It took him three auditions to get a chance, but he'd won by the show's biggest margin of fan votes yet. His play on Southern charm and vocal talents across pop, hip-hop, and country music widened his appeal, and he was rocketing fast up the celebrity ladder. Everything about his image was brilliantly marketed to make the country fall in love with him. Even this return to Nashville to record his debut album was great spin.

Three weeks ago, I didn't know any of this shit. I was grinding along on a project when Rick brought me into his office and said we got the Jesse Storms contract.

I replied with, "Cool. Who?"

My boss called me a dumbass and told me to do my homework. Then he said, "Nick, you're the best damn engineer I've got. It's time to move you up. Storms's label wants authenticity to the Nashville feel, and Storms must have a hell of a lawyer, because he's somehow gotten more control over recording than a debut artist should have. You're the executive *producer* on this project, son. The label will have heavy input, but you're calling the shots." He pushed a check across the desk and smirked. "A bonus. The album should go platinum easily. You do this right, have it wrapped by the end of August and make sure it doesn't sound like total garbage, and you'll be second in command around here. First choice of projects and a *lot* of input. How's that sound?"

"Partial garbage, end of August, and I—holy—" My words broke off when I glanced at the check.

Rick grinned. "You've more than earned it." His one moment of affection hardened into his usual crusty demeanor fast. Clearing his throat, he motioned me out the door. "Don't screw up."

While my fellow employees shook Storms's hand, I reached in my pocket and fingered the key fob to the brand new Camaro 2SS I'd bought with the bonus money. The car was serious motivation to crush this album and give it all I had. What I couldn't predict was how difficult it would be to keep Storms focused on recording over his first summer of stardom.

"...Your audio engineer." At Rick's introduction, I snapped to attention and walked forward. "Jesse Storms, this is Nick Field. Nick's got everything covered."

"Mr. Storms." I nodded, but he grinned and thrust out his hand.

"Jesse," he insisted as we shook. The air of star power that pulsed around him evaporated into a genuine smile. "Great to meet you, Nick. Pete's got our calendar all laid out. Let's go talk." He gestured back to Peter Lawson, his manager, who saluted with his phone and took my contact info as Rick led us back down the hall.

Jesse explored Studio A, including its premier control room and deluxe lounge, while the four of us discussed the recording schedule. He prowled everywhere in constant motion, his attention on at least three things at all times. Despite that and all his self-interrupting questions and comments, the conversation was strangely coherent.

"So, we'll start on the single as soon as you're ready," I said at last. "Do you think we could shoot for next—"

"Tomorrow." Jesse finally stopped moving and looked around the lounge. "I like this place. We can, like, use it whenever, right?" Rick agreed immediately. "Awesome. Peter, let's make this the office. Tell the crew."

Before Peter finished nodding, Jesse's focus jumped back to scheduling.

"Great, so we'll be here by eleven—is eleven good, Nick? I can work late, but mornings aren't my best."

"Eleven is fine."

He grinned. "Perfect. I love it. I'll be here tomorrow."

"If you need more time to memorize the single—"

"I don't. We'll be here in the morning." He gave me a resolute nod and moved to the exit.

I looked at my boss. "He talks a good game. Let's see what happens when the summer gets going."

Rick clapped my shoulder. "You'll make it happen. Don't think about it any other way. That album is all that matters."

"Aye, Captain."

"Smartass," Rick grumbled. We traded a smile before he stalked back to his office, and I took off for the day.

The next morning, I had the soundboard ready, the mics checked, and the backup band busy rehearsing. My blood was up, but I refused to sweat or let the phrase "executive producer" rattle in my head. *It's just a job. You've crushed dozens of projects.*

This was true. Technically, Rick and his partner were the producers at InSight. But when newbie artists paid for studio time out of their own thin pockets, they usually defaulted to the engineer's expertise. I'd developed such an ear for the indie rock sound of the moment that advising those artists was totally natural. So, yes, I'd produced before, but nowhere near on a project this huge.

*Shut up.*

Right.

The interoffice phone shrilled. I glanced at the time: 11 sharp.

"A white Suburban just pulled up. I think Mr. Storms is here," our receptionist gasped into the phone.

"Cool. Show him back." I took a quick breath and headed into the lounge.

The door opposite me opened, and Jesse and Peter walked in. We exchanged greetings while a glamorous older woman and two scruffy dudes in jeans and t-shirts hovered in the doorway.

Jesse gestured behind him. "This is the crew. That's my stylist, Fern, and those are the guys who keep my shit together. That's Seth, and this is Eli, but everyone calls him Steve."

"Why Steve?" I asked as I gripped his hand. Besides the fact that his hair was brown to Seth's blond, these guys were a single entity in my mind. No artist I had worked with before had ever had an entourage. Fern as a stylist made sense, but I had to wonder how those two might keep anyone's shit together. *And what are they going to do all day while we work?*

Steve chuckled. "Well—"

But Jesse looked around and cut him off. "Where's Melody?"

Melody. The name tickled the hair on my neck and made me forget every single name I'd just committed to memory.

Peter said, "I think she was talking to the receptionist." He jogged to the hallway calling, "Hey, Miss Twitter! You're wanted in the lounge."

I scratched my neck to make the tingling stop. "Did you say Melody?" *Shut up. There's no way it's her. Focus.*

"Yeah. She's a hell of a writer and the best damn girlfriend a guy like me could ask for." Jesse shrugged like we shared a joke.

The tingling started to close my throat. "Writer?"

But Peter reappeared, and the woman who followed him in confirmed every ounce of adrenaline coursing through my system. My pulse beat in my ears and muted the scene as her ocean-blue eyes landed on me.

Suddenly I was eighteen again, rocked by nostalgia and memories that had been locked away for a decade.

I saw the shock in her gaze, but she rearranged her expression to a placid mask fast. Her cool stare under those black—*Black? What the fuck?*—bangs made me hold my tongue and remember where we were.

*His girlfriend.* Jesus, I didn't see this coming.

"Hi."

Her soft greeting turned my mouth to dust. I wondered if it was her hand or mine that was so cold when I reached to clasp her outstretched palm. I'm not sure if I spoke, but after a beat she withdrew.

*Easy, man. Calm down. The album is why you're here. Don't make a scene.*

I turned to Jesse. "Should we get started?"

He grinned. "Hell yeah. Let's do it."

While he met the band and started rehearsing, I dropped into my chair behind the sound board and rolled my shoulders. *The album is all that matters. All. That. Fucking. Matters.*

"Ready, Nick?" Jesse called into the mic.

I nodded and echoed his words back to him. "Hell yeah. Let's do it."

# MELODY

Coming Storms @ComingStorms –Just Now
Back in #Nashville and ready to make this single!
Drops July 3rd! More news to come! #HomeSweet-
Home #OnTheGrind #ComingStorms

*Send. Hit send.* My brain knew what to do, so why wouldn't
my body move? Why was I still staring at the tweet I'd
composed in the hall?

"Are you okay, sweetheart?" Fern offered me a cup of
coffee, and I realized I'd been rooted to the same spot while
everyone else grabbed food and got settled. I flashed her an
embarrassed smile and nodded. "Get comfortable. We're
here awhile," she said gently.

"Don't you get sick of working every single second of the
day? You're allowed to chill for a sec, in case you didn't
know." Jesse's buddy—*That's Seth. Smartass Seth and Steady
Steve, remember?*—gave me a teasing grin as he walked past.

Those monikers were clutch for helping me differentiate those two.

*Thanks for the tip, Smartass. Chilling would be nice, believe me, but not if I want to do this right. Luckily, you can chill enough for six people. Have a beer, why don't you? It's 11am and you're still sober.*

I swallowed the retort that itched to fly out. I'd only met Jesse's guys when they joined us in L.A. last week. No way were we familiar enough for me to be myself. Seth didn't wait for a reply anyway, just went to the couch and got lost in his own phone as he did indeed crack open a beer. He didn't see me smirk as I looked down at the screen again.

With the tweet finally sent, I wandered to the desk in the corner and powered up my laptop.

*Nick.*

Over a million people live in Nashville. Of those million-plus, there were maybe three who would really remember me. Of those three, there was one I wanted—no, needed—to never see again. One I needed to remain ancient history. One I hadn't let myself think about in over ten years.

I'd been back in town for 48 hours and had seen no one outside of the crew and my father. What the hell were the odds that he would be the first person I encountered?

The computer came to life, and I gave my head a strong shake. *That's the past. That's not the story now. Get to work, Miss Twitter. You have a story to tell. You are Coming Storms. That's what matters.*

The mayhem of the last year had turned me into someone I never dreamed of being, but that didn't mean I couldn't handle it. The nonstop list of tasks leapt to the front of my mind while I opened my browser. I was off and running again.

# NICK

Melody Thomas.

How had I missed *her* in my research?

After a long day and a surprising amount of progress on the single, I returned to my apartment with a takeout sandwich and a mind that wouldn't rest. I grabbed my laptop and settled in.

Googling "Jesse Storms Images" made me feel like a total creep. I snacked on dinner and scrolled through more photos of one man than I ever needed to see until it occurred to me to add "girlfriend" to the search criteria. That explained a little more of this mystery, because she *was* a mystery. No stories featured her, and in photos she appeared in a hat and sunglasses, usually a step behind Jesse. "Jesse Storms and girlfriend," or "Jesse Storms and his hometown sweetheart," were the extent of her identity according to captions. Her image seemed carefully designed to give Jesse's sex symbol status a bit of balance when the situation called for it.

Brilliant PR.

I moved on to social media, where Storms's presence was

hot. On Twitter, Instagram, Facebook, and YouTube, ComingStorms had millions of followers and a constantly-updated profile. I saw a shot of the lounge posted today, and reluctantly joined the followers on Twitter and Instagram before slapping the computer closed.

The sandwich wrapper landed in the wastebasket when I launched it across the room. I leaned back in the chair and stared at the ceiling. *Be cool. Jesse doesn't know. Not that there's anything to know. That was a different time. Would anything have changed if you'd known about her? Would you really have refused an opportunity like this just to avoid that toaster-in-the-bathtub jolt when she walked in?*

Maybe.

I grabbed my keys and headed downstairs to the garage. One look at my Camaro in its parking space made me smirk. *Bullshit you would've. Now, go chill out for awhile.*

The album was definitely the top priority of the summer, but it wasn't all that mattered. There was always time to unwind. I gunned the engine and let the warm wind hit my face on my way to Bar 40 to meet my friends.

I found them at a large booth in the back, a round of drinks already on the table. Ben and his girlfriend, aka my cousin Celeste, were seated on one side of the bench. On the other, an empty space waited for me beside Liv Milani.

Liv and I traded a close-lipped smile. We had been a little drunk last weekend, and our usual silly banter had turned into flirting. That flirting had turned into making out... and a little more at my place later on. But, hell. Liv was Ben's ex girlfriend and one of my best friends in the world. *We don't have to rehash a silly mistake, right?*

"Hi, honey, how was work?" Liv asked while I signaled for the waitress to bring me a beer.

Her cheeky greeting was exactly what I wanted to hear.

It told me we were cool and let me switch from work to chill. "Not bad. And you, dearest? Did you starch my shirts? Are the kids bathed and in bed?"

"Ha! In your dreams."

"Hardly." My sarcastic tone matched hers, and we toasted our bottles in solidarity.

Beer, friends, and music had Jesse Storms fading fast from my mind. During the set break, Ben glanced across the room and smirked. "Hey, don't you know her?" He nodded toward a woman in a fedora heading our way.

"Shit. Yeah, I did her album back in March. We hung out a little. Damn, what was her name?" I slouched in my seat and turned to Liv with pleading eyes. "Help me out?"

She made a face. "You're going straight to hell, Field."

I couldn't argue, especially since she put her head on my shoulder and her hand on my thigh just in time.

The girl—*Damn, really, what* was *her name?*—approached our table. "Hey, Ni-ck." Her voice dropped off when she registered the scene.

"Hey there. How've you been?"

"Fine. I'm still waiting to hear on my demo." She toyed with her hat.

"Ah, yeah, that can take time."

"Hi, I'm Olivia." My champion buffer lifted her hand off my thigh to shake with the girl. I tried not to wince when she pinched me in the process.

Ms. Fedora glanced between us again and shrugged. "Uh, well, see you around, Nick."

"Take care."

As soon as she left, Liv sat up and shoved my shoulder. "You owe me for that one, buddy."

I glanced around and found a waiter to motion over. "Please hydrate this lady with your best bourbon."

"A double, please." Liv flashed a sweet smile.

"Let's go ahead and do a round for the table." Celeste cackled an evil laugh while Ben chuckled.

I presented my friends with a middle-finger salute that kept the laughter going. As the band started up again and we accepted our very fine, very expensive drinks, I thought of my car and new job title.

"Here's to smashing out of ruts but still living free." I raised my glass in an impulsive toast. The resounding clink was music to my ears.

In the parking lot later, Liv flashed me a casual look. "I was going to get a taxi home unless you'd want to give me a ride?" I hesitated, and she laughed. "Come on, *friend*. It's just a ride. Thought you were living free?"

The woman knew how to make a point. I waved at my passenger door. "Damn right I am. Let's roll."

~

"That's a wrap."

Storms's grin widened at my announcement early Friday afternoon. Take eight of "Would You Mind" had just faded out, and we had our final cut.

"Hell yeah!" He ran around to high-five the band. "Party tonight, guys. Everyone's invited. Nick, we're good to stop today, right?"

"Definitely."

Jesse came into the control room and clapped a hand on my shoulder. "Be at my place about nine and bring friends. Peter will text you the address."

"Ah, I'd planned to—"

He cut me off with an amused look on his way into the lounge. "It wasn't a question. See you there."

Alone for a moment, I texted Liv to see if she'd be game for the party, and then sat back and gazed at the now-empty studio through the glass.

Since landing this project, I'd spent a lot of time cracking jokes about pop divas and mentally strategizing how to scrape together enough material to make a decent album. I anticipated a client who was little more than a voice and a pretty-boy face.

From the first day on, Jesse Storms made me eat my words by the shovelful. Not only was he musically talented, he took directions without question, the douche. What made him an even bigger douche was the fact that he was so damn easygoing and fun to work with. He could make the band *and* me smile through long hours and take after take. Even while I choked on all my expectations, I had to admit that I liked the guy.

His crew was a different situation. Because it was part of the job, I forced myself to learn who was who. The ladies were no problem. Melody I could never forget, and Fern the stylist was elegant and kind. But all Jesse's bros seemed to do was eat, talk, and stare at their phones. Even Peter, who seemed so formal at first, had ditched the suit and tie in lieu of lounging on the couch for hours on end.

It helped when the guys dragged me to a club midweek. There I learned that Peter was born for his manager role given the way he made things happen. Steve was quiet and happy to listen and laugh, and Seth was the smartass of the group.

Life became surreal as I adjusted to Jesse's version of normal. The constant presence of the quiet girl in the corner who could make millions of people talk with a tap of her finger only added to the weirdness. Her girlfriend status seemed to extend to Jesse's arm around her shoulder from time to time. She had *not* gone to the bar with us. Probably for the best; I'm not sure any woman would be thrilled to see their partner flirt with as many women as Jesse did, even if her gaze was on a screen 90% of the time.

I told myself daily that it didn't matter, but she hadn't shown the slightest hint that she recognized me since we first shook hands. How long could the charade hold up? And what would it be like when we finally acknowledged the past?

*Wonder if she'll be there tonight.*

"Done for the day?"

Rick's question jolted me back. I spun in my chair and gave him an update. His eyebrows arched. "Damn, son. Well done."

I twisted my lips. "Thanks."

"Get on home and have a good weekend. And remember, don't screw up."

*Don't screw up. Right.* Thinking about Jesse Storms's girlfriend definitely fell into the category of colossal screw-ups. I nodded and followed Rick to the exit, lighting up my phone to summon Celeste and Ben as additional reinforcements for the night.

Before I could type, a message popped up:

Celeste: Drinking @ Flipside. Wanna join?
Me: Sure, if you'll come w/ me to a party later.
Celeste: ... Come give us the details. LOL Sarah wants to see you.
Me: NO. I've told you I'm not dating your colleagues.
Celeste: Hahaha, maybe better to say she wants to fangirl over your client.

I sighed, but I also turned left out of the parking lot to go meet my friends.

Sizzling chicken made my mouth water when I walked into the restaurant. Celeste and Ben were at the end of a table full of people I knew vaguely. Celeste and her colleagues often came here on Fridays. Since it wasn't far from the studio, I'd joined her a handful of times before. The group was nice enough, but I didn't talk to them much.

I'd just pulled up a chair when a young woman turned bright eyes to me. She twined her long hair around one finger. "Are you really doing Jesse Storms's album?"

"Sarah Rose, the office receptionist." Celeste's whispered reminder in my ear wasn't necessary. Of course I remembered Sarah. An adorable girl, but way too young and innocent to do more than wink at and watch her giggle. She was a sport, though, and definitely the most fun of Celeste's coworkers.

"Who wants to know?" I directed the question to Sarah, flashing a grin I didn't really feel at the prospect of discussing work.

But her eyes disappeared in a smile, and her blush went from pink to red, so I laughed and leaned my elbows on the table.

"I love him," she explained. "I voted for him every week on *American Pop* and jumped up and down on the couch when he won."

Ben and I both chuckled, but Celeste groaned. "You know all that stuff is fake, righ? The producers probably decided he'd win before filming even began."

"So cynical." I shook my head at my cousin in mock-disapproval.

Sarah waved her off. "You always say that, but I don't care. I love celebrity news! It's so fun to escape real life and read about exciting lives. What better than a hot new star from our hometown? How can you not love him?" Still smiling, she stuck her tongue out at Celeste before looking back to me. "Tell me everything about him. Is he nice? I hear he is."

"He's pretty cool. Not as much of a diva as I'd expected. And he's got real talent. He can sing and play."

"What can he play? Guitar?" She barely blinked.

I shrugged. "Far as I can tell, he can play everything in the studio: guitar, piano, percussion."

Sarah clapped and squealed. "Oh my god, he really is perfect. Gah, I'm so in love with that man."

Celeste threw her arms around Sarah while Ben and I laughed again. "Better not let your boyfriend hear that," Celeste said with a grin.

Sarah hugged her tight and giggled. "He'll just have to understand. You can't compete with perfection."

"Well," I cut glances at Celeste and Ben. "We're going to his party tonight. You should come with us. I'll introduce you."

The color drained from Sarah's face. "Oh, I could never. I'd faint dead away to meet him in person! Besides," she wrinkled her nose and looked at the ceiling, "I do actually have a date later, which suddenly seems a lot less fun now. You guys are so lucky."

"I don't remember to agreeing to this party." Celeste gave me a teasing glare.

"Come on, you know you can't say no to family."

"Can't I though?" She swiped my beer and took a sip, and then passed it to Ben—a clear message that I had my reinforcements locked in.

Jesse Storms wasn't the only one who could summon an entourage. My friends were truly the greatest people on the planet.

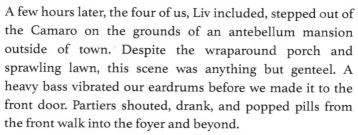

A few hours later, the four of us, Liv included, stepped out of the Camaro on the grounds of an antebellum mansion outside of town. Despite the wraparound porch and sprawling lawn, this scene was anything but genteel. A heavy bass vibrated our eardrums before we made it to the front door. Partiers shouted, drank, and popped pills from the front walk into the foyer and beyond.

We edged our way into the living room and squeezed onto an empty sofa. After watching the scene in silence for several minutes, Liv stood, hands on her hips. "This is boring. Want to dance, Field?"

Before I could agree, I glanced behind her, gaze landing on a chair in the far corner of the room.

*Shit.*

My pulse jumped at the sight of Melody on her phone, typing away while the party raged around her. *Some things never change. You always were the girl on the edge of the action, weren't you Mel?*

A memory hit me with another gut-shot: catching sight of her through a crowd at a high school party, having my heart kick up, and making my way over to her. I'd tried to be cool and clever with my opening line and put my foot in my mouth instead with a dumbass comment. How I got her to stick around for more than five minutes, I'll never know.

Liv's long hair and miniskirt were already blending into the crowd by the time that thought passed. She found a dance partner, and, by the smile on her face, it seemed she was enjoying herself. Ben and Celeste stood as well, so I gave them a nod before striding across the dance floor.

*Be fucking cool.*

# 4

# MELODY

**ComingStorms @ComingStorms**
Major welcome home #party in #Nashville! Thanks
to everyone who came to #celebrate tonight! #VIP
#WorkingForTheWeekend #FridayNight #Jesses-
Home #NashvilleVibes

**ComingStorms** New single is done after only a week!
Time to #party! Tag us in your pics w/ #JessesHome
and show us how you #celebrate! #FridayFun
#NashvilleLove #GetTurnt #NightOut

The hair on my neck stood up. My perch by the window
offered an excellent view of the party, but the throng was
thick at the moment. No matter; an alert caught my attention, and the being-watched shiver was forgotten. When
you're retweeting, snapping, posting, and sharing on four
sites at once, there's not a lot of room for the real world—or
the world of celebrity parties, either.

Jesse moved through the house like a rip current. Voices and bodies swirled in his wake, beautiful women on call to dance whenever he pleased. It wasn't the kind of party to be tied down to a girlfriend, and anyway, I was happy on the sidelines.

Who was I kidding? Like any party in recent memory had been the kind to be tied down to a girlfriend. It was just that the sting of my transition from girlfriend to "girlfriend" had worn off dozens of events ago. My new role meant work, and that kept me going. I called for selfies, shared photos and updates, and generally kept the partygoers talking online as they danced and drank and made sure to be seen.

That shiver whispered over me again, and I looked up to see Nick Field headed my way.

My breath caught at the sight of him, so grown up but so the same. On some guys, hair the length he wore it looked shaggy or sloppy. Paired with his black-framed glasses and well-maintained stubble, he made it work. He edged through the crowd, hands flicking up to adjust his collar in a fluid, confident motion. The subtle gesture clenched my stomach.

*He always was so damn cool.*

I'd giggled at the thought more than once that week, but those were private moments when no one was looking. With his gaze pinned on me, I didn't dare smile.

Peter appeared out of nowhere and snagged Nick's arm, nodding in my direction before disappearing again. *What was that?*

Nick smirked and strolled to stand in front of me. "Hey."

The phone slipped from my hand. "Hi."

"Peter said I should ask you to dance."

I almost rolled my eyes but remembered my role and put on a neutral expression. "No, thank you."

"No?"

*No, Nick, I'm not about to put myself through keeping this straight face while I freaking dance with you.*

I shook my head to reiterate, and he shifted his weight from one foot to the other. "Too bad. Guess I'll leave you alone."

"Would you mind doing an interview?" My words tumbled out before he could retreat.

Nick's brows knitted together. "Here? Now?"

I stood up and cringed as sleepy tingles flooded my legs from sitting so long. "We can go out back. Just three questions. It'll be quick." *Should've let him walk away, but I do need this interview. Dammit, too late to revise now.*

He gestured me to lead on, so I skirted us around the dance floor and through the kitchen. We slipped out to the quiet backyard, where a handful of people dotted the grass. The night breeze was sweet and refreshing.

*"We could be that couple who spends the party talking on the lawn, telling each other secrets until sunrise."*

Good god, when was the last time I thought of *that*? I glanced over at the man beside me—the man who'd said those words to me in another lifetime.

*You don't know each other. We're both just in the crew. He's nothing to you anymore. He might not even remember you. He's certainly not said anything to make you think otherwise.*

"So, an interview?" Nick's gruff question punctuated my reality check.

"Right." I started a voice note and cleared my throat. "How is recording going so far?"

"Excellent. We—what?" He broke off when I frowned at the screen.

"It's not picking you up." I stepped closer and lifted the phone a little higher. "Try again."

Nick didn't speak, and when I glanced up, I understood why.

Inches separated us. This close, I could see the way his pupils grew larger in the low light. This close, I could —*dammit, dammit, dammit*—I could smell him. His scent was fresh and clean, almost minty. It was a perfect match to his cool vibe, but his warm body seemed to beckon me nearer.

Blood was already draining from my arm from holding the phone aloft to someone almost a foot taller than me. My bicep trembled as my feet inched toward him. What should've been a subtle shuffle nearly became me feeding him my phone.

His head jerked back in time to avoid contact. With a grin, he grasped the phone, his palm across the screen. "Here, let me help."

I could've let go, but the heel of his hand landed on my fingertips. He shifted his grip, and his fingers coasted across my wrist and rested there. His touch was far more calloused than in my memory.

And I had plenty of memories of Nick Field's hands on me.

I battled to keep my face from turning crimson. *Questions. Interview. Words...* "How's the album coming along?"

"Great." Nick reported that the single had wrapped already and things were going well in the studio. When he finished answering the third question about goals for the album, I stopped recording and stepped back. My hand still tingled even though blood began flowing again.

"Thank you for doing this." I made a show of checking Twitter like the fate of the planet depended on it, but he didn't leave. At last, I had to glance over again.

His lips curled. "Does that mean I'm dismissed?"

"I appreciate your time."

The formality of my tone erased his amused look. He eyed me once more and disappeared into the house, leaving me staring at the closed door until my lungs burned.

*Revision: "Does that mean I'm dismissed?"*

*"Only if you want to be, Nick Field."*

*He'd smile. This time, he'd be the one to walk closer. He'd take my hand—no, touch my cheek. "And if I don't?"*

*I'd look up at him and step closer on purpose this time. My voice would be throaty and cool as I said, "Then let's stop pretending we're strangers."*

"Don't be silly." I exhaled hard and threw myself back into work.

∾

Near dawn, the house was finally empty. My "JessesHome" hashtag had raged through the party, but the buzz was quiet at last. I jogged upstairs to fetch my purse from Jesse's bedroom.

"Hey you. Where you been all night?"

I turned to find him leaning on the doorjamb. "I've been around, Jess. You look a little tired." Understatement—his eyes were barely open.

He smiled and nodded as he crossed the room and wound his arms around my waist. I rested my palms on his chest, brows arched. "What's up?"

"Why don't you stay a little longer?"

The velvet purr in his voice would have had most women flat on their back before he finished speaking, but I cocked my head. "Stay?"

"Mm-hmm. Come here, baby." Jesse bent his head, his fingers inching under my shirt.

His kiss tasted of champagne and sugar, sickly sweet. *Close your eyes, genius.* Before I could obey my own command, his lips trailed along my jaw to my ear, giving me a view of his neck.

And the lipstick smear printed on his skin. *Big surprise.*

My nose tingled with Jesse's cologne overlaid with expensive perfume. I puckered my lips and stepped back from his embrace, noting as I did how heavily he'd been leaning on me. "Not tonight, Jess."

"Aw, baby, but..." Jesse's mumble trailed off as he plopped onto the bed and fell to his back. His chest heaved with a deep sigh. A halfhearted wave was meant to beckon me, but I shook my head straightened my top. His eyes opened blearily when I pulled the sheets back.

"Come on, baby boy. Time to sleep."

"You're the best, Melody."

"Depends on what you need me for, I guess. Have a good weekend, Jesse." With a kiss to his forehead, I let myself out.

The sun was peeking over the horizon when I got to Dad's house. I shut off the car and said a silent thanks that Jesse had been cool with my plan to stay here. Ostensibly, the goal was to give me space to write and edit my article. Truthfully, what I needed most was shelter from the hurricane that was Jesse's life.

With the birds chirping and the sky a rosy orange, I closed my eyes and took a deep breath. That lipstick stain on Jesse's neck floated to mind, but how could I be mad? He worked so hard, and we'd come to an "understanding" about my role in this empire ages ago. I wasn't really his girlfriend anymore.

*Wonder if Nick had lipstick on his neck tonight.*

I sucked in a breath. Now that was a thought I had no right to feel anything about. And yet, it stung more than the smell of perfume on Jesse's shirt.

My eyes scrunched tighter, picturing Nick's sly smirk dissolving into a ragged gasp of pleasure as I pulled his skin between my teeth—

Wait. Me?

I blinked to find my knuckles white on the steering wheel. Heat flooded my face as I stumbled out of the car and hurried into the house.

Dad had coffee brewing when I entered through the back door into the kitchen. "Hey, party girl. Big night? You're all pink."

He peeled a banana and offered me a chunk, so I leaned on the counter. "Yeah, we had a huge turnout. Just a little tired, I guess."

"Did you have fun?"

"I mostly worked." I yawned and scratched my head.

Dad aimed a pointed look at my hair but didn't comment. "Bet you're exhausted. Still think you can help me in the yard this afternoon?"

I kissed his cheek. "Most definitely. See you in a couple hours, okay?" He smiled and waved me on.

Saturday was the first day in my memory that "Coming Storms" took a break. When I woke, Dad and I tended his garden while we caught up on the past two years of our lives. That night, we made pasta for dinner, drank cold Yazoo beer, and watched *Star Wars* for the billionth time.

My mom left us when I was in middle school. From the moment she walked out the door, I promised myself that I would never become her. Giving up wasn't in my vocabulary, and no way would I let random chance direct my life. Writing was my passion. After she left, it became my *mission*, and no one cheered me on more that Dad. He was my parent and friend. When I got frustrated, he'd listen and promise to buy a hundred copies of my first book. He supported me when I went away to college and then sought journalist jobs across the country, but we missed each other like crazy all the time. A whole day with him, and without a laptop or phone, was the recharge I needed to devote Sunday to my big article.

In L.A., I met Jesse while covering *American Pop* for a popular but small-time entertainment mag. I had a steady readership and a strong blog following, but nothing major. *Pop* had been my beat for a couple seasons by then, but Jesse was definitely the first contestant I'd gotten to know personally. We'd started dating; when he won, I didn't hesitate to give up my day job to work for him. He was going places, and I was ready to move.

With such limited credentials, I was speechless when *Now Playing!* contracted me for a feature. The international magazine wanted a huge retrospective on Jesse's rise to stardom, and they felt my unique perspective of girlfriend and reporter was the perfect angle. My editor said I had the right voice to give the article fresh insight on the world of reality competitions.

The honor and magnitude of such an opportunity had left me giddy since I got the call. However, balancing the deadlines with the nonstop demands of Jesse's media could be a burden. Case in point: 1,000 words on his background were due by Friday. With an article like this, every word was precious, and so far I wasn't satisfied with the draft.

"Don't tell me you're going to be up all night." Dad broke

my reverie with a mug of chamomile tea late Sunday evening.

I put my feet up on the chair and accepted the cup. "I'm nearly done for now. Tomorrow I've got other stuff to work on, so I want to find a good stopping point."

"What's on the agenda tomorrow?"

I smiled. Dad called hashtags the pound sign and still used the phrase, "I'll go online and check that out," but he always asked about my work and listened intently while I babbled.

"Well, there'll be posts to share and news to push as always, plus I've got an interview I want to publish and... stuff." I trailed off, suddenly distracted.

"Sounds daunting." Dad chuckled and patted my head. "Get some sleep."

"Night," I muttered as he shut the door.

A soft breeze snuck in through the window. *We could be that couple who... No, we couldn't. We can't. New story. New rules.*

*God, I've got to stop thinking about him.*

I arrived at the studio hours before scheduled the next morning. The lounge was already stocked with breakfast, so I grabbed a large coffee, popped on my headphones, and uploaded the interview to my laptop. Time to edit.

Ignoring the tickle Nick's voice gave me, I got down to work and had the conversation trimmed to snappy sound bites within the hour, complete with a slideshow of images from the lounge and various shots of Jesse I kept as stock footage. While the file posted to Reddit, Twitter, and YouTube, I stood and turned to refill my coffee.

"Oh, sh—" I checked the profanity before it could fly out. No matter what, Coming Storms didn't swear. That rule didn't stop me from jolting hard, the empty paper cup clattering to the ground at the sight of Nick at the snack tray.

An orange fell out of his hand and rolled across the floor. His lips moved without volume, and I remembered the headphones and yanked them off. "Say again?"

"I was trying not to disturb you."

"Oh."

"What are you doing here so early?" he asked in the uncomfortable silence.

I almost fired the same question back but held myself and remembered my role. Instead, I put on a smile and went for a fresh cup of coffee. He stepped away from the counter, and I wished I didn't notice the way he recoiled when I was near.

"Just getting a little work done." I focused on pouring, all no big deal.

"Anything specific?"

I looked over, surprised he'd asked. He seemed as surprised as me by the way he pushed his glasses up his nose and looked away. "Actually, yes," I said. "Check your notifications. Your interview just posted."

Two taps on his phone, and the recording came through the little speaker. "Oh, god." He groaned and shut it off. "I didn't realize you were going to use my voice."

"It's more dynamic than text. You're in the story now; get used to it. The more we talk about the album, the more buzz we generate."

Nick grunted but didn't answer. I cleared my throat and shuffled back to the desk.

"Uh, I'm about to set up. Do you want to see the studio?

For pictures or whatever. If you want. I don't care, but I thought if you, uh, wanted."

My smile wasn't planned that time. "I'd love that."

We walked into a huge control room. Soundboards and monitors faced a wide window into the even larger studio. Nick began to name the functions of various equipment, so I started another voice note. Gawking had me far too busy to remember anything he said.

He led me into the studio itself, and I looked around the space in wonder. "Hold this and keep talking." I pressed my phone into his hand. The setup was gorgeous, beech wood floors and burgundy walls, instruments and mics at the ready. "God, this is beautiful."

Nick broke off his sentence, and I realized I'd spoken aloud. "I know, right?" He flashed a broad grin, more relaxed than I'd seen him. I grinned back, but when I did, his dimmed. "I need to get started. Take all the photos you want. I'll be at the boards."

No pic could capture the magic in here, but I did my best. I returned to the control room to find him reclining in a desk chair while the monitors hummed to life. He didn't look up, but my feet slowed to a stop. I toyed with my phone. In my periphery, he cocked his head, clearly curious as to what the hell I was doing.

"Could I sit?" I motioned to the couch on the back wall.

He shrugged. "Sure."

Part of me longed to make small talk, ask about the album or his job just to hear his voice. Part of me wanted to make a joke. Was I funny anymore? I used to laugh a lot, but Seth and Steve's cracks made me roll my eyes. Maybe my sense of humor was a casualty of this crazy life I'd bought into.

Part of me wanted to throw my hands in the air and ask

how the hell he didn't remember me. And, as I gazed at the back of his head and spotted the faint scar behind his ear that I'd traced a hundred times, a lot more of me than I should admit wanted to run my fingers through his hair and find out how grown-up Nick Field kissed.

The first time we kissed, that boy blanked my mind. The first time we kissed, and every time after, Nick's teasing tongue and full lips unleashed a need in me that I couldn't control and didn't want to. Over my last year of high school, I spent hours kissing those lips.

I shook my head hard and dove into Instagram. Despite the silence, simply being around him was satisfying in its own way. My private, dreamy smile reflected on the phone's screen.

"You tagged me." His voice cut through my concentration minutes later.

"Uh-huh."

"But I'm not in the picture."

"Hang on, just finishing a couple things." When I found a place to stop, he was absorbed in his own phone. "What did you say?"

"Don't remember. Something more important came up."

"About Jesse?"

He grinned but didn't look up. "Nope. I'm watching a video of a guy strip naked and jump into a hay baler."

My burst of laughter caught his attention. "Please show me."

Nick was beside me in a second. The concept was funny, but the absurdity of the video had me in stitches. His laughter echoed my giggles, both our shoulders shaking as we succumbed to the hilarity.

When the video ended, he lowered the phone with a final chuckle while I wiped away mirthful tears. He flashed me another one of his easy grins, the kind that made my insides shiver.

The kind I could never forget.

We weren't laughing anymore.

The room went silent as I stared up at him, frozen between the rules we had to follow and my racing heart. Nick cocked one brow as if asking a question or daring me to speak. I bit my lip, unable to look away as I shifted to put space between us.

Why the couch cushions chose that moment to go from soft to suctioning, I don't know, but my efforts only served to bump us closer together. "Oh, sorry," I gasped, practically shoving him away.

"No problem." Nick defied the snuggly couch and got to his feet in a single motion. He strode back to his chair.

"There you are!"

Jesse burst into the room. His greeting was aimed at Nick, but he smiled when he saw me. "Baby girl, I missed you all weekend." He summoned me into a hug and kissed my forehead. I gave him a squeeze, but his attention bounced again. "Nick, I've been thinking. Let's hear that single. Melody, stay here. I want your thoughts."

I sat on the arm of the couch while the song cued up. As it played, I watched the two men in front of me. Jesse shuffled on the balls of his feet, head bent in concentration. Nick leaned back in that chair, exuding cool confidence. I admired how he reacted to Jesse, how self-possessed he seemed. Even the studio head and the receptionist looked dazed when we walked in, but not Nick. He was good for Jesse. He was balanced enough to work with him and not get bowled over. He was—

Gazing right at me.

The curious crinkle at the corner of his eyes made me snap my attention to my lap. *Don't notice me. Don't ask.*

"Talk to me," Nick said to Jesse when the song faded out.

"Do you think it's a hit?" Jesse asked.

"Definitely," was the automatic reply.

"Melody, talk to me."

I looked up, my brain clicking into work mode at the tone of Jesse's voice. "What are we thinking, Jess? You don't like the single?"

"No, I like it fine. It's fun, a good summer love song, and my man Nick believes in it."

"But you want more."

Jesse cocked a brow and gave me a look said me I'd taken the words out of his mouth as usual. "I want more."

*You want it all, boy. And we're gonna get it.* I stood and crossed my arms. "Something more artistic. Something deeper. Something that we can drop as a second single with the album that'll make the critics go, damn, he's got range. Then we can talk about crossovers and—yeah, Jess. I see it."

"Goddam, Melody, you're a mind reader sometimes."

"I can get you another song."

Jesse and I looked at Nick. I blinked, crashing down from the zone that only Jess and I could make together. A thousand ideas for spin and possible angles still whirred in my mind as I processed what Nick had said.

"You know someone good? I want art, not bubblegum on this one. Melody can make it fit the image, but I want people to take notice," Jesse said.

Nick nodded. "Let's keep going with the album. I've got a friend who can get you what you want."

"This guy, Melody. He's a perfect addition to the crew, isn't he?" Jesse clapped him on the shoulder, tossed me a smile, and jogged into the studio.

I have never known someone with so much energy.

*Back to work.* I hurried to the door into the lounge, eager to jot down my ideas. "Thank you for the tour. I'm sorry if my working here is intrusive. I'll try to—"

"You can be here whenever you want."

My hand froze on the handle. "Thank you," I whispered and made my escape.

# 5

# NICK

We finished another track in the second week. Rick was thrilled with our progress, even happier because Jesse was thrilled with me. Ben was also thrilled. He said yes right away when I told him I needed a song. His day job was in IT, but he'd written some killer music over the years, and I had no doubt that his sound would be perfect for Jesse.

I was thrilled, too—at the prospect of next week. Jesse had a trip to Daytona scheduled, which meant I'd get plenty of time to finish mixing the single before the deadline. The crew wouldn't be back until Friday at the earliest, Monday if I was lucky.

The time was useful, but what I wanted most was a break from *her*. Why had I said she could be there whenever? She took me up on it, dammit. She was in the lounge most mornings before anyone else. I'd caught the hint that she didn't live with her "boyfriend," which interested me more than I'd like to admit. We didn't talk much, but every time I saw her, my throat tightened, choked on too many things to say and too many emotions to name.

I spent the weekend doing marathon workouts at the

gym and hiding in my apartment, playing guitar. The idea of hanging out with friends felt more like work than fun after the whirl of Jesse's social calendar, and I knew Liv and I needed some space. We'd been getting too close lately, and neither of us wanted to wreck our friendship by caving to a reckless fling.

Distance from Liv definitely had nothing to do with Melody Thomas. Jesse Storms's girlfriend had zero bearing on my personal life, so no way did memories and a ten-minute interview keep me from fooling around. That would be absurd.

With four solid days of work without anyone asking me to take on a side project, I crushed the edits. The single was mixed, finalized, and sent to the record label by Wednesday. While I waited on feedback from that, I went ahead and got a jump on the second track, too. By Thursday night, I'd gotten so much done, I decided to take Friday as a personal day.

That plan went out the window with the text I received just before bed.

Peter: Video wrapped early. J says studio tomorrow after lunch.

Instead of sleeping late and noodling on my own guitar, I had mics checked and the system booted by 10am. The band would arrive at noon to warm up, so I went to update Rick.

He kept it brief when I stuck my head in his office. "Single's solid gold, buddy. Don't screw up."

"Aye, Cap'n." I saluted his wry grin and left without sitting down. My kind of meeting. With a quick detour for coffee in the lounge, I headed back to the boards to—

"I, I, I, I... forgot the next line. You're..."

Melody was in the studio. Even if she'd forgotten the line, she sang her heart out into the microphone. Only half the lights were on, and she clearly hadn't noticed me. I also suspected she didn't realize the mic was live. The coffee burned my hand, so I left it on the desk and crept to my chair, gaze glued to her.

Her clothes were different. Usually she wore a black t-shirt and jeans, but today she was dressed like she'd just returned from the beach—which, I suppose, she had. Melody was small-boned and short, but those tiny denim cutoffs did a lot of justice to her legs. That black-and-white tank had her pale shoulders and breasts on fantastic display.

Good god, she was beautiful.

At the party, standing so close with her phone thrust to my face, I had no idea how I answered her coherently. Part of my consciousness must've been on autopilot as Jesse's producer. The rest of me was intent on her blue eyes, dismayed at how that jet-black hair and charcoal eyeliner changed her look compared to my memories. It was a stark contrast to her pale skin and the faint sprinkle of freckles on her nose, but damn, still sexy as hell. Even when she wore that irritating fake smile, her mouth made my chest ache.

Now her lips parted in a dreamy, faraway expression as she swayed to the tune in her head, and the ache in my chest became tension in my pants. I leaned into my palms on the desk, humor and delight tugging at my lips while I stared.

When her voice faded out, I called up "Lover" and piped it through the speakers. "Taylor Swift just called. She wants you to do a duet remix next time she's in town. Better run it again," I said into the intercom.

Melody jumped and hissed a strangled gasp. Her hands clapped over her face as her shoulders curled forward. With a chuckle, I gave myself a quick adjustment, killed the music, and walked through the door. Leaning against the wall, arms crossed and grin unchecked, I waited her out.

She peeked at me through her fingers but hid again. "Tell me I wasn't mic'd up." Her words were muffled against her palms.

"Mm, loud and clear. I put it through to the whole office."

Wide eyes appeared. "Bullshit," she whispered.

The profanity finally made her sound like a real person, not a shadow figure with a plastic demeanor. I laughed. "Yeah, it is."

She exhaled loudly and dropped her hands, cheeks flushed a fantastic pink.

"Jesse said he'd be here after lunch."

"Yeah." She nodded.

"But here you are."

"I didn't know you'd be here this early."

"*That* is bullshit," I snorted. Her lips parted, then fell into a line. Good thing I'd straightened my dick against my waistband, because her silent admission did nothing to cool my arousal. "Do you really work that much better here than anywhere else?"

She gestured vaguely. "I just—I like it. It's nice, and I can get a lot done without distraction."

"And put on one-woman concerts."

She flushed again, gaze lowered. "Shut up, Nick."

My heart slammed against my ribcage. "That's the first time you've called me by name since you walked in here."

Her mouth formed a perfect circle when she lifted her face. "Oh?"

Three weeks we'd played this game. Three weeks I'd tried like hell to ignore her, to pretend like I didn't feel like a live wire whenever she was around. Now, her cool detachment was gone. This was the Melody I remembered, and I couldn't hold back.

Blue eyes got even wider as I crossed the room. She rocked back half a step, but then shuffled forward until we were face-to-face. Good god, why did she affect me so much? There was no logical reason, but, like that first moment she walked in, my pulse thundered in my ears and muted everything else when her tongue darted out to wet her lips.

I swallowed hard and pulled my shit together. "Tell me something, *Melody*."

"What?"

The tremor in her voice made me smirk. I reached out, pinched a strand of black hair between my fingers, and stared at her over my glasses. "What the hell happened to your red hair?"

## 6

# MELODY

Dammit. Dammit. *Dammit.*

"You—you—"

"I what?" He smirked again, and I wished the look wasn't so distracting.

"You remember me?"

*Fool.* What an absurd question. Of course he remembered me. I'd known all along that Nick Field knew exactly who I was.

The look on his face confirmed the idiocy of my words. "Are you kidding me? Do I remember you?"

"I—I mean—oh, never mind." Seating was limited, but I needed to get off these wobbly knees. The piano bench was my best option. I dropped onto it, palm against my blazing forehead, and closed my eyes to take a deep breath. When I looked up again, he was watching me steadily. I nodded in silent invitation to come sit; he accepted.

His hip rested against mine. It was a light touch, but it made me hold my breath too long. I dazed all over again. Calling me on my bullshit was completely accurate. Our brief encounters were one of my favorite parts about getting to the studio early.

No. They were my favorite part.

But it was one thing to have random moments where we nodded good morning. Even my little fantasies of conversations between us were innocuous. Actually breaking down the wall of denial between us was another matter entirely. How could I possibly pretend now?

"Are the mics still on?" I asked for lack of anything better.

"No, I turned them off. We're soundproof." He glanced at me. "You've done a good job pretending like *you* didn't remember. I almost wondered if you did."

My nose wrinkled with a frown. "Come on, Nick. How could I have forgotten?"

When I said his name, his lips crooked up. *Please stop doing that.*

"Ten years is a long time. Maybe you did."

I forced my gaze the piano keys. "Ten years, wow. Actually, it's almost eleven. Fall of senior year, right?"

His shoulder nudged mine as he gently tapped out a tune. My cheeks heated when I realized it was the song I'd just sung.

Nick kept playing and said, "It started then, yeah. God, I remember that fall. What was that kid's name? The one who threw all the house parties."

"Jason." I laughed.

Nick's hands stilled as he laughed. "Hooking up with you in Jason's mother's walk-in closet. Hell yes I remember."

There was a dreamy detachment to his voice that clenched my thighs. "It was his mom's closet a lot, wasn't it? Where were that kid's parents?"

God, his easy smile was exactly the same. "It's a good

question in retrospect, but back then, I was just grateful that they were gone so much."

I nodded. "It smelled like perfume and baby powder in there."

"Pink carpet," he blurted. "I remember: your red hair and that pink carpet." I blushed to my toes, but he resumed playing. "We had some fun that year, huh? All the way up to—"

"Prom night." We said it in unison. An unbearable minute passed before we both looked away.

"I need real coffee," Nick grumbled. "Want to come?"

"Definitely."

The sun blinded me as we walked to a little spot called Sam & Zoe's in the humid, late-June morning. "Iced coffee with cream and stevia please," I said to the barista while I pulled strands of hair off my sweaty neck.

"Regular coffee, black," Nick added. He pointed at the pastry display. "We should get the coffee cake, too. You won't regret it."

I unzipped my wallet. "I'll buy. Atonement for making you endure my singing." My credit card was out before he could do more than frown.

We snagged a table in the corner and settled in, but the cool metal chair and refreshing drink couldn't ice my nerves. My toe tapped nervously while my attention wandered around the room. His gaze was too much, too captivating and embarrassing and...

Exciting. *Dammit!*

Nick broke the silence. "Thanks for the buying, but you killed that song."

I huffed. "Stop. I was just being silly, playing around when I thought no one was there. How much did you hear, anyway?"

His grin made him look positively rakish. "Almost all of it."

"Oh, god, really? Why didn't you stop me?"

Nick leaned forward, his amusement morphing into a dark tease. "You don't think I'd stop watching that show until I had to, do you?"

Wicked fire licked my spine and made me sit up straighter. "You *watched* me?"

"Yeah." One word, but he drew it out to imply far more than a simple yes. "Maybe you shouldn't know that."

"Probably not. I probably shouldn't like it so much, either."

He gave a small nod, and then broke off a piece of the coffee cake and flipped the conversation. "Where have you been? And how did you end up with Jesse?"

I played with my straw, unsure if I appreciated the break in tension or not. "Well, I went to college in Chicago."

"I remember," he muttered.

I bit my tongue. Of course he would remember. "Right. After college, I stayed and interned at the *Tribune*. Then I came back here for a year, and then out to L.A."

"Why L.A.?"

"Not many openings in journalism here. I sent my résumé everywhere from New York to California. The offer I got was a celeb rag in L.A. I couldn't pass it up, so I went."

"And then Jesse?"

"Yeah. *American Pop* was my beat. We met during the audition process and bonded over the Nashville connection. I could tell he was going to go far, so I stuck with him. We started dating. As he got bigger, I became his media manager, and now here we are."

"Here you are, showing up to work hours before him."

"This isn't the kind of writing I wanted to do. I wanted to

be an AP reporter and travel the world, but it's a start. And with the story—"

"Story?"

"Yeah. *Now Playing!* magazine assigned me a major feature about Jesse and *Pop*. It'll publish in September, same day his album drops. If I can do this well, a lot of doors would open."

"That's so awesome." The excitement in his voice had me thrilled about everything all over again. I smiled in thanks and finally took a bite of the cake, humming with delight at the sugary cinnamon.

"Sounds like ten years have been busy," he said over his cup.

"Stop and start. Busy has been the last year, since *Pop*." I washed a second bite down with coffee. "Tell me about you."

While we finished our drinks and cleaned every crumb off the shared plate, Nick told me about college. He'd spent one semester locally before discovering sound engineering and transferring to arts school in Savannah, Georgia. He graduated and returned to Nashville just as the city exploded with local rock artists. I made him tell me about projects he'd worked on, and we laughed over a few of the crazier moments.

Before I could ask how he landed Jesse's contract, his phone dinged and killed the conversation. "It's Peter. They're on their way. We should get back," he said, eyes on the screen.

I followed him to the studio and into the lounge, but he headed straight for the control room. *Don't go yet.* "I'm glad you remember me, Nick," I blurted.

He slowed to a halt. For a second, I thought all I'd get was a nod, but Nick pivoted on his heel. His strides were long, and so quick that I had the briefest notion he meant to sweep me right off my feet. Before my brain could even try to react— prepare? —for such a thing, he stopped, his face inches from mine.

"I never forgot you, Melody."

Twenty minutes later, Jesse and the guys arrived to find me tucked into my corner, staring at the computer. I smiled up at them and tossed a wave like all was normal.

Like I wasn't staring blankly at the Twitter feed while I daydreamed of a thousand ancient memories.

Like bubbles didn't race from my chest to my brain every time I thought of his smile.

Like I didn't wonder if "never forgot" meant he was thinking of me right now.

*Shit. Stick to the story!*

# 7

# NICK

The Sunday before July 4$^{th}$, I reported to my aunt and uncle's house for the family summer cookout. I almost begged off, but Mom wouldn't hear of it. With everything going on, my down time had become much more valuable. Still, family was never a burden.

I was glad to see Ben's black CR-V parked in the driveway when I pulled up. The aunts attacked me with hugs and questions about work, girlfriends, health, etc. before I could disentangle and grab a beer. Celeste and Ben were on the patio, so I sank into a lawn chair and joined the conversation. They wanted updates on the album and Jesse, but before I could give more than a vague affirmative, Aunt Elle called for her daughter.

With a roll of her eyes and a grumble about gender roles, Celeste excused herself. Ben swatted her ass as she left, which got us both the middle finger.

Once she'd gone, my friend let me sip my beer for a few minutes before he eyed me. "How is it going for real? You seem tense."

"Me?" I sneered and tried to loosen my tight shoulders. "I'm cool as always. Why wouldn't I be?"

Ben gave me a *come on, man* look. "You seemed rattled at Jesse's party. After you disappeared with that girl—"

Just before my molars started to grind, Celeste saved me. She skipped across the patio to us, her fluid motion completely wrecking Ben's train of thought.

I chuckled and shook my head when she sat on his lap and kissed his cheek. "Get a damn room, guys." Giving them hell was much, much better than continuing *that* line of questioning.

Even with that close call, the day did a lot for my state of mind. Celeste told me not long ago how grateful she was to have the family back in her life after she'd lived in New York for years, and I agreed completely. Time with people who freely called you on your bullshit did a lot for your sanity.

Jesse got a summons to appear on an *American Pop* special in L.A. at the last minute. He and his people were gone before I got home from the barbecue, but Peter's message assured me that Jesse would be back in town on Wednesday, which was July 4th, and that I was to join them at a party on Tims Ford Lake.

I cancelled my holiday plans with friends and spent the first two days of the week working at my own tempo again. The single dropped Tuesday, and even in my work zone, I didn't miss the fervor it caused on the charts. Rick nearly grinned, the salty bastard, so I knew for sure I'd done a hell of a job.

The Fourth was beautiful, sunny and hot but with a mercifully manageable level of humidity. I dropped the

Camaro's top and drove out to what was essentially a palace on the water, only briefly considering shirking the invite and just driving all damn day. At the house, I tossed my keys to the valet, walked up a wide staircase through the open front door, and wondered how this had become my life.

Jesse was in the living room, his arms draped around two long-legged blondes, each dressed in metallic bikinis and holding red Solo cups. He whooped when he saw me. "Nick, you made it! Guys, this is Nick. Nick, meet the guys!"

I waved and accepted a passing cup from the waiter, noting that "the guys" were more accurately described as handful of dudes and some insanely hot models. Before I could fade into the background, one of Jesse's girls looked me over. A brunette rose from the couch and stood beside me.

"Who's Nick?" asked the blonde.

"He's in the crew." Jesse's declaration seemed to be answer enough. He tossed me a sloppy wink and gestured between his companions. "This is Alexa and Zelda. From A to Z, get it?"

I laughed with him, but the introduction didn't help me discern who was who. The woman beside me, a beauty in a white miniskirt, gave me a warm appraisal. "Hi, I'm Heaven. What's your name?"

I repeated it. She threaded our arms and guided me to a couch opposite Jesse, where Jesse's buddy Steve sat with a girl of his own. Peter lounged with a couple women on an adjacent sofa, but Seth was nowhere to be seen.

Heaven crossed her legs almost over my knee and sat so close her breasts snuggled my arm. I glanced over, and she batted her lashes. "Comfy, sweetheart?" she asked.

*No, not especially.*

I like casual relationships. "Hanging out" with a girl for a night, a week or two, whatever, was my preferred MO. This was an entirely new situation. I'd never had a girl who was essentially an accessory before. While Jesse held court, Heaven proceeded to do everything from drink from my cup to lick my ear. It was clear that I shouldn't react to her; Alexa and Zelda did the same things to Storms, and he didn't so much as blink. Steve and Peter gave their women more attention, but every word Jesse uttered got an instant reaction from them.

*All my friends are at the pool. I could've spent the day enjoying barbeque, good tunes, cold beer, and all my favorite people. I'm the producer. I never agreed to be this deep in the crew, dammit.*

"Hey! Get over here! Where have you been?"

Jesse's shout came just before I got really pissed about giving up my holiday, but his beckoning brought Melody into the center of our circle. The cool little smile she wore rubbed cayenne on my ire, but, dammit, her dress—hell, the simple sight of her—placated me more than I wanted to admit.

"I've been by the pool." Her professional murmur made me cringe.

"Who's she?" A or Z wondered.

"This is Melody." When Jesse made an introduction, additional information was not invited.

"Should I say hi?" The girl fluttered her gaze over Melody.

"No," Jesse said without hesitation. He pointed to the half of cushion between me and Steve. "Sit down, Melody. Join us."

Steve's girl climbed into his lap when he shoved over to make room. Heaven started to pull me closer, but I gripped her knee gently.

"No thanks," I muttered as Melody settled beside me.

Her posture was stiff but sure. If she was uncomfortable, or if it bothered her that Jesse had failed to mention her girlfriend status, or if the girls who bookended him were of the slightest concern, you'd never know.

Heaven leaned over me to speak to Melody. "This is Nick. He's cute, huh?" She patted my chest, and I cringed.

Melody turned toward us with a glint in her eyes despite that damn placid expression. "Yes, he is."

Her tone didn't waver, but I almost choked on my tongue. My fingers tapped on the couch as I fought the urge to grab her hand and drag her away to the nearest walk-in closet we could find. She had me so twisted up with her cool detachment and that shimmer of fire underneath. I knew I shouldn't think things like that, but *fuck*, I could almost taste it when she licked her lips.

"We can share him if you want," Heaven offered. "You wouldn't mind, would you, cutie?"

"Not in the least." While I spoke, I watched Melody out of the corner of my eye so hard my head hurt.

She breathed a low laugh. "I'm sure you wouldn't." To Heaven, she said, "Thanks. Let's see what happens. Here, let me take your pic."

Heaven struck a dramatic pose. I leaned back to stay out of the shot, which seemed to suit her fine. The party continued, but I quit paying attention to Heaven's perfume in my nose and Jesse's nonsense about rap battles. Half in my head, half obsessed with the slightest movement to my right, I wondered how long I could endure.

Melody at least pretended to care. She laughed on cue and took photos of anyone who preened for the camera. She didn't flinch when Alexa and Zelda tag-teamed Jesse with open-mouth kisses.

She did clear her throat when Heaven turned my head, though.

I'd all but forgotten about the person curled against my left side. But when Jesse's second girl went in for the kiss, a soft hand cupped my chin and swiveled my face. Heaven's cherry-flavored lips opened against mine. Before I could decide whether to kiss back or even close my eyes, Melody's tiny cough tickled my ear and made me withdraw.

"Mmm." Heaven grinned and touched my nose. "I'll be right back." She rose and walked toward the restroom like a model on the runway.

"Having fun?" The question was just loud enough for me to hear. Not like Steve would've cared; his girl was feeding him a brownie.

"I feel like I'm in some kind of dream."

"Fantasy, more like it."

I snorted. "Hardly. The punch tastes like medicine, and this conversation is about to liquefy my brains. What did Jesse just say about Scooby Doo taking Shaggy in a fight?" Her lips twitched, which made me smile. "And you?"

"Time of my life."

"Are you serious? The girl I used to know would've been in the corner, inventing dialogue and giggling so hard she pissed herself."

Melody clapped a hand over her mouth to hide a sudden laugh, but, again, no one cared. She cast a mischievous look at me. "I couldn't invent dialogue as random as the Scooby v. Shaggy debate. Besides, it is pretty cool to listen in. When you listen, you learn what excites people, what entertains them and concerns them. It's fascinating."

She'd lost the cool façade entirely, and it made me smile harder. "Personally, I find this crowd pretty damn far from fascinating. I'd rather hang out with my friends, but *I'm* not 'Coming Storms.'"

Her quick glance sparked with something I couldn't decipher before she looked away. "There's a difference between being in a crowd and observing one. That's what I do: observe and report."

Heaven chose that moment to reappear. She settled on my side again, kissed my cheek, and reached for her cup. Melody inched away, but a moment later, I dropped my head to the right and murmured, "But your reports are so skewed. Coming Storms is always having the ultimate fun, no matter what. It's not true analysis."

"Are you hungry, sweetie? I'll get you a snack," Heaven crooned. I shook my head, and she went back to a brightly colored game on her phone.

After a beat, Melody spoke again. "It can't be analytical. This world is supposed to be beautiful and exciting, and my job is to spin it to get the biggest reaction. The right words, images, details—I make people live the life they dream of through my posts."

"Holy shit, you're out for world domination."

"What are y'all laughing at?" Heaven asked, leaning into me more.

"We're talking about YouTube videos," I said.

"Oh, I always watch—"

"Guys? Let's take this party upstairs." At Jesse's announcement, everyone looked to the foyer.

Seth stood there with a shopping bag in his hand and a wicked grin on his face. He jerked his head toward the staircase, and the entire group rose and drifted that way.

Heaven squealed and brought me in for another kiss. This time, she forced me open with her tongue and shot a stream of juice and vodka into my mouth. I gagged, and she sat back and beamed. "Let's go."

Melody muttered an excuse me and disappeared.

Jesse rose with an arm around each of his girls. "Nicky, get your ass upstairs."

"I think I'm cool down here." I tried to resist as Heaven pulled me to my feet.

"No," she whined.

Jesse cocked his head. "You're sure?"

"I'm sure, buddy. I'll catch you later. Enjoy." I grinned at him while the three women linked arms and headed to the stairs.

"Join us anytime you want." He punched my shoulder and jogged to follow the girls, Seth on his heels. Steve gave me a grin and sheepish wave before he, too, hurried away.

I exhaled hard and fell back onto the sofa, clutching my swimming head. Minutes ticked by as I stared into space. *I'm out. Obligations have been fulfilled. Nothing left for me here. Get up and go.*

"Why are you still down here?"

I jolted upright as Melody walked toward me. The white lace dress she wore hugged her body gently. It was so sweet and sexy that it turned me on, and I was in no mood to be aroused, not after an afternoon like this.

"Why are *you* still down here?" My reply was rougher than she deserved, but damn.

She sat down in the corner where Heaven had been and crossed her legs. Damn the flash of thigh I couldn't not notice; damn the scoop neck of her dress that I wanted to tug a little lower.

"I'm not invited. You are." She put her fist to her temple and gazed at me.

My jaw clenched. Damn, her patient mildness was more

irritating than anything else. "You're his girlfriend. Doesn't that give you an automatic invite to an orgy?"

"What an inappropriate question."

"Is it inappropriate to assume his girlfriend screws him?"

Her fist dropped, eyes flashing as she put both feet on the ground and quit the act. "Watch it, Nick."

"Then stop playing with me, *Mel*."

"I-I'm not. You're the one who... who... you called me Mel."

I was too fried to think ahead, so I didn't plan it when I leaned forward and caged her into the corner with my hand on the arm of the sofa. "So?" I whispered, but I knew exactly what she meant. Damn, her lips were too pink, eyes too blue. She smelled like the faintest hint of... *roses*, I decided after a few deep inhales.

"No one but Dad calls me Mel anymore." She stumbled over her words again, breathless, exactly like I wanted her.

"Do you mind? It's how I think of you." She shook her head at my question, shoulders at her ears. "Mel," I breathed, and her eyes told me she loved it. "My fucking brain hurts."

"Mm-hmm. It's all part of the job, Nick."

I did not imagine it when she leaned closer. My arm was so tense, there was no way I could've moved without knowing, but her lips grazed mine when she said my name. She nodded, letting our noses touch.

"Do you?" My words were little more than an exhale as our lips dusted again. I swallowed a shudder at this slow tease.

"Uh-huh." She nodded once more, her eyes wide and locked on mine in the frozen moment.

*Be careful. You can't screw up, and you definitely can't—Aw, fuck it.*

I kissed her.

At first contact, her jaw set and denied me the pleasure of those soft, full lips. *Failure—retreat!* Before I could obey the mental warning, warm arms wrapped around my neck and tugged me forward. Her head hit the sofa, mouth yielding with a little sigh. Right away, just like our first kiss so many years ago, her tongue touched mine and flooded me with desire. I licked, and she gasped and did it again, that dart of the tip of her tongue just enough to let me sample her flavor.

Just enough to drive me wild.

This was the kind of party where no one cared what anyone did, so I only felt a twinge of guilt about climbing on top of her in the middle of a stranger's living room. Not enough to stop myself from using her teasing tongue as an excuse to let go and throw myself into the kiss.

She held me tighter and tighter, her fists wrapped in my shirt, right up to the moment she twisted away.

"Oh, god, I remember," she gasped.

I crashed backward to the far side of the couch, struggling to breathe against a tide of want and memory. "I know," I croaked. "I *know*."

Mel's kiss was so new and familiar all at once, and I ached for more. I gazed blankly at the cushion. One look at her and there would be no holding back.

"That was a huge mistake," she said. I nodded, not sure I agreed, and she exhaled loudly. "God, such a huge... Follow me."

We hurried down a dark hallway to the master bedroom. She slammed the door shut and flung herself against me, but I was already reaching for her. We fell to the bed side-by-side, locked in another kiss. I flipped her to her back and let my hands run up and down her body, dimly registering how much of a woman she was compared to my memories.

"Nick." She trembled under my touch as her eyes fluttered closed.

Our kisses were long and deep. She fed my need with the fire of her answering pull, exactly like I remembered. Her petite body arched off the bed, pressing into my chest until I fell on top of her. Arms and legs wrapped around me, her dress bunched around her waist. I realized I was starting to soak my boxers with the gentle rhythm of our hips. My shorts were too much of a barrier, but I reached down and palmed her naked thigh to bring us closer together. Her head lolled, so wild and unrestrained that it tore me in half.

She groaned when I flexed against her. "Oh, no, we can't do this."

"I know," I gritted even as I hitched her thigh a little higher and tickled her skin. We moved together, her hands sliding from my face to my hair as she gazed up at me with heavy eyelids.

"We *can't*," she sighed between kisses. "Except maybe... one more." She tugged me closer and punctuated the hell out of that request.

Fuck, it was the sweetest kiss I'd had in ten years.

Mel broke free and shoved me away, so I rolled off and let her stumble to her feet. Her flushed face and bright eyes stopped my breath, even with the guilty look she cut at me.

"I *can't*." She threw me one more tormented glance and ran out of the room.

I watched the door close and decided I would be damned if Mel Thomas walked out of my life again.

# 8

## MELODY

**Coming Storms @ComingStorms:**
Nobody does #4thOfJuly like the Dirty South! Find a
pool, crank up #WouldYouMind, and tag me in your
pics!

**Coming Storms** #PoolParty #LakeHouse –What
better way to spend the #4thOfJuly?

I let the screen go dark and slapped my flip-flops against the
soles of my feet, legs dangled over the edge of the dock.
Behind me chatter and music floated down from the house.
My breath was steady, but I could still feel the weight of his
body on mine. Could still feel it, and didn't want to forget it.

*You are Coming Storms. You are—*

"Mel."

The phone nearly tumbled off my lap and into the lake,
but I didn't turn. "You weren't supposed to follow me."

Nick's feet scuffed the worn wood planks as he came to sit beside me. "Yeah, but I did anyway."

I glanced over. "I tried to tell you."

"We can't. I know. Your boyfriend is my client."

"I have to be faithful to the story we've made."

Nick grunted. "He's not faithful to you. Pretty fucking flagrantly, actually. Jesus, how did you sit through that?"

I flinched at the edge in his tone. Nerves of steel and cold detachment were requisites of my job, but that was my business. "No, he's-we don't-it's different. You wouldn't understand."

"Do you love him?"

*Oh, Nick. So naïve.* "Jesse is in love with being a star. He can't afford to love one person, except maybe himself, if he's going to be more than a flash in the pan."

"Do *you* love *him*?"

"I admire him. That's all I need to do." I hesitated before, "We were never in love, if that's what you're asking. But things used to be... different." I shrugged and looked out at the water. That was the most I'd ever told someone about Jesse and me. The nervous regret I expected to feel at my confession didn't come, and at last I met his gaze again.

Nick's brows creased. "You know he's unfaithful to you, you don't love him, but you *are* faithful to him."

I held up my index finger, a silent request for him to pause. This was something I could talk about easily. "My loyalty is to the story we've created. I have a vantage point, and the angle is as his girlfriend. That's my role for Coming Storms. It's part of the voice I use to write his life and make him famous. Cheating on him would be cheating on my dream. Can't do that."

He sighed. "You have always been crazy driven. I know

this is your break, but it's so calculated. Don't you ever get to live your story?"

"My story?" We turned to face each other, each with one leg bent on the dock and one over. I skimmed my fingers across his knuckles and up his arm. He cleared his throat, and a thrill raced through my bloodstream. I watched as his face went slack, eyelids drooping. I knew that look. It was the same look he'd worn on the couch just before he kissed me. It was a look of *want*.

It was a look I couldn't resist.

I tugged his collar, and he met me halfway. Reason and reality paused for the sweet, hot pleasure of his lips and tongue. God, Nick Field always did know how to kiss me senseless. I squirmed at the ache between my legs when his hand stroked up my neck to my cheek. If he hadn't reached for my hair, I probably would've climbed into his lap. I tensed and batted him away without pulling back, but when he did it again, I had to stop.

We gazed at each other a long moment until Nick grinned and sat back. I smiled and sucked in a deep breath.

*Live my story? I think I just did.*

The dying sun's orange light dipped below the surface of the lake. Before either of us spoke again, the peaceful scene shattered with an echoing boom of fireworks. We startled, but then traded a grin and lay back on the dock to watch the sky blaze. His fingers brushed against mine while we stared into the night, and for a few minutes, I was a kid again.

A sudden silence filled my ears when the grand finale burned out, but the music from the house party soon blasted again. Nick and I sat up together. "Sounds like the night's just getting started," I said as we got to our feet.

"Nah, not for me. I'm leaving."

"Would you take me home? Jesse will be here until dawn, and I don't want an all-nighter."

His brows rose. "Sure."

We walked up the stairs to the pool deck, around the throng of dancers, and into the house. "I'll just grab my bag and—"

"Hey, cutie."

My plan was cut short when Nick was suddenly intercepted by the girl from the couch. She wound her arms around his neck as he nearly crashed into her. Despite her generous offer earlier to "share," my presence clearly didn't register.

I eyed her while she eyed him. Her angular face and big eyes screamed model. A white bandeau top covered her perky breasts while a tiny miniskirt kept her from breaking any decency laws lower down. She was at least 5'10", her willowy height accentuated by four-inch wedge sandals. If I stood beside her, we would've resembled Legolas and Gimli from *The Lord of the Rings*—and I would *not* have been Orlando Bloom in the equation.

"Hey, sweetheart," Nick murmured.

"We're having the best party. There's still time, if you want to come play." She leaned back, forcing him to hold her upright. A sultry look couldn't hide her dilated pupils and dreamy smirk. "I'll play as nice or as naughty as you like."

*Ugh, what a cliché. Revision: Perfect Girl says, "You can make up the rules as we go." Still a little corny, but better.*

My snarky thoughts derailed into a flash of jealousy far stronger than I had a right to feel when Nick hooked her chin and angled her ear to his lips. Her eyes fluttered while he whispered.

"Oh, Nick. You're so sweet." She giggled and turned her face for a kiss.

I couldn't watch. How silly, given all the girls I'd seen kiss Jesse. But this girl's pouty lips against the mouth that had just turned me inside out were more than I could bear. Head bent to hide my disgust, I hurried to fetch my bag in the master bedroom.

The errand should've taken half a second. Except when I walked in and saw the rumpled bedspread where he'd, *god,* he'd been on me, so warm and perfect, all I could do was daydream.

"I didn't bring Heaven. Hope that's okay."

"Excuse me?" I spun to the door.

"That's her name. You didn't really want to share, did you?" Nick chuckled.

I rolled my eyes. "I can't believe you didn't go party with her."

"Can't you?"

I bit my cheek and rummaged in my bag to avoid answering. *Why not? She's hot, she wants you. That's part of this life. Enjoy it. Lord knows the rest of them do.*

Nick came over and gently took the bag from my grip. "Can't you?" he repeated.

I sighed. "Nick, *we* can't."

He shook his head. "I don't care. I won't touch you again if that's what you need. I'd still rather be with you."

I wanted so badly to give him my work face. The mask I'd learned to wear didn't simply allow me to report on a scene. It helped me through raging parties, long hours sitting and pretending to care, and all of Seth's asinine jokes. It had even kept me from falling apart when I first walked into the studio.

But with Nick, my mask was now useless. He knew me

like no one else. He knew Mel, and because he did, I couldn't pretend. I couldn't pull it off, and he'd never buy it anyway.

And so my neutral expression dissolved into a blush—the curse of a fair person, dammit—and heavy blinks. I knew I looked foolishly awed. Having to lift my face to meet his steady gaze didn't help. *Damn, I don't recall him being so tall, so broad shouldered, so deliciously defined. It's not fair he's even hotter than I remember.*

His wisp of smile turned into a smirk. "You know how you were talking about getting the biggest reaction earlier? I think I see what you mean."

"Shut up, Field. Don't get cute." My lips twitched despite my grumble.

He laughed. "Come on, let's get out of here."

I texted Peter to say I'd left—not that he cared, but it was protocol—and followed Nick to the front doors. He gave a ticket to the valet. Seconds later, a black Camaro rolled up.

Nick hurried to the driver's seat and dropped the roof. "Please tell me you're good with the top down."

I whipped out my blue scarf, cinched it around my hair, and slid into the passenger's seat. "Perfect."

We cruised down the country road, my fingers tapping with the Arcade Fire song on the stereo until Nick merged onto the interstate and punched the gas. The car roared, and the music vanished in the whipping wind. I snuggled deep into the rich leather seat, completely content while he focused on the road. The occasional backyard firework lit up the sky as we drove through the dark.

*Perfect indeed.*

Nashville's skyline glowed in the distance when he tilted his head toward me. "Where should I take you?" he shouted.

I spread my hands and shrugged. "I've got no place to be."

"Yeah?"

"Yeah." *Social media's updated. It's a holiday. Have a little fun.*

We took the loop to the south side of the city and pulled off. "We're going to the studio?" I asked when the streets became familiar.

Nick nodded. "Rick texted that I need to send the completed tracks to the record company at the start of business tomorrow. I've got keys. Thought I could do it tonight, so I don't have to get in too early. We can go wherever you want afterward. Swear it won't take long."

Alone in a dark, empty building, my carefree attitude crumbled. Even when he flipped on the lights, the silence made my heart flutter. Nick didn't say a word or give me a look, so I forgot my jitters and buried myself in work while he went to the computer.

About twenty minutes passed before he said, "I'm almost done. Go into the studio; mics are on."

I stashed the phone. "What makes you think I want to sing?"

"Just a guess. Any song you could name is on this drive if you want backup."

His sly smile ended my resistance quick. I heaved a dramatic sigh, stomped across the room to lean over him and type, and then yanked open the studio door.

"I can't believe I'm doing this."

He laughed. "Yeah, you can. Go for it."

Magical energy struck me again as soon as I walked in. The walls practically hummed with the music they'd soaked in over the years. Memories and unlimited potential crackled in the air like ions. With few inhales, the magic was in my bloodstream.

I was no musical prodigy, though, just a girl whose mother taught choir when she was a kid. Instead of tapping talent and creativity, Studio A turned my brain waves from an organized map into doodles and swirls.

I released a shaky breath and walked to the front microphone.

"Ready when you are," Nick said through the intercom.

I took another deep breath and nodded. Music filled the room. The opening line of "Son of a Preacher Man" trembled out of my mouth, but my voice grew stronger the more I sang. Hands on my head, I swished my hips to the beat and almost kissed the microphone as I belted the lyrics to the very last note.

The song faded away. In the silence, I opened my eyes and dared to look through the window. Nick was reclining in his chair, but he leaned forward and spoke into the com. "That was perfect."

"Hush." I snatched my hands off my head, but I knew I'd nailed it.

"What next, Melody?"

I stood behind the mic and watched him watch me. I thought about how my stomach jumped every day when he appeared in the lounge, and how I pretended not to care. I thought about the moments before the party moved upstairs, about Seth's creepy grin and all those girls ready for whatever. Feigned indifference was my MO, but the truth was, it weirded me out. Jesse was always careful with his health, but rock-and-roll wasn't complete without sex and drugs. Since he'd made it big, Jesse's life had become something beyond my comfort zone.

I thought about the warmth that surged my heart when I

saw Nick alone on the couch, how I could've wept with relief for no logical reason.

I thought of his kiss.

To be fair, I'd thought about it nonstop since it happened, but when Nick tilted his head at my silent reverie, I *really* thought about it. Then, I stopped thinking.

"Um, I want..." I whispered with a thick swallow. My hand floated to my skirt, dragging the hem up my thigh with a tickling touch. *Are you really doing this?*

Nick put his fist to his mouth. Even through the glass, I could see his gaze flick from my hand to my face and back again. "Yeah?"

I closed my eyes as the rough, dark sound of his voice washed over me. Without sight, the heavy ache between my legs glowed brighter. My thighs were warm and sensitive to the slightest brush of my fingertips. I tickled a little more, ghosting my breasts with my other hand.

"*Fuck.*"

I heard him, but the word was so soft, and I was so focused, that I didn't react. When the ache started to throb, my fingers inched between my legs. Pleasure made me hum.

Before I went further, I paused. "Should I?"

"Hell fucking yes you should."

*Hell fucking yes.* Pushing the damp fabric aside, I shuddered and bowed to my own touch. I bit down on my lip, but my head tipped back with a soft moan. "Oh, god."

"Don't stop."

I teased my clit and smiled. "I won't."

My moans got louder and less controlled as I spiraled toward climax, rolling my hips in time to the rhythm of my hand. "Oh... yes, please... *Nick!*"

Once the last wave of pleasure subsided, I stumbled on shaking legs to the closest wall for support. My heart raced, but I was too blissed to care. When I could breathe, I straightened my skirt and went back into the control room, surprised to find it empty. My legs were still jelly, so I flopped into his chair and closed my eyes.

The door to the lounge clicked open. I peeked up to see him leaning on the wall. "Where did you go?" My voice was barely a whisper.

"To clean up. Where do you think?" He laughed and walked forward, adjusting his glasses. His eyes, always a fascinating mixture of brown, green and gold, were wide behind the black frames. "Holy shit, Mel."

"You should probably take me home now." There was nothing else to say. I wasn't sorry I'd done it. If anything, the release of tension was incredible. But it was a punctuation mark on the day, not the start of something more.

He nodded. "Probably should."

I gave him the address on the way out, and we took off with the top down again. When we pulled into Dad's driveway, Nick parked and looked at the house. "I remember this." He groaned and dropped his head to the steering wheel. "God, do I remember."

"That was a long time ago," I said, maybe for both of us.

"It was." He cleared his throat. "But it was less than an hour ago that you—"

"Don't you dare." I fell over the console to clap a hand on his mouth. He laughed and tried to pull away, but I threw my other arm around his neck. "Don't say a word, Field— you *dick*!" I shrieked when he licked my palm. Nick tapped my knuckles, so I lifted my hand.

"You're not in control of this moment. Thought I should warn you."

"I'm always in control."

"Oh, really? Because, again, it was barely an hour ago when you—"

I clapped him back to silence, cringing when his tongue flattened against my hand. But he was right, and I didn't realize in time. His arm snaked around my waist and pulled. My hip bumped over the emergency brake, and suddenly I found myself in the driver's seat.

Before, *Oh my god, I'm in his lap*, could solidify as a thought, Nick's fingers dug into my ribs. I dissolved into helpless, furious giggles as my lock on his mouth failed immediately.

"Mercy, mercy," I gasped when five seconds became an eternity. "Please, stop."

"Less than an hour since you sang for me. That's what I've been trying to say. I don't know what the big deal is, Mel."

I pinched him. All he had to do was hover over my ribs, and I giggled again. "Stop, Nick, don't."

"Don't," he mimicked, but he let me swat his hands away.

I looked down as silence fell. *Oh, my god, I'm in his lap.*

My calves and feet rested between the seats, but most of me was nestled on his thighs and cradled by his left arm. I was still hugging his neck while my other palm lay on his chest. His right arm was draped across my stomach, anchoring me with the thick muscle of his bicep.

His cock was hard against my hip.

I forced myself to meet his gaze. "How the hell am I supposed to get out of this?" My body throbbed with traces of orgasm from "barely an hour ago," eager for more. All he'd need to do was slip one hand between my legs. *Good god, woman, get a grip.*

"Well, when you say so, I'll open the door and lift you

out. I realize I already broke my promise about not touching, but you technically broke it first."

I nodded. I did *not* tell him to open the door. Instead, I reached up and traced his forehead. Nick inhaled sharply but didn't move, so I kept going. The kisses of cinnamon in his chocolate-brown hair were hidden in the shadows, but I loved the slide of that soft thickness through my fingers.

Nick shivered when I stroked the back of his head. His face flushed as he shifted his hips. I withdrew, but he caught my wrist and brought it back. "Just a little more torture today," he chuckled quietly.

"I didn't mean to torture you."

"Nah, it's the good kind of torture. Keep going."

I petted him in the comfortable silence for quite a while longer, neither of us moving or speaking. At last I sighed and skimmed down the scruff on his jaw. "Better open that door."

He lifted me out and set me on my feet. My body cried to be so alone again, even though he stood right beside me. I looked up at him, clinging to the moment. "Thank you for the ride. I'm glad we had this time."

"I'll take time with you time whenever, even if you choose not to sing for me again."

"No more singing," I agreed, glad the darkness hid my blush. "I'll see you around, Nick."

He bent, letting his lips graze my ear. "Later, Mel."

# 9

## NICK

I had a new track on my phone, and it was the sweetest sound I'd ever heard.

But I couldn't listen to it yet. Memories were still too potent. I knew her breathless moans in my headphones would be more stimulation than my hand could satisfy, so I let my thoughts and the lingering scent of roses be enough...

Before bed

At three a.m.

After my alarm the next morning.

"Fuck," I groaned after that one, more pissed than pleasured. I hadn't jerked it so much since I was a 13-year-old with my first copy of *Playboy*, and still I wasn't sated. For four orgasms in twelve hours, I was a wreck.

I reached for the tissues and stared at the light on the ceiling. A day with Jesse was the last thing I wanted after nearly spraining my wrist over his girlfriend, but the text that came through as I sat up made me scowl.

> Peter: J had a long night. Let's do Friday/Saturday instead.

With Jesse's recent trips, our recording schedule had begun to unravel. Another day lost to recovery from a hangover definitely didn't help, but it was useless to argue. I sent Peter an okay, texted Rick that I was taking a personal day, and fell right back to sleep.

A few hours later, better-rested than before, I hit the gym to clear my head. As I ran on the treadmill, though, there was only one thing on my mind.

I don't think I ever volunteered to keep my hands off a girl whose tongue had been in my mouth. What would be the point? If we got that far, why backpedal to platonic good times?

But it was *Mel*.

The crazy pop-star world she was wrapped up in was something I wanted no part of. It was also the thing she was making her career on. Writing was Mel's dream, one she'd built her whole life around.

*Her life? How about you?*

Too true. I hadn't asked to be bumped up the ranks at InSight, but nothing would keep me from busting my ass on this project. This taste of creative control was something I wouldn't give up willingly.

But it was *Mel*.

Even thinking about her was a stroll across a minefield. I'd walked that danger zone almost constantly in the past few weeks. Ten years had turned Melody Thomas into a beautiful woman; her enigmatic smile and our secret encounters had me totally captivated. I craved more time with her, even if I had no control over what we did.

And, for all her "We can't," and, "Jesse's story," after last night, I didn't doubt that part of her wanted it, too.

That thought looped me back to tickling her in the car,

which took me back to the studio. Good god, her hand in her skirt, her face as she moaned my name...

I broke stride and hit the emergency stop on the treadmill, gasping from more than the run. After a few gulps of water, I threw the towel over the timer and resumed, determined to clear my fucking head for real this time.

It kind of worked. By the end of my unexpected day off, I started to remember what reality was like again. After the gym, I went to Cellar Door Studios. My buddy Jack Spencer and his group had opened the studio and named it after their band. They let me hang out and jam, which unwound me exactly like I needed.

Dinner with them was another dose of normalcy. They're successful, but not once did someone approach our table or send a bottle of anything over. Beers, burgers, and bullshit conversation defined our night out. So much more my style.

Peter's text confirming tomorrow's session came through right after I got home, and with it my twisted "reality" returned quick. The text was one thing; the damn Twitter feed that I should've never even looked at was another.


**Coming Storms @ComingStorms retweeted:**
Jesse Storms & GF Get Domestic in Franklin. Could They Be House-Hunting Next??


The photo, taken by a local news station, showed Jesse and Mel walking out of a furniture store in the small town just south of Nashville. As usual, she was incognito, but that blue scarf on her head was a little too familiar.

I scowled at the screen, the muscles in my shoulders constricted to a pinch. Bile coated my mouth as I tried and failed to block the mental image of her with him now, her legs around his back, hands in *his* hair.

*Get over it, asshole.*

I launched the phone across the room. It hit the couch and bounced to the floor, but at least I didn't crack the screen. I skulked around, played a little PlayStation to keep busy, and threw myself into bed two hours later. Staring into the dark, I remembered I'd need an alarm the next morning. My phone was still on the floor, so I stumbled through the apartment and grabbed it.

Back in the sheets, I lit up the screen and found two missed notifications.

[Maybe Mel]: It's Mel. 3 questions, but I promise they're just for me.

1. How many times have you been in love?

2. What did you think when I walked into the studio the 1st day?

3. Why'd you pick me for 7mins in heaven at that party in HS?

[Maybe Mel]: Fine, don't respond. See if I text you to avoid writing again.

The first message had come through an hour ago, the second 30 minutes later. Sleep was forgotten as I added her contact. I pictured Mel at her computer, a welcome relief after the vile thoughts of her with Jesse. Yes, it was possible she was writing at his place, but somehow I didn't think so.

Me: Sry, phone was on silent.

1. Zero.

2. Holy shit... no way... damn, she's HOT.
3. See #2.

She replied instantly.

Mel: 1. Hmm.
2. Me too...me too... hmm.
3. BS! Answer for real.

I laughed and typed.

Me: A smart, beautiful redhead? Where's the
mystery? No BS.
Mel: Ugh, I want to talk about this more, esp #1, but
too much to text. Brace for
news tomorrow, btw. Goodnight, Nick.

I put the phone by the bed and rolled to my side wearing
a smile.

"Get in here. Now."

Rick's growl the next morning stopped me mid-stride.
He disappeared into his office. "Shut the door and lock it."

"What's up?" I sat on the edge of the chair while he
glared at his computer for a long, heavy moment.

Slowly, he turned the monitor toward me. "Care to
explain this?"

*Shit. Shit!*

Frozen on the screen was a black-and-white image from
the security camera in the hallway. The time stamp was
10:22pm on July 4th. Rick stabbed a key, and the video

played. All it showed was Mel following me with her head bent to her phone, but still. *Shit.*

I glanced at my boss. "I told you I sent the tracks to the label."

He didn't blink. "You didn't mention you had a guest. A guest who looks an awful fucking lot like your client's *girlfriend*. Please, please tell me I'm going blind. Please tell me you're not—"

I held up both hands. "Stop, nope, no. Come on, Rick, you know me better than that. Do you think I'd be that stupid?" He growled. "Yeah, that's Jesse's media manager— his, uh, girlfriend—but no. No way, man. I told you about the party that day. Well, Jesse stayed the night. She asked for a ride home, that's *all*. She works around the clock, so while I sent the tracks, she just, you know, tweeted or whatever. Here, look." I fumbled for my phone and raced to find proof Mel had been working.

Rick glared at the posts, then at me. "I'm going to erase this video. And that's the last word about this, because if I even think that you—"

I jumped to my feet. "I'm gold, Cap. Don't waste another breath."

Alone in the control room, I dropped to the sofa and put my head in my hands. Nothing like a piss-your-pants reality check to start a day, but I shook off the adrenaline and refocused on the album. By the time Jesse arrived, the band was warmed up, and I'd made a ton of notes on the next track.

As Mel had mentioned, he was indeed full of news. "Nick, pack the bags. We go to New York on Monday."

I'd just entered the lounge to find Jesse ruling over everything from the center of the room. Seth and Steve were hitting the snack tray, Peter was on the phone, and Fern leaned over Melody and her laptop at the desk.

Mel was smiling. For one brief, terrible moment, I imagined crossing the room and kissing that gorgeous mouth. Then I pictured Jesse getting hold of my phone and hearing his girlfriend's crazy hot moans. He probably wouldn't punch me in either case—couldn't risk bruising his million-dollar body on a bastard like me—but one of his guys would take care of it for him. I glanced at the three of them. *Peter or Seth, definitely. Steve's too chill.*

All of this bullshit winked through my head in half a second, but it was enough to ice my blood. I puffed out a breath and snapped my attention to my client. "New York?"

"Yep, NYC. Talk to your boss and find us a studio because we're falling behind. I don't want to fuck up, but a ton of stuff just fell into place yesterday. I'm playing—shit, which show is it? I forgot, but Pete knows. Anyway, I'm playing one of the morning show's concert series on Friday morning."

He grinned and reached to high-five Peter, who slapped hands and went straight back to the phone.

Jesse barely paused for breath as he continued. "But we're going Monday because there will be promos to shoot, and Peter's got me lined up for a bunch of other appearances over the week. I might even drop in on one of the late-night shows. We'll make time for recording in the mornings. I want OJ."

At his abrupt finish, Seth thrust a cup in his hand. Jesse downed it in a couple of gulps and grinned at me. "Let's get shit done."

"Sounds good to me." *A jam-packed week in New York? Perfect. There won't be time for either of us to dick around.* I followed him into the studio.

Jesse stepped up to the mic and grinned at me. "Ready when you are, buddy."

Orgies and furniture shopping must've rejuvenated him, because Jesse was laser focused and showed no sign of fatigue. We dismissed the band per their contract that evening, the crew left, and still he wanted to rehearse. Fine by me; a grueling day left no room for drama.

We finally called the session around 9pm. When Jesse and I walked into the empty lounge, he paused and looked around. "When you get used to having people with you all the time, it's weird to be alone even for a night."

I glanced over. "No Friday plans?"

He shook his head and led us out. "Nah. I was slayed after the Fourth, and next week is sure to be wild. Once in a while, sleep is good." We chuckled together. In the parking lot, Jesse eyed my Camaro. "Sweet ride. Why American though?"

I shrugged. "My uncles owned muscle cars when I was a kid. Guess it's in the blood."

He grinned and circled my baby, asking for more details. I could talk forever about my uncles' GTO and hot rod Camaro, and Jesse was game to hear. He was a fan of Italian sports cars, which didn't surprise me in the least. What did stun me was how easily I shared with him Uncle Brian's days of illegal drag racing.

Jesse tilted his head back and laughed when I told that story. "Fucking cool, man. Very fucking cool. Alright, I'm out. Tomorrow afternoon, we're gonna finish the track, right?"

"You got it. See you then."

Celeste was out of town, so I cruised over to Ben's place to hang out with him and his brother, James. We ate pizza and drank beer while James rambled on about his plan to invent an app and get crazy rich. He'd been obsessed with this idea for over a year, so it was nothing new. More interesting to me was that Ben was almost done with Jesse's new song. We roped a couple of our musician friends in for a polishing session the next night, and then zoned out to *The Empire Strikes Back.*

While we watched, I thought about my brush with disaster. With hours and plenty of distraction in between, I saw things more clearly.

*Mel said that she was faithful to Jesse's story. She said we can't, you said you knew that. You do know it, dummy, and that's the end. Jesse won't have Peter black your eye because there is zero reason to. The job is yours, and the album is good. You and Mel are just a memory. You know damn well her career always came first. She'd never let anything sabotage that, so you're set. If she doesn't screw up, then neither can you.*

*It's fine. It'll all be fine.*

∾

Jesse nailed the fifth track on Saturday. He and the band were in and out, but I stayed to finish the edits and play with a different mix for the fourth track. I never imagined pop music could be such a blast to work with. Headphones on, all my attention on work, the rest of the world swept away for hours.

At last my alarm chimed to remind me to get to Ben's house, so I shut down and staggered out, glassy-eyed.

Only to find Mel Thomas leaning on the bumper of my Camaro.

Panic ripped through me before I remembered that the outdoor security cameras were trained on the building's entrance. The parking lot was unobserved. *Thank fuck.*

"Hi there." Her smile deepened.

I walked to her, all my warnings and discipline beginning to crumble. "Hey. What's up? Jesse left hours ago."

She looked at her hands. "I know. I worked in the lounge all afternoon. I tried texting you. I wasn't even sure you were still here, but I saw your car when I came out, so I thought I'd stick around."

"How long have you been waiting?"

"Twenty minutes?" She scrunched her nose, an embarrassed flush in her cheeks that toppled the last of my resolve.

I looked at my messages.

Mel: FYI, I'm here, if you have a minute.

"I have a minute."

She shuffled her feet. "Do you have more than one? I, ah... maybe this is silly."

"I doubt it. Talk to me."

"Do you want to hang out? I thought maybe we could. That it would be good, I mean, if we spent a couple hours together like two normal people."

"As opposed to two abnormal ones?"

She laughed and rolled her eyes. "No. Two friends. Colleagues. As opposed to, um..."

"Two people who can't keep their hands off each other?"

"Basically." She groaned. "The Fourth was ridiculous. What was I thinking?"

"You weren't." *And it was hot as hell.*

"Obviously. So, um, I thought we could hang out a little and just be... you know. Normal together. I guess. If you want?" She didn't blush this time, but her pitch was a little too high to be cool.

"We can be very normal together." I told myself this was

a smart, mature idea, but nothing about Mel Thomas in my mouth or on my lap seemed the slightest bit aberrant. Still, Rick's warning haunted me. "But Mel, we need to be careful. This could look bad if people found out."

My boss's death glare had nothing on the blue gaze that leveled me then. "Do you think I don't know that, Nick?" Her voice was deathly quiet. "You're not the only one with everything to lose."

I pushed my hand through my hair. "Is it worth it?"

"You tell me."

I didn't think. I didn't speak. And she knew my answer.

Her lips crooked up. "So, what should we do?"

"Uh, I promised my friend I'd help him finish Jesse's new single tonight. Would you want to come?"

"Sure, sounds good."

On the drive, she asked the question running through my head. "What will you tell your friends about me?"

I flexed my fingers and shook off the tension. "I'll tell them you're my friend. They don't care if I bring a girl along."

"Which brings us back to my question about your girl-friends."

"Nope. Not now. I need alcohol for that conversation," I said, half-joking. Mel hummed.

I might've been a little bit tense when I shoved into Ben's apartment and threatened violence if he asked her any questions, but after an hour or so of working with the song and Mel tucked into a chair, everything was pretty cool.

We got it polished and perfect, all thanks to Mel. She helped Ben find the right sound for the bridge, and it took all I had to keep the awe off my face.

When Ben suggested she sing on the demo, it took all I had not to staple his mouth shut.

But once we finished and the group was chilling over takeout dinner, Celeste appeared. She wasn't due back until tomorrow, and Ben's jaw unhinged at the sight of her. He stuttered a comically baffled hello while Celeste eyed Mel with obvious curiosity, but I think my expression kept my cousin from asking too many questions.

We wrapped up fast. It was obvious that we should leave the couple to their reunion. Celeste hugged me at the door and whispered that we'd talk soon. Ben clapped my shoulder and said the same.

Mel and I dropped into the car with a shared exhale. "Sorry if that was too much," I said.

She turned to me and tilted her head. "I had a lot of fun. Ben and Celeste are a cute couple. She's your cousin?" I nodded. "You got them together?"

"No, that was pure coincidence. They worked together. I hadn't seen her since she moved home from New York, even though we were close as kids. Imagine my surprise to run into her at my buddy's party."

"Were you more or less surprised to run into me?"

I laughed and rubbed my eyes, my glasses bumped to my forehead. Mel plucked them from me, cleaned the lenses on her shirt, and handed them back.

"Thanks. You were a bigger surprise... maybe. Maybe just different."

Mel nodded. "Anyone can see they're crazy about each other. His face when she came in was too cute. I like seeing two people so obviously good together." She blinked and shrugged. "Anyway, it was fun to just be Mel for a while. No expectations or image to keep. I liked it."

"If you liked it, then that's good for me." After a pause, I asked, "So, take you home?"

"If you want to."

"If I don't?"

"Then let's see what kind of trouble we can find."

We cruised downtown to prowl among the revelers along Broadway. Live music poured from a dozen different open balconies while patrons smoked electronic cigarettes under awnings out front. Drunk tourists in cowboy boots took selfies and didn't give a damn about crosswalks. Packs of bachelorette parties in matching "Bride Tribe" shirts squealed and shouted from party buses. Mel's hand slid into mine to skirt through the crowds, and I had no problem keeping it, even when the sidewalk was clear.

By midnight, we were shooting pool on Second Avenue with a bunch of guys in Skynyrd t-shirts and drinking beer to battle the humidity. After winning a little money and buying a round for our new friends, we headed to the Gulch for a calmer scene and found a table in a quiet lounge. Her face glowed in the candlelight as we told each other everything we could think to tell.

That was the night I knew I was in love with her. Too bad it didn't make a damn bit of difference with everything else going on.

# 10

# MELODY

He insisted on taking me home when the bar closed and we had nowhere else to go, saying he was sober and no way was I driving. It was the right plan; he'd stopped on a single whiskey at the lounge. I, however, was fuzzy from two glasses of champagne. I asked if we could ride with the top down and cinched my scarf tight when he indulged me.

The wind in my face woke me up a good bit, but a silly smile tugged at me even as I sobered. It had been a great night. No, check that. It had been the *best* night. Living in the moment and letting fate lead weren't things I'd done much of in my life, but this night had made up for a lot of missed experiences.

I stole a glance at Nick's profile in the dark. *And you did it all without laying a hand on him.*

Well, kind of. I did hold his hand while we walked, but that was for safety, nothing else. I also might've touched his arm at the bar to make a point, and *maybe* I hugged him when I sank the eight-ball in the side pocket. And, yes, we sat so close in the lounge that our shoulders were pressed together, but the booth was small.

Not that I noticed any of those moments. Not that my skin still tingled if I thought about them.

I edited the idea. *You did all this as friends. No need to worry. When he gets to your place, you'll get out of the car and go inside. End of story. You certainly will not grab his collar and pull. You will not confess how thirsty you are for his kiss just before his mouth finds yours and you put your hands in his hair while he...*

My stolen glance had become a dreamy gaze. I blinked hard and faced forward again. *You're exhausted. Shut up.*

The sky was periwinkle when he took the exit and navigated the back roads to my childhood home, not needing GPS or any instruction from me. He killed the engine in the driveway and leaned against the headrest. "The whole way here," he yawned, "I tried to think of something else to do, just so I wouldn't have to take you home. That's my last secret."

We'd learned a lot about each other, from fears to dreams to deeds we'd rather not remember, so I smiled at this simple one. "If you'd thought of something, I'd have said yes."

Yet again, nostalgia hit me hard. How many times had we sat in my driveway at dawn, talking just to delay our goodbye? I'd wanted those nights to never end.

I wanted the same thing now. *So the same. But so different, too.*

Because it wasn't nostalgia that kept me in his car. It was the moment, the night, the way he made me feel. Not the way I remembered, but new and different and dangerously addictive.

"NYC is going to be wild, huh?"

I stirred from my thoughts and nodded. "Not to be

condescending, but probably like you've never experienced."

He nodded and flicked his gaze over me with a sleepy smile. "I like that shirt."

I glanced at my The National tee. "It was a great concert."

"Okay, enough. We're just stalling now. Go sleep. I'll see you Monday."

*He doesn't even want to kiss you.* I tried very hard to be pleased at the progress we'd made.

"Melody?" Nick drawled when I looked at my hands.

"Hmm?"

He laughed and adjusted his glasses. "That's code for get out of the car before I try to undo the purpose of this evening."

"Dammit, Nick. Why'd you say that? We're supposed to be friends."

He dropped his hand, glasses low on his nose, and looked at me over the rims. "We're friends, kid, I promise."

I hurtled back in time.

*"Psst. Hey. There's a party tonight, kid. Are you going, or do you have to study on a Friday night?"*

*I broke the lead on my mechanical pencil when the boy beside me leaned over and whispered the question. The teacher glared through the darkness of a classroom watching a movie, and then went back to grading.*

*I ducked my head and whispered out of the side of my mouth. "I might go."*

*"Hey," he murmured, so I made myself look at him. He grinned, and I could see why all my girlfriends had his name scrawled in their notebooks. "You should come."*

That was the first time he'd called me kid, but definitely not the last. That was also the party where we wound up in the pink-carpeted closet for the first time, when he "spun" the bottle and pointed it right at me. I'd been so nervous, but he made me laugh right away. While I was still smiling, he stepped closer and said, "I hope it's okay, but I really do want to kiss you, Mel." By the time seven minutes were up, we were on the floor together.

I shivered at the memory. "Do you call every girl 'kid'?"

Nick laughed again and fired the engine, so I popped the door. "Tell yourself that if you want to."

"Actually, I don't."

"Good. Sweet dreams, kid."

"Back at you." I jogged up the walk, noting that he didn't leave until I was inside, exactly like he used to.

Dad was in the living room, stretching in his wind-breaker pants and a t-shirt. "Good morning, Sunshine."

A thrill of guilt shot down my back, but it dissipated quickly. *You're twenty-eight, not eighteen.* "Up early, aren't you, Dad?"

He nodded. "If I don't get my walk in now, it'll be too muggy later. How is it out there?"

"Muggy, but not quite as hot."

"Walk with me? Or are you too tired to keep up?"

I accepted his dare and went to change from jeans to workout shorts. While I was at it, I freed my hair and pulled it up into a messy ponytail. The air on my legs and head was refreshing after such a long, hot night.

Dad set a brisk pace around the neighborhood. We strolled along, listening to the birds waking in the trees. At last, he said, "That was a beautiful car in the driveway. Camaro?" I hummed a yes. "But not Jesse's." It was more of a statement than question, to which I murmured another affirmative. He didn't press further.

A few blocks later, I couldn't help but say, "No, Dad, that

wasn't Jesse's car. I was out with a friend last night. Not that you asked, except kind of you did."

He laughed. "It's not my business, but you came in looking pretty darn bright-eyed. Usually when you come in from an all-nighter, you're beat."

"Bright-eyed?"

"Yep. Mostly I was curious who drove a car like that."

I smiled. "His name is Nick."

Dad squinted thoughtfully. "Didn't you know a Nick in high school?"

I stumbled on my stride and came to a stop. "How the hell do you remember that?"

"He was a nice kid. We'd talk music when he'd come over to take you out." Dad raised a brow. "Same guy?"

I covered my sweaty face and nodded. "Yes," I mumbled through my palms.

"So is everything okay with Jesse? I thought you were his, uh, girlfriend."

"Nick is Jesse's producer on the album. That's the connection. But," I lowered my hands and walked on. "It's not - I mean, I'm not - I'm still with Jesse, of course. Nick and I were just, um, catching up."

"Got you." Dad nodded.

We rounded the corner back to the house. "Dad? Are you happy?"

He stopped at our driveway and faced me. "What kind of question is that?" he asked gently.

"I mean, do you wish you'd remarried?"

We sat on the porch to catch our breath. "No, Melody, I don't. I'm better off on my own. And yes, I am happy with my life. But."

"But?"

"But I worry that I raised you with too much of that attitude. You're so driven, honey. I worry I trained you to be too independent. I mean, I see you with Jesse and I worry."

"Because I'm with him?"

"Because you don't love him."

"So?"

"So how do you stay with someone you don't love?"

"It's not about that. My career—"

"Is not a substitute for a partner in life."

"Isn't it?"

"That's exactly what I worry about." He tucked my hair behind my ear. "Look at all that fire in you. Don't burn it all up on words and pages."

Frustration and fatigue made unexpected tears prick at my eyes. "Dad, it's what I *do*."

"And you do it well. But there is more to this life, and you need to find that, too." Dad's brows pulled together. "Maybe you should call your mother. She'd be a good person to talk to about this."

"My mother?" I recoiled, tears forgotten. "Why would I call her?"

The line between his brows deepened. "Angela knows a lot about self-discovery." He chuckled. "She's always trying to get me into meditation and yoga."

"Always? You talk to her?"

His frown turned into a sad smile. "Yes, Melody. Your mother and I talk every month or so. And since we do, I know she'd absolutely love to hear from you."

"Maybe if I get some free time," I muttered, perfectly aware that Dad knew 'free time' wasn't in my vocabulary.

He stood with his hand out and pulled me up into a hug that brought on another threat of tears. I didn't know why I was so raw suddenly, but Dad and I didn't need words to understand each other. He patted my back. "Come have a banana and some milk, then go sleep, okay?"

I followed him in, muddled thoughts turning to mush under a veil of sleepiness. Fuel in my stomach helped after such a long night. After finishing the milk, I crawled upstairs and almost fell asleep in the shower. I shut the blinds and silenced my phone, my eyes closed before I hit the pillow.

~

Peter emailed the week's itinerary that evening. The schedule was packed, exactly like we'd hoped. Jesse would play two late-night shows, plus a club, all before Friday morning. We were booked at the Bryant Park Hotel, and when I read the details about that, I left Dad at the grill and slipped inside to call Jesse.

"Baby girl! Ready for tomorrow?" he greeted me.

"Definitely. I just read the schedule."

"It's beautiful, isn't it?"

I smiled at his infectious excitement. "Gorgeous, Jess. I, ah, noticed I have my own room."

"Mm-hmm, a suite just for you, babe. You're happy, right?"

Anytime Jesse and I traveled together, whether on location for an *American Pop* challenge or for a show or interview after his victory, we shared accommodations. I would have my own room in his deluxe suite, or we would share a bed that he was usually never in.

I released a quick breath. "Yeah, it's great, just different."

"Well, I know you'll need space to work, and this week will be nonstop crazy. Besides, it's not like—yeah, I'm coming, I'll be down in a minute," he yelled off the speaker. "It's not like we've been close lately." He spoke with zero accusation, but I winced to recall Thursday, when I declined his invitation to stay the night.

When Jesse and I met, we really did hit it off. He was easily one of the most compelling people on the planet, and our Nashville connection gave us a common bond. The sex was good, the connection obvious, and the professional rhythm we shared magic. But, by the quarterfinals of *Pop*, invites to parties increased, and the "open relationship" conversation came. It hurt, but if the choice was to accept it or walk away, there was no choice at all.

In my heart, we broke up then, and I put everything into our work. In some horrible way, I started to look at the rare times we were together as part of my angle, another job requirement. How else could I endure all the parties and fangirls? How else could I face the bitter rejection?

Since we'd returned to Nashville, though, being in his bed had become something I couldn't stomach. Maybe it was one too many wild moments, one too many lipstick stains, or all the hours spent watching him flirt with everyone in the room.

Maybe it was me.

"Are you mad, Jess?" I asked hesitantly.

He laughed. "Not at all. Are you?"

"Of course not."

"You and me are fine. You're still my girl. We're doing this together, right?"

"Absolutely. Absolutely together."

Jesse hummed. "I always knew we would do big things, and Melody? We're getting *huge,* you know."

The smile in his voice let me say, "Damn right, Jesse. See you in the morning."

But once he hung up, I stood alone in the living room and covered my eyes. Outside, Dad hummed with the Eagles and flipped burgers. If I let myself, I could go straight back to last night, to Nick and his Camaro and that walking-on-air high he gave me.

*Keep it together. You're still Coming Storms.*

Fists and jaw clenched, I refused to fray at the edges and instead grabbed my phone again. First, I updated Twitter and Instagram with some favorite posts. It was nothing original, but enough to stay on people's feed. The notifications started to hum while I added three to-dos to my calendar before 9am tomorrow morning and emailed Peter to get the press details for each show.

"All okay in here?" Dad stuck his head inside.

"Everything's under control."

The week that followed was a hurricane, and Jesse was the gale-force wind driving it all. New York was hot, smelly, and on fire with summer energy. From morning to early afternoon, Nick and Jesse were at the studio. This was the only time the rest of us were free. I cherished those quiet hours in the air-conditioned hotel, writing maniacally as the story unfolded at lightning speed.

Every night was something new. Monday, Jesse made an impromptu guest appearance at a concert in Central Park. Tuesday, he taped a set for a late-night show. Wednesday, he had a gig in Chelsea. Thursday, the busiest day, featured a pre-concert press conference in the afternoon, and then a VIP party at the hotel's club.

The unholy three a.m. alarm the next morning had me drained like I'd run a marathon every day for the past week.

Lifting my arm to paint on under-eye makeup was painful. Thank heaven for the giant cup of coffee room service delivered when I dragged out of the bathroom.

I stepped into my shoes and peeked out the windows at Bryant Park. Even in the dark, I could see the stage crew working and fans already lined up to get in. *Tweet, tweet, tweet.*

**Coming Storms @ComingStorms**
Awake and hyped for the show! See you there! #SleepIsOverrated!

"Really, it's not," I told the screen as the elevator arrived.

The doors opened again several floors down. I retweeted a post— and then gulped the coffee so hard I burned my throat. In stepped Nick with one of the girls from last night's party.

Jesse had been in loyal boyfriend mode through the evening, showering me with kisses and dragging me to dance, but of course we'd been flanked by a crowd the whole time. When I retired, "Goodnight," had barely left my lips before he was on the dance floor with a flock of ladies. This girl had been a fixture at our table, squeezed between Steve and Nick, but I hadn't realized she'd caught Nick's interest.

*Mind your own business, Melody.*

"Morning," Nick said when our gazes connected. I nodded and looked away.

"I am dead," his companion rasped. "I can't believe I actually got out of bed for this concert."

Nick laughed. "At least you had a choice."

"Daddy's so grouchy. I wasn't *that* loud when I got to the room." She laid her head on his shoulder, her dyed-red hair tumbling down his back.

I blanched. *Daddy?*

Nick laughed again and touched her spine to escort her out of the lift. Far too awake and edgy suddenly, I followed and perched on the lobby couch. I pretended to be absorbed in my phone, but my attention returned to the two of them.

He walked her to the door and slipped a VIP pass in her hand. She put her arms around his neck and kissed his cheek. He pressed one to hers before she pushed through the revolving doors, and he ambled back to me with a groan. "Christ, I am the walking dead right now." He spied my coffee. "Can I have some?"

"You have cooties," I grumbled.

He laughed and crossed his heart. "I'm cootie-free, I swear."

Reluctantly, I passed the cup. He sipped with a happy sigh and thankful smile that curled my lips up. It was our first private interaction all week. If not for the circumstances, I'd say I'd missed him.

"Up all night?" I asked while he took several swills.

"Do three hours count as sleep?"

"Did you get that many?" My sharp tone surprised us both, but I cocked my chin. Instead of a retraction, I nodded toward the door. Nick looked from the vacant entry back to me, and I scowled. "Really? She calls you daddy and you completely forget her five minutes later?"

His eyes widened as he coughed on the coffee and fell against the couch. I snatched the cup to save the remainder of my beverage, and he buried his face in my shoulder. The deep, low sound of his laughter tickled my ear.

"Get off me," I hissed, completely lost.

Nick nuzzled his forehead against my neck, and then sat up and shook his head. "Well, now I'm awake. Lana was talking about her father, Mel. She's staying with her parents on the same floor as me. I promised her the VIP pass at the table last night."

My face flamed, so I hid behind the cup. "Oh."

He laughed again and leaned to whisper, "If you've invented a story about how I got her to call me daddy, I'd love to hear it."

"You're the worst." My lips twitched.

"Worst or best with a nickname like that?"

I bit my lip but laughed anyway. Nick's grin stretched, but I wrinkled my nose. "Her hair wasn't really red."

His laughed tickled again, partly from the sexy sound and mostly because he was still dangerously close. "Please, Mel. I know the real thing when I see it."

The elevator doors slid open, and out strolled the boys while Nick and I hurried to our feet.

Jesse fell against me with a kiss and a playful groan. "Melllodyyy, I'm beat."

Over his shoulder, I saw Nick turn away. "Aw, poor baby boy." I patted his back. "Let's go; you need makeup, big-time."

Jesse performed at seven a.m. to a lawn full of screaming fans. By ten, we were back at the hotel, eating breakfast and drinking mimosas in his suite. I reported that both fans and press had blown up social media with love for the show. We toasted once for this morning and once more for every other day this week. No doubt, New York had been a huge step forward for Jess. Next up, a killer album.

Breakfast adjourned with everyone headed to sleep some more. With all those mimosa toasts, we'd be lucky to make it into the rooms. I'd just gotten to my own floor when my phone rang. It was Jesse, summoning me back to his suite. Sleep would have to wait.

∾

Jesse and Peter were the only ones there when I returned minutes later. Jesse looked up at me, all business. "I just got a call," he began. "Ron Fancy—X-Tra Fancy?" I nodded, familiar with the hip-hop artist through my old magazine job. "He just called and invited me to fly to Europe tonight for ten days. He's doing a few shows and asked if I wanted to come party."

I sat on the edge of the couch and nodded. "Awesome, Jess. You're going, right?"

"Definitely. But Peter and I were just talking. I'm thinking of going alone, and I want your thoughts."

"What's the angle?" Always my first question.

He expected nothing less. "High-pressure, fast-moving summer, long hours working on the album and shows to boot. I need to blow off steam. Europe is where I go to relax and let loose."

"Let loose." My mind began to hum. I sat back, and my eye caught on a flash of red in the cushions. Lifting the lace panties by one finger, I gave Jesse a look. He grinned sheepishly and shrugged. I tossed them to the floor and tried to focus, but what came out was, "You're going whoring with X-Tra Fancy."

Both men grimaced. "Melody, that's not the angle," Peter grumbled.

"Yeah, yeah, I get it." I exhaled and started again as the media manager, not the former lover.

"Okay, a lost weekend." They nodded at this direction, so

I kept spinning. "This'll get a lot of attention, which is always a good thing. Press catches you going wild, gives you a little bad boy look to counter the sweet Southerner image from *Pop*. I like it, but I think we need to be ready with humility when you get home. We'll do a statement that you're recommitted to the album, maybe a personal message to followers—oh, I know. You can do a detox facility. Nothing like rehab news."

Jesse leapt into the air and threw a hug on me. "You are *brilliant*. You came up with all that just now? Peter, didn't I tell you this woman is incredible?"

His arms were still around me when I added gently, "Also, we'll need to make some kind of relationship scene." Jesse frowned as he looked back to me. I went on. "Your Nashville sweetheart is patient, but with this level of wild, there will need to be some reaction: a breakup, a fight, a grand gesture to beg forgiveness."

"I didn't think of that."

"That's why I'm here, but we'll figure that out later. Detox and the message can be prepped while you're gone. Once you're rested, we'll plan out the rest."

Peter gave me an uncharacteristically broad smile. "It's perfect, Melody."

We talked out a few more details. Jesse would take over social media with photos of his "vacation," but I gave strict instructions that he ignore the parties and let the tabloids build that buzz. His plane left that night, which left Peter with a lot of details to work through and Jesse with a serious need for sleep.

He insisted on escorting me to my room first, though. "Melody, listen." His tone was low so as not to be overheard in the hall. "While I'm gone, I want you to relax. You've been nonstop with me the whole time, and when I get back, there'll be plenty more to do. Enjoy the break. Okay?"

At my door, I turned and hugged him. "Thanks, Jess. I will, promise." I pecked him a quick kiss before he left.

It wasn't until my eyes fluttered shut that I realized what that could really mean.

# 11

# NICK

Nothing can turn you into an old man faster than surviving on roughly four hours' sleep for a week straight. I had never lived in the fast lane like that, even in my college days. After brunch, I practically needed a cane to get myself back to bed.

Drawn shades and a muted phone blocked the world until I woke from a sweet, sweet slumber, the kind where all you do at first is lie there and listen to yourself breathe. I had no thoughts, just vague ideas of how good a shower and food would be once I bothered to move.

Late afternoon sun glinted off the buildings across the street when at last I was clean and dressed. I turned my phone back on—and immediately wanted turn the damn thing off again.

*DING! DING! DING! DING! DING!*
Peter: Unexpected change. Need to discuss recording schedule.
Ben: Your boy sounded great this am! Call ASAP.
Peter: J wants a word ASAP; departs at 5.

Mel: Have you heard?
Ben: Tried calling. We have news. Hit me back
ASAP.

"I need a week off *ASAP*." I sighed and dialed Peter.

Jesse himself answered. "I'm getting into a limo right now for the airport," he began without greeting. "I'm gone for two weeks, but I swear to you we'll finish before the middle of August. Cool?"

"Uh." I estimated how plausible that was. Fifty-fifty odds at best.

"Okay man, keep the room this weekend. I'll talk to you when I'm back. Take it easy." He was already speaking to someone else by the time the line went dead.

Peter called right back. "We're meeting at the Southwest Porch in thirty."

Good thing I'd gotten some sleep; we were right back on the roller coaster. I forgot about Ben's message and headed outside.

The "meeting" was mostly an excuse for a drink. Predictably, I was the only one in the dark about Jesse's sudden Europe trip. Talk of plans for the next ten days got peppered into lazy chitchat.

Fern was the first to depart, smiling and wishing us well. Mel rose and muttered a promise to meet Peter a week from Saturday. He nodded once, and she vanished. *How the hell does she do that?* It was beyond me how anyone could not notice her, but to all three of the guys, she clearly didn't register as a person of interest.

"Nick." Steve looked at me while Peter and Seth checked

their phones. "We're going to Atlantic City tonight to play a little poker. Want to join?"

If I hadn't gone so hard all week, I might've accepted. As it was, I shook my head. "Appreciate it, but I think I'll see what kind of trouble I can find around here."

"Okay then. Call me if you need counsel." Steve laughed and stood to follow the other two, but he paused at my blank stare. "I'm a lawyer, dude." He looked over my shoulder and took off running. "Wait up, you dicks," he shouted after Seth and Peter.

On my way upstairs, I dialed Mel. "Steve is a *lawyer*?" She laughed and affirmed. "So what is Seth, Jesse's personal physician?"

"Financial manager."

"Shut your mouth."

"You thought they were just bros, didn't you?"

"Why wouldn't I? I could barely tell them apart for weeks, even though they look nothing alike. They're like some kind of entity."

"I gave them nicknames to learn who was who. Steady Steve and—"

"Smartass Seth?" I filled in, grinning so hard my face hurt.

She gasped. "How did you know?'

"That's what I called him." I laughed harder at the delighted giggles coming through the phone. "They're okay, but I didn't think they literally kept Jess's shit together."

"I know, but Jess believes in them. Where are you?"

I stepped into my room and told her as much, then asked her what she thought about the Europe plan.

"I think it's good for him," she said right away. "And it's good for me, too. I need a break."

"From what I've seen, I'd say you've earned it." I stared

out the window, shuffling from foot to foot. "What are you going to do with your free time?"

"I just want to be Mel for a few days," she said softly, and I was way more pleased than it was my business to be. "What about you? Plans tonight?"

My tone was serious even though I grinned. "Yes. I have a date with what Celeste touts as the best pizza in the city."

"That's a good plan."

I took the plunge. "Want to join?"

"I thought you'd never ask." Her smile was audible. "But, ah, how about you pick me up first?"

I stopped shuffling. My pulse changed tempo. "Yeah? When? And would you prefer a dozen roses or just a corsage?"

She laughed. "Now. Forget the flowers."

Out the door in a blink, I stabbed the call button for the elevator and tried to reason through this. *She'd never do anything crazy. It's not what you think.* I could've had it tattooed on my eyelids, and I'd still have damn near sprinted down the hall to her room.

*It's not what you think*, I told my dick again as I knocked.

Mel called to me through the door. "I said I wanted to be Mel for a while, right?"

"You did."

"Okay. Because if you laugh, I'll never forgive you."

I chuckled once before the door opened, and I forgot everything I ever knew.

She stood, hands clasped behind her back. I think she wore a dress, but all I could see was her hair spilling over her shoulders.

Her *red* hair.

# 12

# MELODY

"No fucking way," he finally stuttered. "What the *fuck*?"

"You didn't know it was fake?" I swallowed as much of my nerves as I could.

"I figured it was dyed. Didn't think about it." He still gaped at me, so I exhaled and ran a hand over my head. His eyes darkened as they followed the movement. "Do that again," he said, so I did.

The door banged shut. My shoulders hit the wall. Nick's audible breath fanned my face while his body pinned me in place. Not that I wanted to move. He threaded his fingers into my hair and watched intently as they moved down from my scalp once, then again.

"I know I promised not to touch you, but you didn't prepare me for this." His voice was deep and hypnotic while he fingered the ends on my shoulder. "Mel," he pleaded, both of us knowing he didn't need to say another word.

My eyes burned from the wicked ache in my legs. It was so heavy that I didn't know how much longer I could stand. I arched up off the wall and flung my arms around his neck.

He caught me and swept me off my feet as our mouths fused together.

I'm not sure if I walked, floated, or was carried across the suite to the bed, but we got there still kissing. Nick fell backward, his palms on my thighs to hitch up the dress. My knees pinned his hips. While we kissed, he caressed my bare legs, a soft but sensuous stroke that tickled and thrilled me all at once. It sank into my consciousness that the rhythm of his touch matched the rhythm of our kisses— and the rhythm of my hips rocking over the ridge in his pants.

We were a song.

That crazy, romantic thought heated my blood even more. I reached between us and flipped the button on his fly. We both groaned when I flexed against him. His warm body through only the thin material of our underwear was *so* much better.

I flexed again and found myself on my back. He slung the waistband lower on his hips and teased himself against me. "You're so fucking *warm*."

"Why do you think I called you?"

He laughed. We fell together, his hands all over my body, his kiss making my toes curl like it always had. His tongue dared me to open to the delicious taste of his mouth until I could barely breathe and didn't really want to.

Like always.

Nick's glasses bumped my cheek when he sucked on my neck, his body rolling gently against mine. My face was fire, and I knew I was crimson from my hair to my chest. Between my legs, we were both wetter by the second.

*Be careful. You can't lose control.*

Slowly, my eyes opened. I rolled away to sit up and get my head together. "Just once."

Nick propped up on his elbows. He pushed the frames up his nose as his eyes focused again. "What?"

I began to unbutton his shirt. "We need to—take this off." I interrupted myself when I finished the job. He grinned and obliged. "We just have to cut the tension and—god, you grew up."

My point was never going to be made at this rate. How could I concentrate on anything but his biceps and lats, the cut of his abs, the hair that dusted his chest and whispered a line down to his jeans? My gaze walked over his body and back up. *Damn.*

Nick touched his glasses again, his lips curled in the closest thing to shy I'd ever seen from him. "Thanks?"

I resisted a flutter of nervous giggles and swallowed hard instead. "Um, I was saying that we need this. Just once, and it'll—"

"No." Nick's jaw set. He stood and crossed his arms.

I scrambled to my knees. "No?"

"No, Melody. Not a one and done. You don't get to control this story. We have as much as we want, or not at all."

"I can't."

"I know." He softened and knelt to face me. "But you can for tonight. If we do this tonight, we do it *as much as we want*. No rules but that."

My pulse raced again. Nick hesitated, and then reached out both hands and traced my jaw, down my neck and out to flick the tiny straps of my slip dress off my shoulders. The blue silk sheath slid down to reveal the satin of my strapless bra. Slowly, he lifted his gaze back to my face and waited for an answer.

*You don't get to write this story. Can you handle it?*

"Only tonight. But we—"

I tumbled to my back, knees untucked and wrapped around his hips all in a fluid motion. Nick kissed me deep and hard, but then jerked his head up. "Do you trust me, Melody? Do you trust me to drive you wild but stop the second you say?"

I nodded, zero hesitation.

"Good. If you want me to stop, let me know. Otherwise, the next words you say will be, 'please Nick, just like that.' Understand?"

*You are out of your league.* It was my last thought before everything turned to mush and want. "Uh-huh," I whimpered—I, Melody Thomas, *whimpered.*

Suddenly, Nick was off the bed and hauling me to the edge. I watched him drop to the floor and ghost kisses on the inside of my knees until I shivered. He tugged my underwear down my legs with a mischievous glint in his eyes. "As much as we want. As much as you can take."

I screamed when his tongue slid between my lips. My hands flailed wildly as I grabbed for the bedspread, his hair, my hair—anything to find some steadiness to my rocking world. "Oh, please, like that, like that, Nick, yes."

*Mm-hmm,* he hummed and added two fingers.

I got still, eyes closed, chest heaving at the steady pulse and gentle kiss that made the ache in my abdomen heavier and heavier. When his tongue flicked rapidly against my clit, I went off. Nick didn't let up until I shivered and tensed, but when he withdrew, I wanted him back immediately.

"Mel." My name tickled my thigh.

"Hmm?" I sighed, buzzed and blissed.

Nick stood up and gazed down at me. He ran a finger across his mouth and blinked. Pinching his thumb and index finger, he held up a single copper-colored hair.

I groaned and hid my face, but Nick smirked and leaned against the wall. "Take the fucking dress off, Melody."

The rough command in his voice would've had me walking on coals if he suggested it. I struggled to sit up but paused to see him reaching into his boxers.

"Show me," I whispered.

He crooked a brow and dropped everything, fist gripped firmly around his... *His perfect...*

I could've come again right then.

My legs wobbled when I stood to shimmy out of the dress. I couldn't take my eyes off his cock in his hand. Between the sight and the post-orgasmic bliss, *blank* was the best word to describe me.

"Your bra, too, gorgeous."

"Oh, right." Shaking fingers finished the job before I plopped down on the bed and beckoned him over. When he stood in front of me, I reached out and palmed him, leaning forward to trace his crown along my bottom lip. Tasting him woke my body from its clumsy stupor. My grip tightened as I opened my mouth.

"Sweet fucking lord."

Triumphant pleasure surged through me at his ragged groan. Finally I wasn't the only one undone. I licked from base to head, closed my lips around him again, and began to suck. Nick flexed to me. Another groan from him through the room, and my blood ignited.

"Shh, shh, wait," he strangled as the tang of come on my tongue intensified. Nick cupped my jaw and pulled back gently, smiling down at my bewildered frown. "We've got a long way to go."

*We do?*

We did.

Nick tossed his glasses on his jeans and lowered on top

of me, our naked bodies together, so much to touch and kiss and learn. When we'd explored each other in depth, he kissed the curve of my breast and murmured, "Just let me know when you need to come again."

"I need to come again."

He laughed and touched my nipple with his teeth, making me shiver from head to toe. My request went unheeded in lieu of more kisses, but saying the words had built an urgent ache in me. *Don't whimper again. Play with him.*

I raked my nails through his hair and watched goose bumps break on his shoulders. He answered by pressing his knee between my legs, and I caved. "I need it, Nick."

Why would I expect anything but a smile? He hummed and pressed again, so I reached between my legs to ease the ache myself.

My hands slammed above my head, his cock slammed into me, and we both shouted with relief. "I wondered how long you'd hold out." He slid out and in with a groan. "I don't have a condom, dammit."

My nails cut into his ass when he started to back away. "Stay unless you shouldn't. I've got an IUD and am perfectly clean."

"I'm good," he gritted between his teeth. "I don't without protection, and my last test was—"

I rolled my hips and shut him up. Hunger for release built quickly as we began to move. "Harder... fuck me harder," I wailed, even hotter when he roared at my pleas.

But it wasn't just talk. I did need it—and I wanted to ask for it. I wanted him out of control and in command; I wanted all he wanted to give, and my body knew without question that he wanted to give it all.

He grunted and sat up, hooked my ankle on his shoulder

and reached between us. I gazed up at his flushed face set in concentration as he thrust harder and tapped his fingertips against me.

"*Nick*," I screamed when I went off from deep in my core and my clit at the same time, both points of release glowing white-hot. Pleasure had me bucking up to his hand and cock, greedy for all I could get while I rode this wave to the end.

"Christ," he said hoarsely when I went slack, spent like I'd never known before.

I reached for him with rubbery arms and wrapped my legs around his calves. My parched lips sucked little kisses on his neck while he went harder, faster, wilder, until sweat slicked his back. "Now," I rasped, and this time, he obeyed.

# 13

# NICK

*Fuuuuucccccckkkkk*

The word scrolled in all caps through my brain while I caught my breath in her arms. With every heartbeat, it alternated between a cry of total elation and a groan of complete, well, fuckedness. I almost couldn't bear to see what came next.

She tapped my shoulder, and I lifted up. Her eyes were still hazy, her smile a dopey expression I didn't know Mel could make. "I'm so thirsty. Could I have water? Or maybe whiskey?" she whispered.

My muscles were as loose as her smile, but I stepped into my boxers and went to the mini bar. Mel wrapped my shirt around her and accepted the water. I sat on the edge of the bed and watched her apprehensively while we swapped drinks. The bourbon brought a little sharpness back to her expression; she cleared her throat and palmed her forehead.

"That's better." She laughed softly. "God, that was a lot."

*A lot? You think, Mel?* I'd never been that turned on or held out that long. I'd never known a sound, sight, or taste sexier than unleashed, ecstatic Melody Thomas.

I shoved my hair back and exhaled. "That was..."

Her lazy smile flashed under pink cheeks and told me I'd said all I needed to. She hugged the shirt tighter and sipped the whiskey again before passing it back. I drained it and tried to think.

"I'm starving," she said at last.

"Right. We were going to have pizza about two hours ago. Do you still want to go? I need a shower." I smirked to acknowledge that I was covered in her from my knee to my nose and licked my lips. Traces of roses and her desire had me ready to reach for her again, but I made myself stand up and get dressed.

Her brows knitted. "I know the pizza's supposed to be good."

"Amazing, Celeste says."

"But maybe we could get room service or takeout instead."

My hand froze above my jeans on the floor. Mel curled her arms around her bent knees and gazed up at me.

"We could do that," I said slowly.

"We have tonight. I don't want to..." I twitched a brow, and she finished her thought: "To leave the room."

*Fuuuuucccccckkkkk.*

She fell back against the pillow when I crawled across the bed. "My shirt's going to smell like roses," I said against her lips.

"I'll have it laundered."

"Not on your life."

"Is the smell too strong? I only wear a drop or two."

I nosed her neck, and she giggled. "It's perfect. Where do you put the perfume?"

"Not perfume, essential oil. I put it here." She pointed where I'd kissed. "And here." Now she pointed to her heart.

I lifted my head and looked down at her intently. No doubt could she feel my cock stir between her legs, but I tried for reason. "We should order food, right?"

Mel's arms wound around my neck and tugged. "We will. Soon."

Twenty minutes later, I was on my back and shouting as she sheathed me inside her again. My shirt fluttered while I ran my hands up and down her body. Mel let her head loll as she rode me. Her hair rippled like silk, puffy lips parted intently while her hands rested on my chest. "Oh, Nick, so good," she breathed. "I, I just..."

"I know." I pinched her nipples and grinned when she thrust into my hands for more. Alternating between pinches and a light tickle drove her *wild*, bouncing harder with frustrated grunts of pleasure that had my orgasm ready to unload. Faster and faster, harder, her body arched for my touch as her face turned dark red before that single moment where the world went mute.

I stared, mesmerized by all that fire flying behind her when the threw her head back. The sound of her satisfaction finally registered, hoarse and perfect and a thousand times more potent than her studio performance.

Mel slumped forward, and I caught her and rolled us over. The satiny skin of her thighs hugged my hips. She lifted her knees and drew me inside as deep as I could go. I thrust with a slow, lazy rhythm just to savor every inch— and every second. Mel's eyes opened, cloudy again but wide and happy.

"Your hair makes me so hot," I panted, braced above her. "It makes me want to fuck you even more than I did before."

"You are fucking me."

I barked a laugh. "I'm trying to talk dirty. Help me out."

A beautiful smile broke on her face, which was exactly

what I'd wanted. I bent my head to steal a kiss and picked up speed, mumbling explicit truths about how desperately I wanted her, what I wanted to do to her. Her eyes fluttered shut as she wound up, nails sunk deep in my shoulders. Release pooled low in my gut, and I ground hard against her open body. She stuttered my name, and we both let go.

"Damn, Nick." Her voice was muffled against my chest. I lifted up slowly. Mel shook her head. "For a second, I thought you were serious about trying to talk dirty—what did you *say*?"

Honestly? I couldn't remember. I shrugged, and Mel began to laugh. She swung her legs off the bed and teetered to the bathroom. "Well, it was hot," she said over her shoulder.

I scraped enough brain cells together to find my glasses and boxers. She returned, dressed in nothing but panties and my shirt, and I dropped hard to the mattress. "You walk around like that, and I'll never get off this bed again."

God, her smile was radiant. She pulled her hair up in a messy ponytail and walked barefoot to the table for her phone. "We need to eat. What should we have?"

"Whatever will deliver fastest. I'm fucking starving."

Mel leaned in the doorway between the bedroom and living room and laughed while she looked at her phone. "We'll be eating in fifteen minutes. How about Middle Eastern?"

"Works for me."

The dial tone hummed, and Mel stared at the ceiling until—"Good evening," she purred in her work voice. "I need dinner for two delivered to the Bryant Park Hotel for Jesse Storms... As soon as possible, please. Your best dishes will be fine. Appreciate it so much." She hung up and wiggled her brows at me. "And now, we tweet."

The food arrived in ten minutes. Mel worked her media magic again while I spread the steaming dishes out on the table. "What are you saying?" I asked.

"Just checked Jesse in at the restaurant and shouted out their food."

"They didn't even charge us."

"Nope, but they'll make it up in business when they're rushed with fans for the next twenty minutes."

"This life is crazy." I dove into the shawarma and quit my muttering.

We didn't talk much over dinner, we were so hungry. Stuffed with rice and meat, I reached for a piece of baklava, but Mel swiped it first. I glared at her, and she cocked her head—then straddled me and held it to my mouth.

"I'm feeling ridiculous tonight," she said, licking honey from her fingers.

"You can feel however you want, as long as you sit in my lap to do it."

"You look at me, and I feel... different."

"Aroused?"

She glared, but then blinked guiltily. "Yeah."

I reached around and let my hand follow the curve of her ass between her legs. Her pupils dilated as she inched forward. "Don't," I murmured. "Push back. Let it feel good."

She took a slow breath and did as I said. I pressed harder, saw the blush creep up her cheeks. "How much more can you take, Mel?"

"I don't know," she sighed. "But I really want to find out."

We didn't leave the couch. I kept her on my lap, helped her ride her pleasure to the end and then help me get there, too, marveling at the depth of desire between us. *How did we ignore this all those weeks? How did we not jump each other the second she walked in?* With her head on my shoulder and her breathless gasps in my ears, the idea seemed perfectly plausible.

Mel kissed me gently and stumbled to her feet with a low groan. "God, my legs."

"You're welcome." I smirked and followed her back to the bedroom just as an alert on my phone went silent. Glancing at the screen, I hissed a breath. "Ben's tried calling three times tonight."

"Call him. Meanwhile, I have to clean up. Again."

My smirk deepened, and she poked her tongue at me before disappearing into the bathroom. I sat against the pillows and returned the FaceTime call.

Ben picked up after two rings. "There you are. Been trying to reach you all day."

"Yeah, sorry about having shit to do."

"Dick." He shook his head. "How's it going?"

I pressed my mouth into a line that dissolved into a sloppy grin. "It's—uh, yeah." I laughed, unable to get rid of this ridiculous feeling. "It's good, man. Pretty damn great."

His brows went up. "You look like you've been deep in the bottle. Partying hard with Storms?"

My cousin appeared over his shoulder, her eyes narrowed at the screen. "He's not drunk," she declared. "He just got laid."

I put my finger to my lips, and they both laughed. "Was there a reason you two called me fifteen times? Or are you such a boring old couple by now that you're living vicariously through me?"

"Hardly, douchebag. We've got news, and Celeste insisted we tell you first—" Ben's words cut off when she thrust her left hand at the camera.

An elegant diamond winked at me. I recognized it immediately. Months ago, Ben dragged me along to help choose it. *About time you got the nerve to ask, bro.* Why he'd been nervous and stalling for so long, I had no idea, but now wasn't the time to give him shit.

The ring and my cousin's broad smile made me whoop. "Hell yes! Congratulations, guys!"

Celeste glowed. "You had to know first. We're having the family over tomorrow, but," she rolled her eyes, "favorite cousin and all."

"Damn right." My face ached from grinning.

Mel emerged from the bathroom and climbed onto the end of the bed. I glanced up with a silent promise to be done soon.

"When did he finally ask?"

I think Celeste said, "Saturday night," but my attention drifted to Mel. She wasn't doing anything really, just sitting there toying with her hair, but tonight she was mine and—

"Earth to Nicholas," Celeste shouted.

I jumped, flashing them a guilty smile that earned me two middle fingers to the screen. Celeste huffed. "What's the deal? You go off with the pop star, and now you're banging groupies? What happened to Mel?"

"Who?" I barked. Mel clapped a hand over her mouth to muffle a little squeak.

Celeste pursed her lips and ignored my snarl. "Uh, hello? The quiet girl from last week? She was nice. You seemed to really like her."

I looked up. Mel's palms were pressed to her cheeks. Rolling my eyes, I returned to the screen. "I do really like her." My admission got a tiny smile from Celeste, but I shook my head and lightened my tone. "Who cares about me? You two are getting *married*."

That broke the mood. I promised Ben a bottle of expensive whiskey when I got home and made Celeste vow to defend me to the family and not let them strategize about setting me up with a bridesmaid. Just the mention of wedding stuff had her over-the-moon happy, which had me the mirroring her mood as we said goodbye.

I tossed the phone aside to see my red-headed angel on her back, legs crossed in the air. She turned sleepy eyes to me. "You like me?"

"You didn't hear that," I grumbled as I lay down beside her.

She stroked my jaw. "I thought I did. It sounded nice. And anyway, I like you."

My heart skipped. To hide it, I grasped her wrist like I was going to kiss her palm—but licked instead.

"Jerk." She slapped my chest. "God, you make me laugh. You made me laugh during sex. Who does that?"

"Who doesn't?"

Her voice and smile turned wickedly saccharine. "What happened to Mel? She was a nice girl, Nicky. So very *quiet* and *nice*."

I laughed and rolled her to her back. "She's not quiet *or* nice. She's loud when she comes, and she let me go down on her before I even got her clothes off."

"Wait, no I—" Mel slapped my chest again, but she squealed when I gripped her ribs. "I'm not... *stop*," she wheezed, thrashing underneath me.

I let go and settled beside her again. "You are the most ticklish person I've ever known. And a pretty bad liar."

Her hand rested on my jaw as our breathing quieted. "It's late, and you're sleepy," she said when my eyes closed.

I denied it though a yawn and lifted my head to look at the clock. "Eleven-thirty." I raised a brow. "Does tonight end at midnight?"

Those blue eyes said enough.

I reached for her, suddenly alert again. "Hmm, I think you want me to stay."

"You can go if you want." But her fingers were in my hair, and her voice was the sexiest tease I ever heard.

I laughed. "I think we'd both rather come, kid."

## 14

## MELODY

I woke the next morning with my leg thrown over both of Nick's, my head on his shoulder. He was sound asleep. *No wonder, when you woke him for sex at four a.m. God, how many times did we even do it?* Although certain delicate muscles felt like they'd been through an Iron Man competition, I acknowledged the fact that more sleep was impossible— and that I really, really needed to clear my head.

I made my way down the block to a nearby gym and set the elliptical to a "rolling hills" workout, but the real rolling terrain was in my mind. Ideas, excuses, and ways to angle this situation for the best damage control bounced around and left a queasy knot in my stomach until my phone chirped.

Peter: J's great. Enjoy your time off.

After that, everything got a lot smoother. What I wanted became a lot clearer, too.

I don't know why I was so disappointed to return to an empty room. The "only tonight" rule was my doing, but the silent suite and rumpled bed still made me frown. Doubts gathered at the edge of my new plan, but I brushed them away and went for a shower.

At the gym, I'd refused to entertain even the vaguest memory of last night, but now, under the stream, I closed my eyes and let my mind wander.

*Sweet fucking lord... I do really like her.* I shivered despite the hot water at the memory of his words. Too eager to stand still any longer, I shut off the shower, blew my hair dry, and hurried to the closet.

My work look was usually all black, either jeans and tops or dresses. But one perk of the job was that no matter where I went, Fern kept me stocked with a wardrobe. She knew my motif, but she liked to sneak in styles that I normally wouldn't consider in case the occasion arose. I told her once that she really didn't need to bother, but she just patted my cheek and laughed.

The blue silk slip dress from last night had been one of those alternative options; the white chiffon wrap top and designer shorts I stepped into then were another. It was elegant, kind of preppy and perfect for a summer day in the city. It would've looked absurd with the black hair, but I smiled when I saw my reflection.

"Now, go be Mel," I instructed the girl in the mirror.

I thought about that on the way to the elevator. My roommate in L.A., another journalist covering *Pop*, always marveled at me. "How can you be so sure of everything?" she'd ask. "I can barely choose which shoes to wear."

For her—for most people, maybe—decisions needed time, support of others, and second-guessing. It never made sense to me to waste time thinking when I could be doing, but I also knew this was exactly what Dad meant when he said he worried I was too independent. Once I had a story, I never looked back.

*Like now, for example. No big deal; you're just going to knock on his door and... and...*

Nick opened up right away, dressed in nothing but a towel slung so low on his hips, he might as well have been naked. I managed to keep the drool in my mouth, but there was no way I could stop my eyes from sweeping over him a couple of times.

He patiently endured my ogling, a smug smirk growing more wicked. "Yes?" he drawled at last.

"Get dressed," I grumbled. "Who answers the door in a towel?" He winked and strolled back into the room while I followed behind, admiring the lines of his back and—

"Wait."

Nick stopped at my request. I reached out and skimmed a finger over the curve of his left shoulder blade, along the tattoo that followed the bone there.

"The opening notes of 'Across the Universe.' It's my favorite song."

I bit my lip and traced the music staff again. "You...You have a melody on your back."

Nick tensed, but then began to laugh. "Don't read too much into it, kid. I'm in the business." He glanced over his shoulder. "Still want me to get dressed?"

I glared and nodded. He went to the dresser while I sat on the bed and tried not to watch him drop the towel and step into a pair of shorts. He pushed his glasses on and came to stand over me. He smiled, but his shoulders were tight. "I didn't expect to see you so soon. Please don't tell me you came down to give me the old, 'It was a mistake' speech. Too clichéd to even bother with, right?"

I rose and crossed my arms to mimic his posture.

"Totally. Actually, I'm here because I ruined your plans last night. Still want to go try that pizza?" My neutral expression masked a surge of triumph when he blinked rapidly, clearly unprepared for the suggestion.

He recovered quickly as usual. "You did ruin my plans, didn't you? Yeah. Hell yeah, let's go."

We decided to walk even though it was pretty far. The day was hot, but it was nice to be outside with no agenda. We took the Highline, an elevated park, down the west side for most of the journey. When we exited into the West Village, Nick plugged the place into his maps. Kesté was a small spot on a side street, but from the moment we walked in, the smell of Neapolitan pizza had us both ravenous.

Conversation was minimal for the walk and throughout the meal. I had a lot on my mind. Stepping out of the story I'd been living for so long gave me a different perspective. One that, honestly, I wasn't sure I wanted. The questions that came with it could've kept me busy all day.

One thing I was sure of. As I sat at that table and regarded the man across from me, I knew for certain that I'd made a good plan, one with minimal risk but exactly what I needed. *We'll spend the day together. We're just two people in this massive city, no hats or cameras or crew. I get to be Mel. And later...*

# 15

# NICK

"I'm getting married," I declared when the waiter cleared the plates, leaving us to finish the bottle of wine we ordered. "This pizza is definitely my soul mate."

Mel smiled. "Do you think we could have some kind of joint arrangement?"

I drew my brows together. "I'll have to consider it. I might get jealous." We traded another smile before she went back to toying with her glass, and I went back to gazing at her.

She was a vision. It was hard to get my head around the sight of her like this in the daylight. Her lips were fuller, her eyes an even brighter blue, and her hair... oh, man. Just looking at it made me stir in my shorts. Mel's hair was a rare, true red, dark and straight. She was a fire that smoldered rather than flared, and it was fucking hypnotic.

For weeks in the studio, I had had the impression that Mel was hiding. It wasn't a nervous or shy thing; her ability to blend into a scene was how she reported on it so well. But sitting across from me in that restaurant, it was like she'd thrown off a cloak. Her energy was different, hotter and brighter, and it pulled at my soul more than ever. This was the real Mel, the Mel I remembered from so long ago.

On top of that, every other thought in my head was of last night. That probably had more than a little bit do to with the pulling sensation.

Mel opened her mouth, but hesitated before: "Is this okay? Are you, I don't know, having fun?"

"Do I seem uncomfortable?"

"No. Just, I thought maybe we could play tourist together this afternoon, if you were free. If you wanted."

I arched a brow. "Like *normal* people?"

But Mel didn't smile. Her expression fell before she looked at her lap. "If you don't want to, just say so, Nick."

"Name a time I didn't agree to your plans."

She fluttered her hands. "Maybe you shouldn't. Maybe you should say it's lame, and it would be better if we didn't. Maybe you should remind me again of how careful we need to be."

*Yeah, maybe you should.*

If we were in Nashville, if Rick and his security camera hadn't been a thousand miles away, if Jesse hadn't winged off to Europe to party, then *maybe* I would have.

Instead, I reached for her fingers. "But you keep making plans. And, to that logic, maybe you shouldn't do that." She looked up, and I dropped the casual act. "I don't know Mel, but *dammit*. Of course I want to spend the afternoon with you, kid."

The spark in her eyes, in her smile, had my blood pumping. Mel drained her wine and stood up. She kept my hand and walked us out onto the sidewalk.

We wandered up to Union Square, and then hopped the subway to Central Park. Our feet grew tired as we explored from the Pond all the way up to Strawberry Fields. By the time we bought exorbitantly priced bottles of water and sat down in Sheep Meadow, it was nearly dark.

She lay back in the grass. "Can I ask a question?"

"Shoot." I reclined on my elbows and looked over at her. We'd talked all afternoon, light stuff and commentary on the city, but this was clearly deeper.

"Am I a freak?"

"Nah, not really. I guess I was a little surprised how *much* you wanted. Not that I'm complaining. And not every girl is comfortable letting a guy go down on them right away, but it's not that strange. I didn't even spank you or—what?"

She'd turned crimson. "I didn't mean in bed," she hissed. "Jesus, Nick."

"What did you mean, then?"

Mel hid behind her hands and huffed. "I meant how I act, the life I live, how I've always been. You were so sweet back in school. We weren't even officially a couple."

"You wouldn't let me commit to you. You always said it would be over too soon, and you didn't want strings tying you down when you went to college." My throat tightened; those were details I hadn't thought of in ten years.

"Exactly." She nodded, her gaze to the sky. "And then you told me last weekend that you prefer casual dating, that you don't really 'do' girlfriends. Is that my fault? Did I screw you up?"

"Screw me up?" The tightness crept into my shoulders, but I tried to laugh it away. My confession on our epic all-nighter hadn't meant to be up for analysis. She'd accepted the information, and I thought it had been smart to let her know I wasn't trying to sneak into anything serious by spending time with her. But in this context, the implication changed.

*Did she affect me that much?*

"I'm very happy," I assured both of us. "I have family, friends, and a job I love. My relationships work for me, too. If anything, it's better to stay casual than ask someone to put up with all the other stuff I have going on." I shrugged. "Guess if I ever find someone I want to rearrange my life for —who wants to be in it with me—I'll know it."

She nodded and bit her lip as she looked back at the sky. "I'm sorry, that's not my business."

"It's fine. Keep talking."

"I was just thinking about everything. Sometimes it all feels normal, but then, if I look at it another way, it's like what I'm best at is getting men out of responsibility. Ten years ago, I told you no strings and set you free. Now, you're all about casual relationships. Meanwhile, I play girlfriend when the need arises and fade into the background when it's 'not the time' to be tied down. Hell, I singlehandedly set Jesse up for a week of debauchery. I sit there, night after night, invisible while he sucks face with..." She took an uneven breath. "Maybe it's *me*. Maybe I'm a freak."

I exhaled hard. "The Jesse thing is pretty crazy, Mel. I guess the real question is, what do you want?"

"You know the answer to that. I want my words to make people think. I want to describe the world in a way that makes my readers see it like I do. I want the ultimate story."

I stroked her arm and smiled as chills rose on her skin. "It doesn't hurt to watch Jesse with other girls?"

"Of course it hurts." Her tone confirmed the pain, and I winced. Mel glanced over at me and twisted her mouth. "Jesse isn't mine, Nick. He belongs to the world. It isn't jealousy, it's... I enjoy being the eyes on a scene, but I'm not so cold-hearted that being totally invisible doesn't sting a little."

I chuckled. "Melody? Maybe you don't know—maybe you don't want to know—but I see *no one* like I see you."

Her lips parted. I leaned in, but she got to her feet. "Let's get going."

We exited the park on the east side and rode two subway stops down to 42$^{nd}$ Street. While we swayed silently with the train's motion, I let go of the tension and got okay with the moment. We'd had a night, and now we'd proved we could spend a together like "normal" people. It didn't change how I felt about her, but it worked.

We were sweaty and grimy as we climbed up from the belly of Grand Central Station. I was mentally in the shower already, but Mel had more plans in mind.

She grasped my wrist before I could turn for the exit. "Can I show you something else? Promise it won't take long."

I followed her into the main concourse, where the sounds of people hurrying to their trains echoed across the giant marble space. Our feet slowed, heads tilted up to take in the beautiful ceiling.

"I love this," she said.

"It's awesome." I gazed at the constellations on the green background. "I saw it on my first trip to New York years ago, but it's even better at night."

Her fingers laced into mine. "One more thing. Come on."

With a tug on my hand, she led me down a sloping corridor toward the Oyster Bar. We stopped on the landing at the entrance. Hallways led off in four directions from a square intersection, each corner tiled with L-shaped columns supporting the low, arched ceiling. Offhand there was nothing remarkable about it, but she looked up at me with excitement in her eyes. "Have you heard about this?"

"Hallways? Yeah, modern science, huh?"

Mel shook her head and led me to one of the corners. She made me face the wall. "Stand here."

I looked around, glad no one was watching us. "What is this, time out?"

Mel just winked and gripped my elbow to square me to the column again. "Don't move." She disappeared and left me to study the marble.

"This, Nicholas, is the whispering gallery."

I whipped around when her voice tickled my ear, only to find her peeking over her shoulder in the corner diagonal.

Her eyes crinkled before she faced away again. "Would you care to make a confession?" Again her words came through crystal-clear, and I realized the acoustics of the arched ceiling were responsible.

Despite my decision to relax, her voice in my ear was insanely erotic. Maybe I was crazy to think so, but I flirted anyway. "I'm not sure I should," I said, pleased to hear her throaty laugh. "How about you go first?"

"Okay. You make this look when you're going to tease me. You kind of squint on the right side and smirk."

"Interesting details you've noticed, but that's not a confession."

"Hmm, well, the confession is that every time you've made that look today, all I can think about is seeing it from between my legs."

*Fuck.* Sweat pricked at my neck as blood surged to my dick. Reason went lights-out as I said, "And did you like it, my tongue in your pussy, teasing you until you came all over my face?"

She gasped, and I turned and caught eyes with her across the way before she whipped back to the corner. "No, Nick, I *loved* it. Say something else."

In a few moments' time, we'd gone from "having a nice

day" to the dirtiest version of telephone imaginable. I pressed my palm into the corner so hard it left a mark, but the pain kept me sharp enough to be coherent. "I can't think of anything else. All I can think about is the way you taste, and how your thighs felt against my head."

I glanced over my shoulder. She stood on one foot, the other wrapped around her ankle, her head bent to the wall. Even in the low light, dark fire dusted pale shoulders, contrasting sharply with that soft white shirt. She clasped her hands behind her back, and something about her innocent stance had me ready to tear her clothes off even more. *Mel, don't play with me. If this isn't real, this is cruel.*

"Then I'll go again." Her murmur commanded my full attention back to the corner. "Confession: I'm stalling. I've known all day what I wanted to say, and now I'm ready to say it." She took a quick breath. "We said one night. I wanted us to get past the tension we'd built. Now, we're past it."

I closed my eyes.

"And I want *more*," she said in this husky, needy voice. "I get to be in my own story for a few days, and I want to be me, with you, as much as I can. I had fun today; last night was unreal. I know it's crazy, but I want you, Nick. A lot."

"Sorry, I didn't hear that last part?" I clenched my teeth and tried not to laugh.

"I said…" Her hand suddenly gripped my elbow to spin me around. I turned, grinning despite all the lust in my system. "I said I want you, Nick."

"I thought I heard you say a lot."

She glared, lips twitching. "I want you a lot."

My skin heated over my whole body, but I looked around. Although no one paid us any mind, plenty of people were inside the restaurant, and an occasional traveller hurried through the corridor. I jerked my head up the hall. "Let's go."

I made it to the shadows of Bryant Park before I locked her in my arms and bent her backwards so far she had to hold on. Her fingers dug into my hair, jaw softening for my kiss. "That's what I think about being part of your story," I rumbled against her lips.

"Say no if you—"

But her caution was forgotten with another kiss which started in the park and didn't officially end until we both passed out on her bed.

Standing with my face in that corner, I'd known I would say yes to anything Mel Thomas had to give me. I didn't think about it, because if I had it would've freaked me the hell out. Instead I decided I'd stay in the moment and not think about the future. I told myself that whatever we had would be enough, but deep down, I knew that the moment she said goodbye would be one of the hardest things I'd ever face.

Harder, even, than it had been the first time she'd done it.

# 16

# MELODY

I woke tangled up in Nick Field for the second day in a row. This time, I simply sighed and let it be.

He stirred. "Ugh, how are you awake?"

"Sorry, should I go back to sleep?" I traced his eyebrows. He mumbled a yes, so I dropped my head and shut my eyes.

Nick breathed deep and began kissing my bare shoulder. "Are you asleep, Melody?" I smiled and nodded. He crawled over me. "Good. Keep dreaming," he said before his lips and hands went to work on my body.

Oh, what a dream. His gentle laziness left me breathless, blushing, and completely docile. I kept my eyes closed, dreaming indeed. Dreaming that we had all the time in the world. Dreaming that he was mine.

"Nick," I cried when his fingers pushed me over the edge. My eyes snapped open to see him wink at me as I choked on the pleasure.

"Good morning," he murmured as he lay beside me. "Sleep well?"

I collapsed against the pillow and laughed.

When we were finally out of bed and showered, Nick

offered to fetch breakfast. While he was gone, I powered on my laptop for the first time since Friday. An eternity in the world of media. Information poured in. My brain whirred, processing so much that I didn't flinch when he returned.

Nick set a large iced coffee and bagel by my elbow. "Zone face."

My attention snapped up to him. "Want an update? Jesse's already getting attention. He's done pretty well with posting stuff. Last night, the press caught him at a club in Mallorca." I showed him the picture: club lights, metallic miniskirts, and Jesse with X-Tra Fancy and about six women.

Nick twitched his brow and grunted, so I continued. "Fans are asking about a concert, but I think it's good to leave everything unanswered for now. My editor at *Now Playing* got wind of it, too, so I just emailed her back. She's supposed to call any—"

On cue, my phone rang. I went to the bedroom and shut the door. "Jan? What's up?"

"So, he's tarnishing the old reputation, hmm?" she greeted me.

"A little bit, yeah." I gave her the outline of our plan.

Jan hummed. "It's a good angle for the summer, especially with all the pressure he's been under. While he cuts loose, what are you doing, Melody?"

"Following the story. Prepping for the fallout. And, um taking a personal break."

"How will this work into your article?"

We talked for at least half an hour. She quizzed me, drawing out ideas I didn't know I had. When we were done, I wandered out to the living room and found Nick on the couch with a half-eaten bagel. The ice in my coffee had melted on top of the milk. I stirred it and sipped, noticing with pleasure that it was sweetened just like I like, and then went back to the laptop.

"Should I leave?" he asked when I completely failed to acknowledge him.

"No, you should wait."

I made notes and arrangements, and then finally closed the computer and shook myself out of the zone. By then he was lounging on the couch, watching the end of *Dazed and Confused* on TV.

"Great movie," I said with a stretch.

"Come watch." He held out his arm, so I tumbled down and let him spoon me. When the credits rolled, we yawned and sat up. "Status report?" he asked.

"Right." I got up, restless again. "Jan gave me a lot to think about. She coached me on angles for the story and inspired me to write this week while I have time. A friend of hers has a lake house about three hours upstate. It's secluded and perfect for writing. I can go there anytime, so I rented a car for this afternoon and cancelled my flight tomorrow." I twisted my fingers together and deliberated whether or not to finish telling him my thoughts.

Nick's shoulders hit the cushion behind him. He fixated on the bagel remains and nodded slowly. While the words stuck in my throat, he sighed and stood up. "It sounds perfect. I guess if you're leaving this afternoon, I should—"

"Come with me," I whispered before I could chicken out.

He dropped back to the sofa, eyes wide.

"I need this time, Nick. I'm always on the go, always busy. I could write, get some quiet, and be alone."

"With me."

My stomach dropped at the enormity of what I'd just asked. The impropriety of it laced with the tiny thought of, *yeah, exactly,* but I couldn't let that take hold. I turned away and checked my phone. "Oh, god, you're right. I can't believe I just said that. Edit. Delete. Forget it. I completely retract that statement."

Nick's hands settled on my hips. His lips landed on my neck, and I broke out in chills all over. The gentle suction of his mouth turned me on as if he'd simply flipped a switch. I moaned and melted into his body; he melted right back into me. "Problem with that is, there's no backspace button with you and me. We may have history, but I want you now. And I really like being able to tell you that."

I spun in his arms and hugged his neck. "I like it, too, but to ask you to go away with me for a week, and then come back and face reality is too much."

He dipped his head and stole my breath with a kiss. "Go away with you for a week, have sex whenever we want at a lake house, and *then* face reality. That's what you're asking."

"No, I'm not."

But Nick pulled me to his lap on the sofa and began to inch my shirt up. "Oh? Then what are we going to do, play Scrabble?"

"Stop that." I bit my lip to keep from grinning and kept his hand from going any higher. "Think about how pointless it would be, knowing that we can't keep this up—"

Nick silenced me with a dry laugh. "Then it's a good thing I'm a man of few scruples and an aversion to commitment. And, judging by the look on your face, it's pretty damn clear you want me to come."

I tried so hard to glare, but his lips just curled deeper. I sighed and leaned my forehead against his. We kissed again. "I really do, but it's foolish."

"I'm prepared to face the consequences of my actions later."

The rental car arrived a couple hours later, and the valet took our bags out to the bright blue Mustang. Nick eyed the car with distaste but insisted on driving, which was fine by me.

*This is crazy,* I chanted silently while we inched through Manhattan traffic. It was a pathetic attempt to stay rational in the face of the giddy excitement that I couldn't shake.

We crossed into the Bronx without talking. I found a nail buffer in my purse to keep my hands busy, but finally had break the silence or risk falling deep into doubts and questions.

"What are you thinking?"

Nick didn't blink from the road, but he grunted. "I hate that question. That's the kind of question that tells me it's time to part ways with a girl." I held my breath, and he glanced over. "I didn't mean you, kid."

His casual assuredness, as if it went without saying that he'd never mean that about me, made my heart flutter. "Well, what did you mean then?"

Nick tapped the steering wheel. "Usually when a woman starts asking that question, there's a right answer I'm supposed to know. Honesty doesn't work. 'Nothing' never satisfies, and the truth is usually something random like mic checks or jumping naked into a hay baler." We both laughed. "She wants the answer to be her. If it's not, it's like I've done something wrong."

"I find that many people gain confidence from being a touchstone of reliability. If you're thinking of her, she's validated as significant to you."

"I don't like that. Someone can matter without me thinking of them at any given moment."

"Another classic pattern," I agreed. "And, of course, absolutely true. I don't know, I think if she asks and you're honest, the true measure of personality is on her. If you say 'nothing,' and she calls you emotionally unavailable, then that tells you something. If you say mic checks and she's disappointed, well, that tells you something, too. Do you really want to be with a woman who needs your brain bent to her all the time?" He didn't speak, so I buffed my thumb and stashed the file. "What are you thinking, Nick?" I asked sweetly.

"What the hell is with the Bermuda Triangle?"

"What are you thinking?" I repeated, grinning now.

"Do you have to slay the dragon to be a hero? Or is the dragon inside of you?"

"The dragon's inside you." I counted to five. "Now what are you thinking?"

He laughed. "What kind of porn does Mel watch?"

I gasped loudly, but then smirked. "Why would I need porn when I can make up my own fantasies?"

"Fuck, that's hot," he rumbled. "So, what are *you* thinking, Mel?"

"About porn... Wait, no. Now I'm thinking about that pizza we ate yesterday."

"So, food porn."

"Exactly," I said between giggles.

We went on about nonsense well after the parkway traffic cleared. I asked the now-magic question again, but my humor vanished when he chuckled and said, "I ran into Seth and Steve when I got breakfast this morning. Seth saw us last night."

His conversational delivery didn't stop my blood from running cold. "*What*? Oh, god, he didn't see us in the park, did he?" Mentally I tried to spin, to find an explanation—

"No, right before we got to the hotel."

"I'm not sure why you're smiling like this is funny." I grabbed one of the complimentary bottles of water in the cup holder and sucked down half of it.

"It's funny because he had no idea it was you." Nick swiped the bottle and took a long drink. "He said—what the hell is wrong with this water?" he interrupted himself, lips wrinkled as he thrust the bottle into my hand. His tongue lashed out twice in a comical picture of disgust. "It's molded or something."

I looked at the label. "It's cucumber infused."

Nick shuddered. "Cucumbers are disgusting. How dare you poison me with such a vile tonic?"

I dug in my purse and found a stick of gum to feed him. Laughter was perfunctory by then. "It's a small penalty for scaring the hell out of me. Are you *certain* he didn't know?"

He snorted. "Absolutely. The gist of the conversation was, 'Damn, dude, where'd you find that redhead?' There were a few follow-up questions I'm too much of a gentleman to repeat."

I groaned and palmed my forehead. "Ugh, douche chills. Seth is the world's biggest bro. I can imagine the rest."

"Go on."

"Please. Redheads get the same crap all the time. Is that your real hair? Ooh, you're made of fire, huh? I bet you've got a temper. And always, always the coup de gras: does the carpet match the drapes?"

Nick laughed so hard I had to grab the wheel for a second. "Uh-huh." He rubbed his eyes and took control again. "That one definitely came up, along with the temper question."

"Because of course they did." I smoothed my ponytail.

"Did you know that blue-eyed redheads are less than one percent of the population?"

"Hmm, I knew you were one in a billion." He kissed my hand.

"Cute line, Field." It still made me blush.

He glanced over. "For someone who wears a wig, you sound pretty proud of who you are."

I frowned. "The wig isn't because I'm ashamed. It just, I don't know, I wasn't having any luck finding work, and on impulse I changed my look. Next thing I knew, I had a job and got assigned to *Pop*. It became my work identity. Now, there's no way I can ditch it. A good thing, given what you just said."

He nodded. "Does Jesse know?"

"Yes. None of the rest of the crew do, though." I shifted in my seat. "What are you thinking now?" I teased when he didn't speak.

His smile was beautiful, even in profile. "You asked if you influenced my relationships? I'll tell you one thing you did impact is my fucking affinity for redheaded women. But," he glanced at me again, voice lower. "I've never known a woman who can compete with your natural beauty, Mel Thomas. That's the damn truth."

"I don't believe that for a second," I muttered.

He shook his head. The speedometer inched higher as we merged into the left lane. "Put on some tunes and make them good. Then tell me whatever is on your mind."

I didn't tell him any of the things I was thinking while I toyed with the Bluetooth and cued up The Lone Bellow on Spotify . I didn't tell him that no man ever took my breath away like he could, that no one could make me feel so beautiful with just one look. I didn't tell him that no one ever turned me on like he did, or that sex with him was the most amazing connection I'd ever felt to another human being. I didn't know how, couldn't set it up to be sweet and light enough to be safe, and we were already on such dangerous ground with this trip. Instead, I told him about my latest segment, sang along with the music, and took his words and put them deep, deep in a safe place in my heart.

# 17

# NICK

I told myself I went for the sex. She was incredible. Her rose-scented, satin skin was so delectable that when I was with her, I lost the ability to think of anything else. After two days of such intense lust, it was easy to reason that the promise of a week of sex was what had me standing on the second story porch of this house. But, as I stared at the dark water below and thought of a purple prom dress from a million memories ago, I knew damn well that it was so much more than that.

"Thinking of mic checks again?" Her voice broke my thoughts; the sight of her affirmed everything I didn't want to know.

"Not this time," I replied, trying to shake my conscience. "More like... how deep this is."

"The water or the situation?"

How did she know so much? Why did she have to be the girl who got me like no other? Or, conversely, why did she have to be the girl I had no business messing with?

My conscience was a stubborn bastard lately.

"A little of both," I admitted.

She brushed a strand of hair off her face and leaned on the rail with me. "It's a beautiful house, isn't it? I didn't realize it would sit directly on the water." Her voice lowered. "Are you sorry you're here? It's okay if you are."

"I'm not. But." I didn't know how to finish that thought succinctly.

"Yeah, I know."

I knew she knew. It had taken so little effort to find that connection to her again, and not just the physical part. I'd noticed Mel because she was smart and beautiful; I'd fallen for her the first time because being with her was effortless. And now, a couple of evenings hanging out—okay, and making out and masturbating in the studio—and that effortlessness was right back. It helped, knowing that she understood what I couldn't put words to, but then again it made everything worse, too.

I shook my head to clear it. "Well, only one way to learn. Hold these." I pressed my glasses into her palm and stripped down to my underwear. Mel's eyes widened, a question forming on her lips that I ignored as I climbed over the porch rail.

"Hell no!" Her voice defined shrill when I sat on the rail and looked down. "You are not going to jump."

"Why not? I already did." I don't think either of us missed my double meaning.

She grabbed my arm. "Don't! It's not safe."

"Who said life was safe?" I blew her a kiss before leaping out.

Cold water blasted my worries away as soon as I hit the lake. My jump plunged me deep into an even colder thermocline that tightened my lungs. Exhilarated, I broke back to the surface, gasping and whooping.

"I take it you're alive?" she shouted.

"Incredibly," I called back as I swam to the dock. "Your turn!"

"Not a chance. I'll be right down." I couldn't see her up on the balcony without my glasses, but she appeared in a moment from the side of the house with a beach towel. "You're out of your damn mind," she scolded.

"That's part of my charm."

Her upper lip curled in a scowl, but then she laughed. "Dammit, that's true."

I set the towel and my glasses on the deck chair and stepped to her. Mel backed up, but I advanced. "You love that I jumped. You love that now you're thinking about it, too. You're afraid, but you're wondering how cold the water is. You're thinking of how it would feel to—"

Her shriek pierced my eardrums when I swept her into my arms and threw her off the dock. She hit the water on her ass, the skirt of her sundress the last thing to submerge. I jumped in after her.

"You fucking bastard, it's cold," she gasped. "I hope you get hypothermia on your dick for this."

I laughed so hard I worried I'd drown while I swam to her. "You're adorable when you curse."

She screeched and lunged to shove me underwater. I went easily so I could cop a feel of her body as I resurfaced. "I meant every last word," she vowed.

We treaded water together, my mirth and her ire both subsiding. When she blinked, the droplets of water on her fair lashes made her eyes bluer. She spit a mouthful of water at me and swam for the dock. "What am I supposed to do now that I'm all wet?" she called as she hauled herself up the ladder.

*Aw, hell yeah.*

"*All* wet, Mel?" I asked in her ear the moment I was on

the planks and had pulled her close. She nodded, so my fingers went to work on the tiny buttons of her dress. "Are you still mad at me?"

"Uh-huh."

Chills broke out over her bare skin when I peeled the top of the dress away, but Mel smirked. "What can you do for me when your dick's frozen, kid? You're getting pretty fresh for someone with literal blue balls."

"Hmm, let's find out."

Lips locked, tongues tangled, we made it to the living room before we hit the floor. Our cold, damp skin warmed fast, especially when I put her on the couch and knelt between her cool thighs to find the pure heat of her pussy. Her breasts rose and fell under labored breaths, fingers in my hair, tugging with growing insistency as she twisted her hips.

I realized she was talking.

Then I realized what she was saying.

She begged for more, told me what she liked and how she liked it, described what I did to her. Curses and a fucking gorgeous tapestry of obscenity fell from her lips and had me sweating with want.

I pulled back with a roar. "Goddam, Mel," I think I said before diving back to taste her ocean-sweet want again, adding my fingers this time and getting her over in a blink.

The moment she was still, I pushed her knees open wide and lifted her ass to shove a pillow underneath. I needed to be in her as deeply as I could. "Keep talking, gorgeous," I said against her neck.

She hiccupped a laugh and put her lips to my ear. "You're adorable when you fuck."

I have no idea why that made me come so hard. I didn't even know you could laugh through an orgasm.

Mel yelped when I fell against her, but then she held me lightly, stroking my back. "I'm glad you came with me," she said softly.

"Me, too."

That set up the week. She wrote, I read, and we hiked, ate, talked, and fucked whenever we pleased. Meanwhile, Jesse slowly unraveled his clean image over in Europe as planned, and the few texts I bothered to check said that my people were clearly concerned I'd lost my mind—which, in a way, I guess I had. Whenever the world got too close, we would look at each other and laugh, a general up-yours to reality, and then it was just us again. It was kind of like a weeklong Seven Minutes in Heaven, which is both amazing and completely unsustainable. No matter; it was without a doubt the best week of my life. I would've been fine if Saturday never arrived.

# 18

## MELODY

"I just can't handle it."

My mother said those words before she left. From that day forward, it was my mission to be her opposite and face life head-on. I discovered writing as a child. After she left, it became my passion, the place I could control the world and prove what I could be, a challenge I never tired of meeting. Part of why Jesse and I bonded so well was because both of us thrived on pushing hard to get what we wanted. I'd often flattered myself with the notion that not everyone could keep up with him like I could.

For someone who spent most of her years climbing the rungs of a life she created, my complete contentment at that lake house was a new feeling for sure. I didn't have to even think about letting go to make it happen. I didn't decide how it would be; it just *was*.

My writing flowed for hours each day, infused with fresh life thanks to the attention I could give it. I turned off my phone when I was done working. I was liberated.

Maybe the trip would've been that way without Nick. Then again, maybe I would've sat at the computer until I went blind and passed out on the keyboard. Honestly, that was a very real possibility.

He gave me all the writing time I needed, but when I wasn't in the office, we just merged. Over the week, we talked less and understood each other more. It was a subtle graduation in intimacy, but, as an observer, I noticed. I wanted to worry about the implications—but maybe I didn't. Maybe all I wanted was exactly what I got.

Friday came too soon. We took a hike before breakfast, and then I went to work. Over the course of the week, I'd revised and resubmitted the first half of the article per Jan's suggestions and was almost finished with the final two segments. Jan's feedback had become more and more posi-tive, which thrilled me all the more.

But I didn't want to get into the writing zone on our last day. After a quick skim of my latest paragraphs, I checked email and packed up the laptop. The house was quiet as I jogged to the bedroom for my swimsuit and some SPF 50. I knew where I'd find him.

Nick looked up from his book when I stepped out onto the second-floor patio. He was clearly surprised to see me so soon. *How are you not used to that smile yet?*

Even if I saw it every day, my stomach would still dip at such a greeting.

He slapped the book shut and rose from the chaise. "You've come out just in time."

I groaned. "I always come out just in time. If I'd come two hours later, or twenty minutes earlier, I'd still be—"

"Precisely on time. It's uncanny, isn't it?"

I plopped onto the end of the chair while he sauntered

to the railing. Every blessed day, we'd gone through this routine. I begged him to not jump, and he laughed and threw himself off anyway. After the second time, it had become a game. The more creative I made my pleas, the more dramatic his jump. It really did terrify me the first time he did it, but it fascinated me, too.

"Care to join?" Another part of the routine, but this time, I chewed on my lip and frowned. Nick turned and cleared his throat. "Now you say," he prompted. Still I didn't speak. "I can't see the face you're making without my glasses. Everything okay?"

I shuffled across the deck to where he stood. "What's it like?"

His brows lifted. "Exhilarating."

"That means terrifying." I hesitated before admitting, "Heights are my fear. Nothing freaks me out like they do."

"Cucumbers." He pointed to himself, and I laughed despite my adrenaline. "No, but really, it is a high jump. Terrifying might be accurate. The drop is long enough that you have time to think about it. Also, the water is cold, and you hit a colder layer thanks to the impact."

"Does it feel like you're going to die?"

"No, but I don't think like that."

I peered down again and took a shaky breath. "Would I get hurt?"

"Unlikely but possible. That's life, isn't it?"

"Not if I can help it."

"Mel." Nick laid his hands on my shoulders. "Sometimes we can't help it."

I didn't answer for a long time. "And sometimes we have to jump." I rolled my eyes at the absurdity of my tight throat and pinched voice. "I'm not missing the metaphor."

He shook his head. "You're overthinking. It's an adventure, not a metaphor."

"Push me."

He inhaled sharply and stepped back. "Now *that* might be a metaphor."

I leaned on the rail with a challenging stare. "Nope, it's literal. I want to try it, but I'm a baby about heights. I don't mind admitting I need help with this."

But Nick shook his head. "Pushing you would be dangerous. If you don't leap out, then you'll be too close to the house. I could throw you, but if you freak out and land wrong, you'd get hurt that way, too. No, Mel, you've got the only option I've ever offered. I'll jump with you."

"You'll hold my hand?" He nodded, and my pulse began to race. "You'll make sure I get to the dock?"

"Of course. What kind of question is that? Even if I have to drag your unconscious—"

"*Nick*, good god. Don't say that, you jerk." I buried my face in his bare shoulder and slapped his chest. He hugged me like I knew he would. I breathed in the scent of his sunscreened skin, and my pulse eased a bit.

"I'm sorry kid, I was just teasing." He nuzzled my hair and squeezed a little tighter.

I thought about kissing him and forgetting the whole thing, but this had become a challenge suddenly, and I was ready to see it through. I stepped back and stripped to my swimsuit with shaking hands, then turned to the water again. My teeth started to chatter. "It's the last day. It's now or never."

"You're sure?"

I nodded and exhaled loudly. "Holy fuck, I'm afraid."

Cold all over despite the hot day, I clutched his fingers and let him help me climb over the rail. We stood on less than a foot of deck, my toes curled over the ledge.

"Breathe, Mel. I'm with you, okay?"

I tore my gaze from the dark water to his eyes. The color always shifted, but the warmth and reassurance in his gaze was a constant that never ceased to captivate me. I bit my lips into a line and nodded.

Nick stroked my knuckles. "Good. Now, we'll go when you say, but listen to me. You can't freeze up here; it'd be unsafe for both of us. Once you say jump, you have to jump. Understand?"

"I understand," I gritted out. "Don't freeze."

"Count down when you're ready."

"N-n-no. I can't. You count." I stared down at the water again, trying to prepare for this. *It's just a moment, just a few seconds. It's not even a whole page in the book of your life. Do it.*

He squeezed my hand. "Look out, not down. Don't think about the drop. Think about everything you're jumping into. See how pretty it is?"

Nick gestured, so I dragged my gaze up to look around. The beauty of the sky and trees soothed me a little bit. *You're jumping into this scene like stepping into a painting.* That thought helped me draw in a full breath for the first time since I stepped out. "Count us down. When you say three, I promise I'll be ready."

"Leap big and leap out. I have to trust you, too."

"Promise."

Together we took a deep breath. "Here we go," he muttered. "One. Two." We bent our knees. "Three!"

The sun glittered on the lake as I flew through the air, his hand still locked with mine. I think I screamed, but sound and sight vanished before my ears registered it. The cold lake swallowed us up, and I plunged down deep until ice gripped me to the shoulders. Glad for Nick's warning that kept panic at bay, I released his hand and clawed for the surface.

I broke the water with a gasp, numb with shock.

"Swim." Nick turned me to the ladder.

I looked without seeing, but my legs started to kick. Nick reached the dock and hauled himself out. He spun around and grabbed my shaking arms to pull me up. I tumbled to the warm planks and stared at the sky while my pulse tried to slow down.

My teeth still chattered when he stroked my cheek and turned me to meet his gaze. "Are you with me, kid?"

The thrill of flying, the icy plunge, and the unflinching way he'd done it with me all set in at once. Pride, fear, and joy hit me so hard, words wouldn't do. Instead, I broke into a euphoric, face-aching smile.

Nick watched me and laughed. "Guess you're okay."

I was more than okay. I was in love with him.

~

I had never been in love. I'd wondered vaguely how one would know, how it would be different from enjoying someone or caring about him. Lying on that dock, the difference was unquestionable; I wanted nothing but him.

Of course, I didn't say any of that. Nick not only had no place in my life, his presence could undo everything if I was foolish enough to let it. Putting voice to such a dangerously perfect feeling wasn't an option.

But, since we were still in our bubble of vacation, putting action to it was definitely acceptable.

I climbed onto his lap and tilted his chin. The heat of our mouths spread from my lips to my cheeks and down my back. Adrenaline, fear, and the icy lake melted away.

*I love you.* I imagined my body whispered its secret to his, the biggest secret I'd ever had. I imagined he answered with, *I love you, too,* and that I knew it and accepted it as real.

∼

*"Valentine's Day is the world's corniest holiday." I leaned against Nick's chest, my legs stretched down the couch in his parents' living room.*

*"It's the worst," he agreed and flashed a wicked smile. "But it's your birthday, too, so the day isn't all bad."*

*"How did you know?" I scrambled around to face him.*

*"Robin told me ages ago. She said she knew you'd never mention it, and it was her duty as your best friend to let me know. What, you thought you were the only one who could investigate?"*

*I buried my face in his neck. "I'm eighteen. An adult. How anticlimactic."*

*"I got you a present."*

*I lifted my head so fast, I nearly gave myself whiplash. Nick reached for the little table behind the couch and picked up a long box. Mute, I opened it to find the daintiest silver chain with an amethyst pendant smiling up at me.*

*"This is a girlfriend kind of present." I looked up and swallowed hard.*

*"Uh, yeah?" He gave a nervous shrug. "I mean, we've been, um, together since before Halloween."*

*"But we're not a couple," I whispered.*

*"Aren't we?"*

*My stomach churned. "I meant we're not long term. This'll be over after graduation. It isn't a permanent thing."*

*"It's not an engagement ring, Mel."*

*"I just don't want you to feel like you need to commit to me. I*

*like how we are; I don't need more than that. Does that make sense?"*

*He scratched his neck and didn't meet my eyes. "Sure. I guess that means you don't want the necklace."*

*I closed the lid. "It's too nice. I wouldn't feel right."*

*He took the box from me and stared at it an eternal minute. Then, with a deep breath, Nick tossed it back on the table and flashed a grin. "Whatever, kid." He pulled me closer and turned on the TV.*

My eyes opened in the middle of the night. On the edge of sleep and wake, that memory had unlocked itself. I groaned and looked over at Nick. He was sprawled out on his stomach, one arm across my ribs.

I brushed the hair from his eyes. "I'm sorry I was such an asshole. But it was only because I was so scared of you. You made me want to stay. I'm not scared anymore—but I still wish I could stay." I glanced around the moonlit room and the bed we'd shared for the week. "Guess I should take what I can get, huh?"

"You want to get some?" he mumbled into the pillow, smiling with his eyes closed. Turning, he flexed his hips against mine. "Get on it, then. I'm asleep, but hop on if you're ready."

"Shut up." I giggled. "I can't believe you just said *get on it*."

He laughed into my ear. "You love it."

I really did.

I also loved his feathery kisses down my neck. "What were you saying?" he whispered.

"Oh, I was just thinking about what a jerk I was to you when we were young."

His lips paused. "You were not. You were the best."

"I was so stubborn. I thought I knew everything."

"You're still that way," he teased. I pinched him, and he pinched me right back. "You were the best, kid. Do you not remember how many hours we spent together, just doing homework and bullshitting? Or how you'd come hang out at the store on Fridays and wait around until I closed? My swagger was ridiculous. I rubbed it in to every dude I worked with that you were with me."

I laughed again and kissed his cheek. "But you worked at Tower Records. I was mostly there for your employee discount." He gave me a sharp dig in the ribs for that. "I was brokenhearted when they went out of business," I added, and he agreed. We lapsed into a comfortable silence while memories floated through my head. "I'm glad that's how you remember us."

"Well, you've given me about a thousand orgasms in the past week. That'll gild anything, right?"

I pinched him again and flipped so we were face to face. "Remember when we first had sex?"

Nick was smirking before I finished. "Hmm, trick question. Of course I remember a week ago."

"See? I didn't even put out. I wouldn't commit, and you... you just... said okay. Why?"

"Mel, I'm fucking crazy about you. Haven't you got that yet?" He crawled on top of me and nuzzled my nose. "Or, put another way, *you are enough*. Just exactly who you are, how you are. You're so damn great. I understand, Mel. I know what you want out of life."

"But—"

"Shh." He reached between us, slipped my underwear down my legs, and unbuttoned the silk pajama top I wore. "I understood you were in transition back then, and I understand this week is almost over. So, let's make the most of the time we have left."

We'd had so much sex that my hips were in a permanent state of fatigue, but every time our bodies connected, I felt like I couldn't get enough. Words collapsed into whispers, and then grunts and choked breath when I clenched in climax. He thrust harder, and I raked my nails across his scalp and wrapped my ankles around his back.

Nick groaned. "Mel, you... are... *everything*." With a shudder, he fell on top of me. "Fucking everything," he sighed.

We passed out in each other's arms.

The plan for Saturday had been made before we left the city last week. I was meeting Peter for a check-in and flying home later that night. Nick was on the midday flight back to Tennessee, so he would drop me off and return the rental car. We agreed not to talk right away when we returned to try and get used to being on our own again, but I'd promised to text him any news on Jesse that I got from Peter.

Nick pulled the Mustang up to the corner of Bryant Park and turned on the emergency flashers. We gazed at the hotel across the way. "You still look better red," he muttered.

I fingered the black strands by my chin. After a week of being Mel, glancing in the mirror and seeing Melody Thomas, aka Coming Storms, was supremely strange.

"I'd better hurry." It was the only answer worth giving. "I'll see you later, Nick."

Twelve hours ago, we'd been tangled in bed together. Twelve hours ago, he called me everything. Now, we didn't even look each other in the eye as I stepped out on the sidewalk.

# 19

## NICK

My phone rang before I could open my front door. "Benjamin is on his way over. He comes bearing Jameson and a Penicillin shot," Celeste announced while I fiddled with the key.

"Can you ask him to get some cortisone cream, too? I've got the worst rash on my..." Our combined laughter interrupted me. "I'm fine, I swear."

"Mm-hmm. He'll be there soon."

I tossed my bags in the bedroom and barely had time to grab some pretzels before Ben was at my door. We traded a tight smile in greeting as he proffered the Jameson.

"How was New York?" he asked while we poured.

"Interesting." I winced through the initial alcohol burn and offered no more insight.

"I see." He nodded, clearly prepared to wait me out.

We drank and snacked in silence. My poker face held; so did his. Only after I refilled the whiskey and gulped some water did I motion to the living room. "Come on."

Ben dropped onto the couch while I took the recliner. He spoke first. "No bullshit, I really just want to know you're okay. You've been weird since you started this project, and then all we hear is you're out of cell range for the week. Meanwhile, your client is all over the tabloids, partying in Europe. You can see how anything from a week-long bender to wearing paper robes and sitting in a sweat box were options, right?"

I leaned back and smiled. "That's fair."

"Celeste wants the whole story, but you know I—"

"Want it, too."

He grinned and shook his head. After a pause, he said, "We were out at Cellar Door's show the other day. Liv was there. She asked if you were alive. Said she wondered if she'd done something wrong with the way you disappeared. I knew you two were pretty tight back in June—wasn't sure what to tell her."

I threw my head back and laughed. "Subtle."

"You know Liv never is."

"No, you dick, I mean *you*. Telling me that story when you knew I'd been with someone in New York."

Ben smirked. "You have to admire the creativity."

"Fine, I'll talk." I groaned and leaned forward to rest elbows on knees. I was ready to share—I needed to get the story out of my head, because it seemed too crazy to be real otherwise—but there was no way I was going to let him think that dishing was anything but a chore.

Ben lost the smirk and assessed me. "You look like you've been on vacation."

I nodded. "I have. From everything."

"So, you're good?"

I considered that. "Might be better to say I'm perfect, and perfectly fucked." He narrowed his eyes while I rolled the glass in my hand, unsure how to begin. "Before you gave your balls to Celeste, you may recall times past when we got drunk and talked about our all-time favorite girls."

"A, fuck you, and B, of course."

I flashed a smile. "Then maybe you remember this conversation usually featured me reminiscing about a redhead in high school."

"Every damn time. It takes about three drinks before you mention her."

I laughed and held out the glass for a refill. "Right. Well, two drinks in now, that girl is Mel."

Ben froze, bottle in hand, eyes narrowed in confusion.

"Not her hair," I said before he had to ask.

"But—but," he stuttered, then took a gulp of whiskey. "Last Saturday you were banging a groupie in—"

"No, I was with Mel. I've been with Mel at a lake house in upstate New York for the past week. That's the perfect part." I took a deep breath. "The perfectly fucked part is the rest."

I told him the rest.

When I finished, Ben stared at me forever. At last, he drained his Jameson, poured another, and jumped up to pace around. "Holy shit, Nick," he exclaimed, uncharacteristically animated for someone so even-tempered. "I mean, *holy shit, dude.*"

"No kidding."

Ben dropped back to sit. "Jesse left Friday. You didn't waste time."

My lips twitched. "*She* didn't, actually."

"Nice," he chuckled. We clinked glasses. "Guess it was as good as you remembered."

I didn't bother with the technicality that, as kids, we'd never gone past third base. Instead, I pushed my hair away and sighed. "And then some."

"*Nice,*" he repeated.

"Yeah."

"You're in love. Holy shit."

I lifted my gaze, throat suddenly dry. "Yeah, holy shit."

Ben pushed the glass away and scrubbed his face with both hands. "You're fucked, buddy." I collapsed and nodded my agreement. "All I can say is, I'll be glad to get drunk and play PlayStation with you if you want, because I don't think there's a lot you can do about it."

I laughed. Drunk PlayStation with James and me had been Ben's coping mechanism when Celeste left him for a short time last fall. "I might take you up on it when Jesse comes back."

Ben nodded. "Cool. But we're going to play now, because I've had far too much whiskey to drive home."

A couple hours of gaming and tacos for dinner were nice distractions, but when Ben left and I stumbled from a doze on the couch to my bed, I had to admit it was weird to sleep alone again.

Mel emailed the crew an update on Saturday night. The press was buzzing, and "Would you Mind" sales had surged. Jesse would return Wednesday and go immediately to a detox facility in Maine; I could expect to see him the following Monday. That meant another week without a single take, but there was nothing to say about it. I didn't bother to reply.

By Sunday afternoon, I started to find the usual groove of life again. I'd worked out, stocked my fridge, and emailed Rick. A bunch of friends were going to open mic night at Bar 40, our favorite hangout. The lounge was cool and intimate, the drinks generous, and the acoustics superb. We weren't supposed to meet until seven, so I spent the afternoon noodling around on my guitar to keep busy.

My phone dinged while I ate dinner. Expecting it to be Ben, I didn't look until I'd put the plate in the sink.

Mel: I haven't heard from you.

Me: What did you want me to say?

Mel: So is that it? We're done?

My gut clenched.

Me: Are we?

Mel: Can we talk?

I texted her my address, and then skulked around for thirty long minutes before she knocked at my door. The flash of red I glimpsed through the peephole made me grin.

Mel turned her face up to me with that mesmerizing light in her eyes. She licked her lips while I leaned in the doorway, and that glimpse of her tongue over her painted red mouth nearly undid me. Mel didn't wear makeup daily, but when she did it was noticeable—and *hot*.

"Are we done?" I asked, but the smiles on both our faces told me all I needed to know.

Inside, she surveyed my place. I surveyed her. Her breasts in that strapless gray top made me salivate. *God, what I'd give to run my tongue along that neckline while she—*

"Stop staring at my boobs."

I blinked, completely guilty and not at all sorry. "But they look so good."

Mel tried to glare as she walked closer and slid her hands up my shirt. Her palms rose and fell with my breath while I held her waist. "Nick, we've got to stop this," she whispered, but she began to unbutton me while she did.

"Yeah, we probably should." My words were tight through a held breath. *Don't move. Don't assume.*

Her gaze grew troubled. "We have to. It's dangerous now that we're back."

"I know."

"It's just..." Her fingers ran down my chest and back up to my shoulders, and I prayed for a good end to that thought. "Just... I can't yet."

Before I could react, she grabbed my collar and pulled. Her arms wrapped around my neck. I lifted her off the ground and groaned when her tongue found mine.

We were in my bedroom in seconds.

A round of knowing smirks greeted me when we slid into the booth at the bar an hour later than I said I'd be. I caught Celeste and Ben's jolt when they saw Mel with her red hair, but of course they had the class not to say anything. The others simply assumed this was my latest girl which, I guess, was true enough.

Except that holding her hand under the table, and the way she fit in so naturally with our group, was better than any other girl I'd ever known. As we chatted and drank away the last hours of the weekend, life felt so damn good. With her next to me, everything felt a little more *right*.

Things would've been perfect if not for the voice in the back of my head reminding me of reality.

We decided on a final round before calling it a night, but the servers were hard to catch between sets. "Come on, Mel, let's go get the bartender's attention," Celeste said when we'd waited too long.

"I want to wear your girl's hair," Aaron announced as we watched the ladies stroll to the bar, chatting the whole way. I shot him a look, but he didn't recant the statement. "Would it be wrong if I asked her to let me stand behind her and try it on?"

"It would be you getting a punch to the neck," I agreed. "Redheads get shit all the time; don't be that person."

He kissed his teeth. "I'd be nice about it," he grumbled, then grinned. "But the way you defend her is pretty satisfying, too."

"What do you think they're talking about?" I asked Ben, not bothering to acknowledge Aaron's last quip.

He laughed. "No idea. How do you think they're going to get the bartender's attention?" He wiggled his brows, but I shook my head.

"Knowing those two? Pointed stares."

They had vanished into the crowd by then, so we turned back to the table. Because I was so aware of her, though, I realized quickly that it took far too long for them to get back. At first I dismissed it as a busy bartender, but when they returned fifteen minutes later with arms full of bottles and twin grim expressions, my stomach tightened.

"Everything okay?" Ben asked Celeste.

I turned to Mel, brows up to echo the thought.

She took a deep breath. "Everything is the same as it has been."

*Perfect and perfectly fucked.*

# 20

# MELODY

I couldn't have scripted a more perfect summer night. A balmy breeze kept the heat comfortable, not oppressive. The drinks were cold, the music was hot, and the company was delightful. Nick's hand stayed curled around mine, but even without his steady presence, it was easy to relax among such an amazing group of friends. They were all so laid back and shared an easy camaraderie that let me be Mel and forget everything else.

Until Celeste and I went to get drinks.

We were the only women at the table. All night, I admired the way she interacted with the guys. She seemed so comfortable and at home with them. It was hard not to envy such a sense of belonging.

On our way to the bar, she said, "I'm glad to see you again."

"Yeah?" I hadn't missed her and Ben's shocked looks when we arrived.

"Definitely. I like how you make Nick smile."

"Nick always smiles," I argued, my own lips curled.

She laughed. "Exactly my point. He does, but he doesn't

smile like *that*."

I bit my tongue and chose my words carefully. "It's been nice to be with him and meet his friends. I've enjoyed this time."

We leaned on the bar. "You sound like it's over. Are things really that temporary?"

*She knows.* The look on her face told me for sure that Celeste was aware of my complicated situation. Not that I was surprised. "Very temporary." I held her gaze, refusing to wince.

"That's not my business, but it is too bad." She shrugged. "We can only do what we think we're able to do."

"Yeah." I didn't how else to respond without telling her my life story.

While Celeste flagged the bartender, I studied her and decided she was a confident woman with a long shadow. Something in the way she spoke told me she knew about choices. Since I knew that she had recently relocated back to Nashville, I was sure change was a concept she was familiar with.

She caught my stare and arched her brows. "Let's do a shot. The boys can wait on their beers. You game?"

I smiled. "Sounds good."

She ordered Jameson; I ordered Bulleit. We eyed the side-by-side glasses, both smirking as we assessed the other's choice. "Bourbon," she muttered at last, and I laughed.

Celeste's smile faded when we lifted our drinks. "I know what it's like to see no future in something that feels right. But, here's to life working like it should."

"Like it should." I clinked her glass. We each drank our shots before I said, "Even if that means that there really is no future in it."

"None at all, Mel?"

"Not if I don't give up everything else."

She eyed me and nodded, lips pursed. "Then still to as it should."

"Speak of the devil!"

We dropped our empty glasses and turned around to see a pair of women. The blonde wore an easy smile, but her companion tossed her pink ombre hair and flashed a tight grimace.

"Oh, hey, Megan," Celeste said to the blonde. "Liv," she added with a noticeable edge.

Megan laughed. "Skip the hello and show me the hardware, lady."

Celeste morphed from a composed, confident whiskey drinker into a literal blushing bride as she held out her hand. I watched, fascinated by their shared delight and the way both women's voices pitched higher to exchange congratulations and thanks.

*Talk about getting a reaction. Show a diamond, and people go nuts. Well, some people do.* I didn't miss the way Liv stared at the bar without a single glance at the ring.

"Who are you with tonight?" she asked abruptly as soon as compliments ended, turning to scan the room. "Maybe we'll join you. Is Nick here? Where the hell has he been, anyway?"

Celeste stiffened, but I found my voice before she could answer. "New York."

No way was I invisible then.

Megan's eyes widened, but Liv fixed a narrowed gaze on me. "And you are?"

"Mel." I felt no need to offer more.

"Let me guess. You guys have been 'hanging out' lately."

"If you want to put it that way." I didn't flinch, but *damn* her stare was intimidating.

Her lip curled as she barked out a laugh. "That asshole. That *asshole*."

Megan touched her arm. "Babe, you said y'all weren't really a thing."

Liv flung her off. "I don't care," she hissed.

"Come on, Olivia," Celeste tried. "You knew it wasn't a relationship."

She didn't seem to hear. Her gaze fixed on me. "He could've at least called. He could've at least been a *friend* and answered my texts."

The bitterness in her voice reflected a deep hurt. Loathing that Nick was to blame, I clenched my jaw in nothing but sympathy for this woman. "I'm sorry this is awkward. If it helps—"

Both Celeste and Megan pinned me with shut up looks, but too late. Liv's pain transformed into venom with a toss of her hair and a nasty snarl. "Do you think I need your help? Do you seriously believe you're that special? In a few weeks, you'll be just another what's-her-name. Get over yourself. I don't need your sympathy."

Redheads and tempers are synonymous for a reason. I ignored the fact that she had half a foot of height on me and cocked my jaw. "Do *you* think," I growled right back, "that I'm a big enough fool to not know the truth of a situation?"

She blinked, but then snapped, "You'll be history in no time. Deal with it."

"Sweetheart, with Nick, I'm already history." With my arm full of beer bottles, I marched around her and back to the table.

Celeste was by my side in a second. "Sorry about that. Liv is one of those people who hides behind a big front, like having a smart mouth makes her edgy or tough. The longer

I've known her, the more I think she really just doesn't know what she wants." She laughed. "She and I got off on a bad foot, too. She gave me the third degree on Benjamin."

I paused. "Both of them?"

Celeste shrugged. "Not exactly. She and Ben were a couple. I never got the whole story, but from what I understand, she and Nick mostly blurred a few lines of friendship." The way her lips puckered told me exactly what she thought of the situation.

"They weren't serious?" *Nick isn't serious with anyone, duh.*

"I don't know exactly what happened. All I know is they're close friends. Not that my opinion matters, but I think it was foolish for them to put their friendship in jeopardy. Liv isn't jealous as much as she misses her buddy, I think."

"I can't blame her," I admitted, and Celeste commiserated.

Back at the table, Nick knew right away something was up. "Everything is the same as it has been," I told him, not sure how else to respond. It was the truth. My heart still fluttered whenever I saw him, and my brain still knew this was a dead end.

The evening was over. Neither Celeste nor I could shake our tight shoulders, so when the beers were gone, the group vacated the bar. On the way out, she caught my arm. "Don't worry about Liv. She'll be fine. You said the right thing."

I didn't want to relive that anymore. "I'm glad we had a drink together," I said instead. "Even if you are a Jameson girl."

She smiled. "Likewise. I hope I get to see you again. Here, give me your phone." She keyed in her number. "Call me if you want. If you ever need a friend."

Nick leaned on the Camaro when I jogged toward him. "Conspiring with Celeste?"

I shrugged and slid into the car, annoyed at how much Liv still bothered me. Being the invisible, nameless girl-friend of a man desired by thousands of women was easy compared to facing a jealous "friend" one-on-one, but why?

While we backed out of the parking lot, I found the answer: vantage points.

As Jesse's girlfriend, I could observe and evaluate. I was good at that angle because it didn't require me to invest emotionally. Facing Liv meant I had to face my feelings and my situation. Where reality was usually work, work, work, suddenly I had this personal agenda that was the opposite of impartial or scripted. The depth of it scared me to death if I looked too hard.

Nick killed the engine and turned to me. "You haven't said a word the whole ride," he said gently. "Again, are you okay?"

I tore away from my thoughts and looked at him. "I'm okay. I'm... okay," I repeated for my own benefit.

"I want you to come upstairs, but I think you'll say no. Much like I think you're not telling me the truth right now."

"I'm not lying," I said stiffly. "But I do want to go home. I've got too much on my mind."

He couldn't hide the hurt in his eyes. "Okay. Call me tomorrow?"

"I'll call you. If not tomorrow, soon." I exited the car without waiting for his reply and made my way to my own driver's side.

"Goodnight, Melody." Nick's voice was flat as I reached for my door.

I paused. Without looking up, I called goodnight and left.

# 21

# NICK

When I dropped into the last seat at the conference table for the Monday morning staff meeting, I struggled to remember when this had been routine. Surely I'd been gone two years, not two weeks. Rick's drone about budgets and new projects was oddly comforting; it allowed me to zone out as usual, so I stared at my dark phone and thought of a dozen random things to text Mel, just to make her smile.

I also thought of at least half that many questions that I didn't want the answers to, but knew we needed to discuss. In the end, I sent nothing.

Rick assigned me a small project over the week. On top of that, the record company wanted more edits on Storms's third track. Busy was good, but all I really wanted was to talk to Mel. She said she'd call, but Storms was scheduled to return on Saturday. That meant our time was short. That meant, I reasoned, we had no time to waste.

I called Celeste on my way home.

By the time I got into my apartment, I wanted to punch a hole in the wall. I was furious at Liv and ready to call and unload on her, but, before I dialed, my conscience gave me a swift kick. Telling Liv what I thought of her smartass mouth would be a powder keg. She'd give it right back, call me out for ditching her without a word, remind me we've been friends for years and she deserved better than that. And she'd be right.

It didn't stop that itch to punch the wall, though.

I gazed at my phone, debated, and finally tapped the contact I needed. The one that mattered.

"Hello?"

"I know you said you'd call me, but fuck that," I said in a rush. "Come over here, *now.*"

Mel sighed. "Give me an hour."

It was a long hour until she knocked on my door. My tension was palpable, and her shoulders were up, too. I paced around the living room while she perched on the couch and tracked my movements. "Why didn't you tell me?" I burst finally. "What exactly did she say to you? Christ, Mel, If I'd known, I would've—*why* didn't you say anything?" I whirled to her, my fingers threaded into my hair.

She jumped up and crossed her arms. "Why would I? What would that have sounded like? Me, all boo-hoo like a pitiful little girlfriend, and you yelling at her? Nope. Me angry, and you desperately trying to make me feel better? Nope. Us both awkward about the fact that she's right? Bingo."

Her words slapped me straight. I reached for her, but she stepped backward. "She's all talk. She doesn't know shit about us."

"True. But she's also right. There's no future here. I'll be history in a few days, which works well for both of us."

"Excuse me?" I barked, far harsher than either of us expected.

Mel pointed accusingly. "Be real, Nick. I've a job to do, and, as you, me, *and* Liv know well, you don't see the point in commitment, which makes my situation a perfect out all around."

I wanted to un-hear all of it. My eyes burned, throat closed, as I absorbed the wrecking-ball impact of her words. When I was able to draw in a breath, I strangled out a single question. "Do you believe that, Mel?"

She dropped her hands and turned away. "I don't know."

"If that's true—if being over will *work well for both of us*—then tell me one thing." I walked forward and gripped her by the shoulders. She lifted her gaze. "Why the hell are you still here?"

Her eyes sparkled, lips open on a ragged breath. "Because I'm a fool." She hid behind her hands and dropped down on the couch.

I knelt and brushed her hair off her face. "No. You're here because you know that there is nothing good about you and me apart. No matter how impossible it is for us to stay together, you *must* know that's true. Look at me, Melody."

She lowered her hands. "Liv said she and I were no different."

I chuckled. "You know that's bullshit."

"I know. But I also know what type of man you are. You never lied about that."

I blinked and sat on my heels. "Mel, I've never lied to you about anything. Yeah, I usually prefer casual relationships. And, yes, I'm a wrong step from blowing the biggest chance of my career by being with you. I don't give a damn. I'll take the risk. You're different than every other girl I've ever known. What do you want me to say? That I'd be more than willing to commit to whatever you wanted us to be? That I—"

I wanted to say it: *that I love you.* But my tongue got stuck, and before I could, she spoke.

"No, Nick. I'd never ask you for that."

"You don't have to, because it's all true. The only trouble is," my voice broke to name the other half of the truth. "It doesn't matter, does it?"

Tears spilled down her flushed cheeks. "No."

I bowed my head and buried my face in her jeans as reality crashed down on us. Mel bent over me, her arms around my back and her face against my hair, her body trembling with swallowed sobs.

"This is worse than prom night," I said into the fabric. Her cheek bobbed in a nod.

A frozen moment stretched forever. Mel sat up, but I kept my head down until she tugged my hair. My eyes hadn't opened before she pulled me to her. I found her lips open and waiting, so soft and warm against the harsh, cold reality we were finally acknowledging.

Desperate suddenly to get as much of us as I could, too aware that this was all going to evaporate faster than I could handle, I kissed her deeper and deeper. When I reached up and palmed the back of her head, she lay back against the cushion and spread her legs, inviting me to fit against her.

"Tell me," she said between kisses. "Tell me everything's okay."

My passion hit pause. I drew back an inch and opened my eyes. "I can't. It's not."

Her ocean blues went round, then fell to a pained squint. "I know."

I took a shaky breath but never got more words out. Her mouth found mine again, drowning me, and all I could do was surrender to every moment we had, no matter how hard it was getting to breathe without her.

# 22

# MELODY

If the week at the lake was about hiding from reality, then the week in Nashville became about stalling it. Nick and I saw each other every night. When Jesse texted me en route from the airport to the detox resort, I was sprawled on Nick's couch, watching TV with him draped over me. When Peter called and left a voicemail to confirm all was well the next morning, I was in the middle of a screaming orgasm in the shower.

I began scheming about how to keep seeing Nick once Jesse returned. I told myself that if Jesse could have women whenever he liked, it made sense that I could pursue my own interests, too. In my daydreams, I'd work hard all week, and then knock on Nick's door on Friday night and fall into his arms. Monday morning, we would kiss goodbye, and I'd do it all over again.

Of course, it was pure fantasy. That's not how I work, and Jesse Storms was *not* a 9-5 kind of gig.

On Friday, our last night before Jesse returned, Nick and I lay on his bed. We weren't asleep, just dozing and petting each other. He yawned and tickled my shoulder. "Two weeks to your deadline, right?"

"Yes. I've got to be done by the twelfth of August."

He smiled. "That's my birthday."

"Hmm, Jesse's birthday is the day before. A pair of Leos. Big surprise."

Nick perked up. "How old is he, anyway? In my research..."

I laughed; Jesse's age was a mystery. According to sources, he was anywhere from 19 to 40, and he liked to keep the public guessing. He wouldn't throw a birthday bash for exactly that reason—even the date was up for speculation.

"He'll be twenty-six, but if you tell anyone, I'll ruin you."

Nick kissed my knuckles. "If anyone could, it's you."

I steered us away from talk of Jesse, not ready yet to think about him too much. "What will you do to celebrate?"

"Not sure. What will *you* be doing that day? What happens after the deadline?"

I swallowed hard. He'd never say it, but I knew Nick wanted me to find an angle that would let us be together.

I didn't want to lie to him.

"I have no idea. *Now Playing* collaborated with Jesse's record label to boost album and copy sales. It's a special edition publication. Everyone wins. But, what it means for me personally, I'm not sure. I don't want to think ahead. It'd be amazing if my writing was well-received, and they wanted me to take on another project—" I twisted my lips, fully aware that I was, indeed, getting ahead of myself. Nick wiggled his brows, but I regrouped and focused on what was known. "Jesse's tour starts at the end of September. He's booked across North America through the spring. If things go right, he'll tour worldwide for at least a year."

"Which means *you'll* be gone for at least a year."

I didn't tell him my secret wishes, didn't dare say aloud my dream that *Now Playing* would staff me or connect me with one of their sister pubs so I could quit being Coming Storms and become Melody Thomas, Journalist-At-Large. That idea was as much a fantasy as anything else.

"I don't have any other options on the table right now," I said.

"I understand."

"And what about you? What comes after the album?"

He sighed and rolled to his back. "Another project, and then another. Life will go on."

*Will it? Will life go on when I lose you again? What does it feel like to know there's someone in this world that you love when you're not with them? How does life simply go on when you carry someone so deep in your soul?*

We didn't talk more, but sleep didn't come for either of us easily, either.

The crew was to meet in New York the next day. Jesse had an interview scheduled, an exclusive to clean up his image, before we returned to Nashville Sunday night. Would he know how much had changed? Would he care? Living my own story was so much less controlled than I liked the world to be.

Saturday morning, long before the sun rose, I slipped out of Nick's bed to catch the red eye to LaGuardia. I kissed his cheek, and he yawned and opened one eye. "See you soon, kid," he mumbled and dozed back off.

*Yes, that, at least, is true.* "See you soon." I smiled and hurried out.

# 23

# NICK

Letting her go was easy. After that moment on the couch, I thought every day that passed would wake us up to reality more and more, but it didn't happen that way. Every minute with Mel confirmed how right we were together. Yeah, there were a lot of details to figure out, but when she left on Saturday morning, I had no doubt that I would see her soon, back in my bed. I spent the day doing chores and recalling our time together, all Mr. Cool.

All Mr. Idiot.

In retrospect, I see how badly I fooled myself, and not just that day. From the moment I opened her hotel room door and saw that red hair, I'd lived in a dream. All the warnings, all the times I said I knew our time was short, they were bullshit. Truth was, I had let myself think that, this time, we might really work out.

∼

Sunday afternoon, I went to Ben's. The three of us were

going to hang out, maybe catch a movie if the mood struck. When I rang the bell, Ben greeted me with a critical eye.

"How're you doing?"

"All good." I held up the six-pack of Yazoo in my hand.

We went upstairs and cracked a couple beers open in his living room, waiting for Celeste to get back from running errands. He chuckled while I reclined on his couch, my legs sprawled wide in front of me.

"Getting laid has chilled you out."

"You'd know about that." I laughed but couldn't disagree. After all those up and down weeks, it was good to be so relaxed.

That easy feeling lasted until the door banged open, and Celeste raced up the stairs. "Oh, my *god*, are you okay?"

Ben and I jumped to our feet at the same time. "What is it, babe?" he asked, but she crossed the room and folded *me* into a hug.

"I'm afraid." I tried to make it a tease.

Celeste pulled back and looked up at me. "Wait, don't you know?"

Celeste was always intense, but she was also the last girl who'd make a scene. It wasn't how our family worked, and it was one of the reasons she and I were so close as kids. I didn't have to worry about making her cry if, for example, I shot her with a water gun.

In that moment, the anxious concern she radiated, from her too-bright eyes to the frown that creased her forehead and lips, told me to be seriously worried. My stomach clenched while I shook my head, knowing I didn't want to hear whatever it was she was going to tell me.

She winced and squeezed my arm again, then grabbed my phone from the table and thumbed the screen. "I'm sorry, Nick."

**Coming Storms @ComingStorms retweeted:**
Big news on the Brooklyn Bridge! Jesse Storms
ENGAGED to longtime GF in front of hundreds of
fans!

**Coming Storms @ComingStorms:**
Did you see the proposal?? Tag us in your pics and
check it out at Instagram.com/rr/kouu459 #truelove
#shesaidyes #goingtothechapel

My thumb touched the Instagram link. A picture filled the
screen. Jesse knelt on the wooden planks of the bridge, prof-
fering a box to Mel. Her head was bowed, one hand
covering her mouth, face veiled by that damn black hair.

Ben and Celeste shouted their disbelief, but everything
bounced off my brain. Dimly, I registered their grips on my
arm and shoulder, guiding me to sit, but my feet tangled and
my stomach lurched. I spun around and stumbled down the
hall to the bathroom, where I vomited up the one beer I'd
drunk.

Celeste appeared while I slumped on the tile. She
hugged me tight, and I wondered why she was crying.

Eventually, Ben drove me home in the Camaro with
Celeste following in her Toyota. They talked to me as I
settled onto the couch, but I don't remember anything they
said. I guess I convinced them I was okay to be alone
because the apartment got quiet while I stared at the wall
until I passed out.

The clock said 4:50 when I woke in a dark room, bile in

my mouth, neck stiff from sleeping sitting up. In a matter of hours, this hideous situation would stare me down in the studio, and I had to pretend to be a functioning human being when it did. I rolled off the couch and went to the shower.

Under the steam, I woke up and knew for damn sure that I wasn't ready to face this. After the last two weeks, I couldn't process the idea that my Mel was going to be some pop star's *wife*. The word made me shudder.

I made it to work and went straight for Rick's office. He was on the phone when I pushed in and threw myself on the chair.

"Let me call you back," he said while I rubbed my sandpaper eyes. "Morning, Nick! How's everything? Ready to finish this album? The record company loves the edits you made last week. I had no doubt when I gave you this project, but I have to say, you've really blown it out of the water, son. So, what can I do for you?"

"Finish the album."

My request filled the room with dense tension. Rick's brows slowly knitted together into a single line. "Come again?"

"I-I'm in over my head, Rick. I can't handle it. The deadlines, the pace—it's too much pressure."

"Well that's a load of bullshit if I ever heard one. Next you're going to sell me some oceanfront property in Arizona, huh?"

I winced but didn't speak.

Rick banged his fist on the desk. "Dammit, Nick, what's this about? I've seen you handle three projects at once. I just finished telling you you're doing a hell of a job. What the fuck?"

"It's more than I can take. I thought I could handle it, but—"

A growl deep in his throat cut me off. "This doesn't have anything to do with that thing that never happened on the Fourth of July, now does it?"

I didn't blink.

Rick's quiet, steady voice was far scarier than his usual bark. "Goddammit, Field, keep it in your pants for five minutes."

"It's not—I just—"

He rose and pointed at the door. "Better get your ass to Studio A and set up. Your client arrives soon, and you have an album to finish. If you don't like that option, you know where the exit is. But be damn sure of this: if you walk away, I will see to it that your career in the music business is over as soon as your feet hit the pavement."

My heart thudded a slow, painful cadence. I wouldn't have minded too much if it had just given up altogether in that moment. At least that would've been a choice. As it was, Rick had left me with none.

"Aye, Cap'n." I sighed and hauled my ass to Studio A, per my orders.

Jesse arrived right on time. The bastard practically glowed, he was so rested and triumphant. "Nick, how are you? Did you hear? I'm engaged!" he crowed as he stepped into the lounge, hand out.

I shook it and forced a smile. "Yeah I saw the news yesterday. Congrats, man. Uh, where's...?"

"Melody? Ah, she called me this morning, said she had a migraine. I told her to stay home."

"Uh-huh. Well, we've got to finish this album, so whenever you're ready." I congratulated myself for staying so level. Between the disgust and anger roiling in my chest and the fact that I had had his fiancée screaming my name for two weeks straight, I considered it a success that I was able to look the man in the eye at all.

Jesse bent all his focus to the album from that morning on. His vocals were incredible, infused with energy and pure determination. The band fed on it and upped their game, too. I was swamped with material and spent long hours mixing when we weren't recording. Melody didn't return to the studio, which helped me shove my personal shit to the backburner. It also helped anytime Rick appeared in the lounge. I knew he'd upped the frequency of his check-ins on Jesse's satisfaction. Without Mel around, at least he quit growling anytime I was in his line of sight.

By Friday afternoon, we only had two tracks left. One of them was the single Ben had written. Playing the demo for him damn near killed me with visions of that night and Mel tucked into a chair in Ben's living room, but Jesse was thrilled with the song and confident we could have it done in a day.

I downloaded the demo and lyrics to his phone so he could learn it over the weekend. When the track ended, Jesse nodded and removed his headphones. "Come on, buddy. Team meeting," he said when he walked into the control room.

Jesse stood in the center of the lounge and filled us all in. He told the crew that studio time would be over within the week, and then told me to be at his house for an engagement party next Friday. The wedding, he said, was scheduled for the first Saturday in September, right after the article and album drop.

Jesse looked around at us and finished with, "Oh, and if anyone has a good photo or news, text Melody. She's so busy with wedding planning and the upcoming releases, she'll be working from home next week."

*Thank god.*

With my birthday on Monday, my weekend schedule was packed with festivities, but when I got home, I messaged my friends and cancelled everything. All I wanted to do was veg on the couch.

A barrage of texts would've been more than sufficient acknowledgment of my 29th birthday, but Donna, InSight's receptionist, was a little too good at keeping track of things. On Monday morning, the much-recycled, "Happy Birthday!" banner adorned Studio A's door, and a box of doughnuts sat in the control room. I took the banner down, but luck wasn't on my side. Donna must've felt an oral report was necessary, too, because Jesse burst into the lounge wearing a grin.

"Why didn't you tell me?"

I waved him off and remembered in time not to mention his own birthday. "Who cares? It's no big deal."

"Well, it will be now. Seth, get us a table somewhere good tonight. Or we could fly to—"

"Album deadline," I said in a rush.

"Fine." He laughed. "Seth, the best table you can get."

"My place for the after party?" Seth was already on his phone. "I'll call the housekeeper and—"

"Yeah, the works." Jesse paused. "Shit. No. Album deadline. We can't pull an all-nighter. Just dinner and drinks. Sorry, Nick. Rain check, okay?"

*Yeah, we'll reschedule a day past never.* I didn't want to

begin to imagine what an after party at Seth's house would look like, but a smile was my reply.

I tried my best to work Jesse so hard that he forgot the whole thing, but, for a man who could talk about four different things in under twenty seconds, he didn't miss a beat when he strode out of the studio and slung an arm around my neck.

I'll admit, it wasn't the worst night of my life by a long shot. We had a four-course dinner at a place where reservations were booked months in advance. After that we walked into Citizen, a members-only club in the Gulch, and were shown straight to a private table. I didn't open my wallet once, and food and drink were in my hand whenever I wanted. It was a guys' night out to the max degree.

While we drank and bullshitted at the club, Peter disappeared. He returned with a string of ladies in tow and pointed at me. "It's Nick's birthday." My smile slipped, but the girls squealed. In a flurry of satin and perfume, I was flanked on both sides and tag-teamed with sugary kisses.

By the time I reclaimed possession of my face, Seth and Steve were on their way to the dance floor, and Peter had his arm around a pretty blonde. Across the table, Jesse grinned at a—

Fuck. A redhead. Not a real one, but gorgeous and perfectly aware of it. "I heard you got engaged," she purred at him.

"You heard right."

She smiled and grabbed his shirt. "Hope she's not the jealous type," she said before their mouths sealed together.

I was on my feet before I knew what I was doing. Jesse was far too busy to notice, but Peter stared coolly up at me. "Something wrong?"

The girls saved me from a reply. They stood up and

tugged my hands, begging for a dance. I smirked at Peter, who grinned and let his attention drift back to his girl. On the dance floor, they sandwiched me tight and bestowed another pair of birthday kisses while we moved.

*Half an hour. Then I can say I'm beat and remind Jess of work tomorrow.* I gazed down at the pink miniskirt grinding against my crotch and stifled a yawn.

The limo dropped me off less than two hours later. I thanked Jesse about four times, but he just laughed and called me a dumbass. "Promise we'll do a bigger party next time, okay buddy?" He clapped my hand before I exited.

Once I was showered and in bed, I thought about Jesse and Mel. There would always be girls, parties, and next times for him. Meanwhile, Mel would... what? Work herself to death, or at least to a life of eye strain and isolation?

The one person whose future I chose not to consider was my own.

~

I suspected that Jesse Storms operated on no sleep more often than not, but whatever he and his guys did after they left me, he was back on the grind on Tuesday. Jesse had matured as a recording artist with every song on the album. The final two tracks took far fewer takes than the early efforts had required. By Thursday, we had all we needed. Final mixes and edits would be smooth enough; Labor Day was an easy deadline. We'd done it.

Rick popped a bottle of champagne that disappeared fast. The crew and I shook hands and promised to keep in touch, and with that, the whirlwind of Jesse Storms lifted from my life.

I embraced the peace as long as it lasted, but the engagement party loomed. All of InSight's employees were invited, and everyone simmered with excitement. Rick had come in while I was editing after Jesse left to tell me in as few words as possible that I'd done a hell of a job. Since then, we'd started trading nods in passing again. Not the usual rapport, but I no longer worried that he had my picture on a dart board in his home. I didn't want to risk a backslide by hedging out of the party.

I considered bringing a date, Celeste at least, but decided against it. She'd question my emotional state all night, and any other girl would just get on my nerves. Alone it would be.

The vibe was very different than my first Jesse Storms party. This one was far more refined. Waiters in black coats served cocktails to well-dressed guests. A string quartet played on the terrace. No pills or Solo cups in sight.

I made straight for the bar and the first cluster of coworkers I spied. An hour of small talk, canapés, and bourbon was an hour closer to going home as far as I was concerned. Still, the liquor was top shelf, the night was pleasant, and Rick can tell a hell of a story if he gets a couple cocktails under his belt. I was actually smiling when a waiter summoned all the guests into the living room.

The music stopped, and a hush settled over the party. Collective attention turned to the top of the staircase.

Jesse and Mel appeared.

Chilly panic gripped me at the sight of her. She was a vision in purple, that ridiculous black hair shining in the low light. Her strapless gown started as a deep violet at the top and grew incrementally lighter down to the powdery hue around her ankles. She was perfect. Her real hair would have made her deadly.

Jesse beamed at the guests. "This is the quietest party

I've ever thrown." His cheeky tone elicited the laughter he clearly wanted. "Hope everyone's having fun. We're so honored that you came to celebrate with us tonight. Let's eat, right?" Applause and cheers guided the happy couple down the staircase, arm-in-arm.

The crowd parted for them as they made their way outside to the tent on the lawn. I realized too late that I stood directly on the edge of their path. Jesse's attention was everywhere, but Mel's face lost all its color when her eyes found me. She bit her lips into a line, but I didn't flinch—I couldn't move—and, in the next breath, she was gone.

"Everything okay?" Rick's low growl rumbled behind me.

Colleagues surrounded me again, this time with worried frowns that told me to fix my face. "I'm fine. Just a little over it," I said as we strolled toward the tent.

Rick guffawed, but I had no doubt it was fake. "Over what? Churning out platinum albums while superstars tell me they love working with you? Christ, man, stop being such a doggone diva. It's not your style." He clapped my shoulder so hard I coughed.

"True. Sorry, guys." I grabbed a seat with my back to the head table, flashed a grin at my colleagues, and did my best to be myself.

Problem was, I didn't feel like myself anymore. I felt cut open in the best kind of way, and patched together in the fucking worst.

When the plates were cleared, Jesse tapped a knife on his glass and quieted the room. "I have a few people to thank. First of course, my brilliant bride-to-be. Melody, baby girl, you know what you are to me. Thank you. And Peter, my manager, thank you for looking out for me when I start to go crazy. Thanks to the rest of my crew for enduring the long hours and wild schedules.

"Guess everyone knows this party has two purposes, though, and it wouldn't be right to ignore the folks from InSight Studios." All around my table, faces beamed at the applause as Jesse continued. "And I have to thank the baddest-ass producer a guy could ask for. Nick, where are you dude? Stand up and take a bow."

Rick's gaze nearly froze me in terror, but I took a quick breath and plastered on another smile before I got to my feet. Jesse grinned at me and raised his glass. "To Nick!" he said, and the guests echoed.

I raised my glass back at him. "To Jesse!"

Everyone shouted and clapped their wholehearted agreement, and I felt like utter shit. Jesse Storms was a decent guy. The pursuit of fame and a crazy celebrity life made little sense to me, but I admired him a lot. I would've been proud to work with him again—if I weren't willing to sell my fucking soul for one more hour with his fiancée.

After dinner, the party moved back to the house for dancing and champagne. On my way across the terrace, a voice behind me stopped my strides. "Nick?"

I turned and faced a middle-aged man in a black suit, a bottle of beer in his hand. He was familiar, but recognition was just out of reach.

"Sorry to bother you, but I had to say hello. You probably don't remember me. I'm Scott Thomas—"

"Mel's father." I beat him to it. Of course those sharp blue eyes were familiar. His warm grin prompted my first genuine smile of the night while we shook hands. "Yes, I definitely remember you, sir. It's so nice to see you."

"Lord, call me Scott, not sir." He pumped my arm once more. "It's good to see you, too. Congratulations on the work you did for Jesse. Looks like you really made something of that passion for music you always had."

We stood off to the side as people streamed by. I laughed, impressed at his memory. "Yes, sir—Scott—I guess I did. I forgot you and I talked about music when I'd come pick up... uh, Mel." The weirdness of this situation suddenly struck me hard.

"Mm-hmm, I was always impressed with your knowledge. You got me into a few bands I'd never heard of. I still follow Pearl Jam thanks to you." He dimmed the smile and gazed out over the lawn, a little too casual. "I won't take much of your time. I just couldn't resist the chance to catch up, even in this rather strange situation."

"Cheers to that," I muttered, and then cleared my throat. "How did you recognize me?"

One brow rose. "You haven't changed that much, son. And besides, I had advanced warning. That was a tough-looking car you pulled into my driveway a few weeks ago."

I mirrored his look. "I didn't know Mel told you."

"Hmm. Yeah, she said she'd been with an old friend and explained how you were working with Jesse." He turned back to me, a too-familiar, too-*familial* sharpness in his gaze. "What she didn't tell me was where she kept herself while Jesse was away."

Heat crept up my neck, but I maintained eye contact. "Oh?"

"Nope. Even so, I have to say that whatever she was up to up North—and all those nights once she was back in town —sure made her happy. Happy like she looked that morning you brought her home. Can't help but notice that she doesn't look that way when she's with Jesse."

"Mm-hmm." I wondered if this man knew how much he just twisted the knife in my heart.

"Anyway, like I said, I wish you and I could've spoken under different circumstances. But I'm glad we got to talk. Thank you for your time, Nick. Good luck to you, son."

We traded another firm handshake, but I barely crooked my lips into a polite smile before taking my leave. Inside, I skipped the great room, where dancing had begun, and headed through the house to the restroom. I washed my hands and stared in the mirror. *This is not my life.*

As soon as I stepped into the hall, a hand gripped my arm and pulled. I stumbled through a door to my left, into a small study. The light flicked on, but I didn't need it to know what I was facing.

Why did her cheeks have to be so pink? Why did she have to wear purple? Why did I have to run into her dad? Most importantly, why couldn't I have just stayed home?

"Shh," she hissed, eyes wide and wild as she reached around me and snapped the lock.

"I don't want to talk with you, Melody."

"Please." One word made my heart jump; it was the first time I'd heard her speak in two weeks. "Please, just listen. Oh, god, Nick, I'm so sorry." She covered her mouth with a purple-manicured hand.

"You're sorry? You're *sorry*? You're fucking *engaged*, Mel. What does sorry have to do with it?"

"No, just listen because I—"

I waved at the giant rock on her hand. "Because you what? Didn't walk out of my bedroom and into his?"

Her eyes flashed lightning, but I didn't give a damn. She opened her mouth but seemed to change her mind and sneered. "What would be the point in trying to explain?" she asked bitterly. I didn't answer. I didn't want the story. "What's done is done. I... I just couldn't let us end without apologizing."

"I have to say, that means very little to me."

Her chin lifted. "You knew I was going back to Jesse when I left for New York. You knew the deal."

"I didn't think you were going to *marry* him! That makes things quite different."

She blinked but kept that stubborn lift in her jaw. "Be that as it may, you knew from the start our time was short. We both knew it was over before it began. You aren't part of the plan, Nick."

I flinched like I'd been sucker-punched. "The plan? You mean your scripted life that you've created in order to avoid taking any real risks with yourself? Is that the plan you're referring to?"

"My plan," she whispered. "My story."

"Your story? Your story? Mel, you *are* the story. You don't get to write it; you have to live it. And when you do—when you do—two things." I stepped closer, backed her against the wall, and held two fingers an inch from her nose. Her sweet scent and the tremor I could see in her lips made my voice fall to barely a whisper. "When you're not too busy reporting and observing all the damn time, you are radiantly alive. And when you're like that, you know we're supposed to be together."

Her cheeks were wax. She shook her head. "No. No, we're just nostalgia and lust."

I barked a laugh through the pain. "Nostalgia and lust? Is that what you're telling yourself? It's *us*, Melody. It was always us. And you know it."

I whipped my phone out of my pocket and lit it up. Keeping one eye on her, I found what I wanted and hit play. *"Oh... god it's so... yes... please... Nick!"*

She grew impossibly paler listening to herself moan. I bent until our lips almost touched, drew her exhale deep into my lungs, and said, "I told you. And I'll tell you this, too, since you're getting married, and it doesn't matter one bit whether I say it or not."

"Nick," she whimpered.

"Mel," I breathed. "I fucking love you, kid."

## 24

## MELODY

He dusted my trembling lips with a single kiss and stepped back. I looked him over, so handsome in his suit but with his smile twisted up in sadness, torment in his hazel eyes. "I never said that to anyone before," he muttered. "Probably for the best it's so meaningless now."

*Come kiss me again. Hold onto me and let me tell you every-thing that's happened. No one will believe it except you.* My heart wept with pleas that had to go unsaid, a small fraction of all the words I had to swallow in that miserable moment.

I wanted to tell him about how Jesse had ambushed me with the ring on the Brooklyn Bridge in front of hundreds of onlookers, essentially requiring my yes. I wanted to explain how he'd told me not to come back to the studio, but instead put me on wedding planning and a lot of media tasks. I wished someone would help me figure out if this was some kind of trick, or better yet, nightmare, since I'd barely seen Jesse or the crew since we got back from New York.

More than that, I wanted to tell Nick how much I loved him, and how desperately I had tried to figure out a way out of this and back to him. Back to us.

But there we were, face to face, and none of it would have made any sense. Nothing I said would undo the predicament I was in, and he was right: being Jesse's girlfriend and being his wife were not nearly the same. I couldn't explain, and I couldn't tell him I would fix it, or that it would be over soon.

I said nothing.

After a long moment, he shook his head. "I've always been stupid for you. I told myself when you walked out of my life in high school that I'd never let a woman do me like that again, and what did I do? I let *you* do it again. And you know what? I still don't regret it. You were worth it, both times." He took a long breath and looked at the ceiling, then dropped his head. "I'm out, and I'm done. I can't take this anymore. Good luck with your story, your life, and everything else you decide is more important. Please, don't ever contact me again. Delete my number and, *god*, don't tag me or some bullshit like that. I just want to forget you as best I can, understand?"

"Yes," I choked.

He nodded, gave me one last look, and was gone.

I balled my hands into fists and sat on the couch, yards of gauzy purple fabric swirling around me.

I was devastated. I'd never been devastated before. Angry, disappointed, frustrated, and sad, sure. But devastated, like *in love*, was a brand-new experience, and it was horrid. I wanted to throw myself on the floor and sob until there was nothing left, but two hundred guests and an army of journalists would certainly have questions about that.

If I learned anything from watching singers give their all for *American Pop*, it was how to handle disappointment. Their dreams were dashed when they were dismissed from the show; my heart had been smashed to pieces and shoved into a velvet box. *Breathe. Just breathe. Life will go on. It always does when someone leaves.* Eventually, I found the strength to stand up and float back to the party with a polite smile masking my bleeding soul.

God, how did all those contestants do it?

This was my debut as the future Mrs. Storms, and I barely knew how to pull it off. I wasn't the center of atten-tion—that was Jesse's role—but I wasn't allowed to observe and analyze, either. I was an accessory, a classed-up version of so many girls at clubs and parties who hang on the guys' arms just to be in the circle. It was boring and awkward and eternal, and the added burn of heartache made every second worse. By the time the last of the guests left, I was a hollow shell on aching legs.

Jesse slid his arm around my waist. "Come upstairs with me," he murmured in my ear.

"Jess," I sighed.

"Mm-mm," he dissented as we climbed the staircase. "It's our engagement party. Let's go be a couple."

I'd managed to avoid this moment ever since he got back from Europe. First, I insisted he get tested. Everything came back clean, just like I'd expected, because he *is* ridiculously careful. Still, I'd caged the issue and cited my schedule and his fatigue from recording as valid excuses.

*He's your fiancé. This is your life.*

When he pulled me into his bedroom, though, I knew I couldn't go through with it. I sat on the bed, my arms crossed tight across my chest.

He eyed me. "You okay?"

"Um, yeah, just a little tipsy, I think." I rubbed my fore-head and prayed my nauseous look sold the story. "Could I lie down for a second?"

"Sure."

He stripped to his boxers and pulled back the sheets, lying next to me. I stretched out, stiff as a board on top of the blankets in my ball gown. *Don't touch me, Jess, please. I can't do it right now.* Even his scent, expensive soap and cologne, made me long for Nick's familiar, fresh smell.

Silence filled the room forever, but my head was full of a very different sound: my own voice on Nick's phone. I didn't know he recorded me. Hearing the desperate desire that underlined my pleasure had been horrifying—and hot. So hot, the thought of it made my thighs clench and quiver.

Jesse stroked my arm. I nearly seized with guilty terror, but his touch didn't wander. "I'm proud of the album, Melody." His voice had lost the velvet purr he used when he was "on." The comment was just him, tired and thoughtful and honest.

The Jesse I met a lifetime ago.

I exhaled and nodded. "You really should be. How did Ben's-uh, the second single-come out?"

He missed my flub as he yawned. "It's my favorite track. The tour's going to be incredible. Peter says Beijing, Tokyo, and Melbourne are talking about multiple shows."

I tangled my fingers in his to show support, but his words exhausted me. "So proud of you, baby boy."

He changed subjects. "Well, if you're not feeling up to anything, I think I'd better sleep. Your room is stocked with a new wardrobe. I want you to move in Monday, okay? Stay with your dad this weekend, but it's time. Our wedding is in a few weeks."

I kept my gaze on the ceiling. It had been ages since we'd had a real talk, but, in that moment, I felt safe to ask, "Jess? Why did you propose?"

Jesse rolled on his side, so I did the same. He smiled. "You're good to me, Melody. We're a team, and you've kind of given your life up for all this. I want you to have what you deserve."

"You pay me well already." I touched his cheek.

He laughed. "Baby, as my wife, you'll *cash in*. Besides, you keep my image clean, and it gave you a hell of an ending to your article, right?"

I nodded. Oh, boy, had it ever.

"I'm pretty beat. Your room's ready for you." He gently kissed my forehead.

I stood and looked down at him. "Will we share a bed after the wedding?"

Jesse lifted his head and frowned. "Did you want to? I didn't think—"

"No," I whispered. "See you Monday."

My room was huge. The closets were stocked with new clothes, the bed was a California king complete with canopy, and I had my own private bathroom. The whole setup sent a clear message about the opulence and comfort that awaited Mrs. Jesse Storms.

I fell into the pillow-top mattress feeling like I was living someone else's life and thinking only of the man I had lost.

No, not lost. Thrown away. Twice.

*Fool.*

## 25

## NICK

When I left the party, I hit the road and drove nowhere for most of the night. Driving was good. It gave me something to focus on just enough to preoccupy my thoughts, but not enough to require too much energy. The Camaro's growling engine soothed me better than chatter or even music could.

When I finally went to bed, though, sleep still didn't want to come. Instead, I lay there and let my mind go where it shouldn't.

Prom night.

Such a big deal when you're eighteen years old, but it was going to be *our* night. We were a week away from graduation and had spent the last eight months practically inseparable. She was a virgin and had been hesitant to go all the way, but we kept each other satisfied plenty.

Days before the dance, we'd been at her place doing homework when she said, "Maybe you should buy condoms for Saturday." She blushed a perfect scarlet, so I grinned and played it cool, but I was on pins from that moment on. I bought the condoms as soon as I left her house and obsessively planned the night. Her corsage was white roses and violet ribbons; I had reservations at The Melting Pot and a hotel room booked at Doubletree downtown. I blew a whole paycheck on that hotel room.

Everything was textbook perfect. I'd slept with a girlfriend junior year, but I felt like such a *man* when we walked into the hotel lobby. She was radiant in a purple dress, blue eyes cutting to me every few seconds on the elevator ride to the room.

Before we got anywhere, she sat me on the edge of the bed. Her smile quit showing her teeth. "Nick, I want this."

"Me too," I said quickly.

"But." She looked down. "Tonight's our last night together. It's time we moved on. We're too close. You know I'm leaving right after graduation for a summer internship in Chicago. I don't want to be up there thinking about you or my next trip home, and I don't want you down here thinking of *me* when you should be moving on, too."

I'd known about the internship, of course. "I don't need to move on, Mel." I still felt every bit like a man. Only by then, I felt like a man being swept away in a tsunami. "I'll have work and school. I don't—"

"No," she whispered. "Long distance is bullshit, and anyway, I don't want to come home every break. Nick, it's time. We're done. I'm history." She bit her lip and tried to smile again. "After tonight."

Looking back, I have a certain amount of pride in my teenaged self for being the one to end the night right there. I still wanted her, had been out of my skin with desire and anticipation, but I stood up and walked to the door. She was stunned, but she followed without question. Silence grew between us all the way to her house. I couldn't look at her as I said, "Goodbye, Melody."

I guess I moved on. After a year or so, her name popped

in my head only randomly. After two years, Mel Thomas quit being a thought at all.

Not that I ever forgot her. It was just that her stamp on my soul had become something I didn't need to think about anymore, in the same way you don't think about breathing.

My eyes opened in the dark, lips curled in a nasty sneer. All these years later, and she'd done the same exact thing to me. And this time, like she said, I knew it was going to happen before we started. "What a fucking idiot," I whispered aloud, still unable to feel what I'd call regret.

My last words to her tonight had been the absolute truth. She was worth it. Worth the pain and the humiliation and the process of moving on. She was worth all of my worthless heart and then some.

But did she realize how different *her* situation was this time? The question eased my self-loathing sneer into a frown. Did she see how scripting her life had led to a marriage that would essentially erase her own story completely? As Jesse's wife, everything she was would be about playing that role. Did she see it that way?

I sighed heavily. "Goodbye, Melody."

When I woke around midday, I was blank. Not good, not bad, just blank. The kind of blank that made me itch for activity. I started with the gym. While I was there, I missed a call from my Uncle Brian.

"Nicky, I need a favor," he said when I returned the call. "That dueling piano bar I bought last year, remember?" Brian owned several venues around town. This one was in the heart of downtown, one those places bachelorette parties often ended up. It wasn't a serious music club, but it could be a good time with the right act.

"Yeah, what's up?"

"One of my pianists backed out tonight, dammit. Could I convince you to play? The other guys knows how it works, so he'll show you the ropes. Help me out, will you?"

Something to do that was guaranteed not to feature talk of Mel or questions about my emotional state? "I'm in."

I arrived early to get instructions and meet my partner, a tattooed hipster named Colin. "It's pretty easy if you know how to play," he told me. "If neither of us knows the song, we toss out the request. If you need lyrics, use your phone. As far as playing goes, it's usually a by-ear thing. Tips are split fifty-fifty. The more of a show we put on, the more we'll make. Cool?"

"Sounds great."

Colin grinned. Oh, and you'll get all the ass you want. Trust me."

I raised a brow. "Good to know."

We took the stage. As Colin greeted the crowd, I peered past the lights to see a full house of all sorts of characters. Tourists, college kids headed back to campus, clusters of girls, and a few quartets of older couples filled the tables. Colin introduced us, and high-pitched shrieks answered him.

*Yeah. This is exactly what I need.*

Our first song was "Twist and Shout." While we screamed out lyrics, I warmed to the role fast. My hair shook on my forehead as I mimicked the Beatles. By the end of the number, a wide grin split my face.

Hours whizzed by while we sang, flirted with the audience, and swilled beer and water in equal measure. The room called for more when we wrapped the last song, but we hopped off the stage and headed to the bar.

"Fan-damn-tastic, man. You were a natural." Colin high-fived me as I gulped more water, unused to singing so much for so long. He counted the tips, and we each pocketed $150. Not bad for two hours' worth of work, even if I did have to play "Wagon Wheel."

Brian arrived and clapped us both on the backs. "Nick, I knew you wouldn't let me down. My usual guy called back and quit, the douche. You want to pick up a few weeks while I look for someone?"

"Sounds like fun. Is that cool?" I asked Colin.

"Hell yeah, it's cool."

We high-fived again, and I excused myself to the restroom to empty the gallons of liquid I'd consumed. When I reopened the door, a girl leaned with one foot propped against the wall opposite.

"Hey," she said in a throaty voice, looking me up and down.

"Hey." I returned the once-over.

"Great show." She flipped her blonde hair over her shoulder and stepped closer. "Nice shirt," she added, undoing three of my buttons.

*Whoa, hold up. Are you sure you're ready to... Ah, screw it.*

Before I could overthink it, the girl pushed me into the bathroom, wrapped her arms around my neck, and angled my lips to hers.

But when I tasted strawberry lip-gloss, I broke away and narrowed my eyes. "How old are you?"

"Twenty-one today," she said with a proud smile.

"Oh, god, you're a baby."

"I'm no baby. Now, how about you give me a birthday present? I'll give you one."

"It's not my birthday, honey."

Those strawberry lips curved into a smile. "That's not a problem for me."

*She's not Mel.*

*Shut up. Mel is gone.*

She reached for my jeans, and I drew a shaky breath.

∾

Colin was chatting with two girls at the bar when I returned minutes later, red-faced and sweatier than ever. He took one look at me and burst out laughing. "What did I tell you?"

"You were one-hundred percent right, thank you very much," I replied with a wicked grin.

"Hang out with us. I'm sure these ladies won't mind."

I shook my head. "I'm wiped. Think I need to work on my stamina. See you next Saturday, okay?"

"You know it." Colin tossed a wave, and I took my leave.

*Sappy geek. Sentimental fool.* My smile slipped the second I turned away. I jogged down the stairs trying to shake the girl's look of bewilderment when I'd jumped back before she could unbutton me. Certainly looking like a panicked loser, I'd babbled something about her being too young and bolted.

*You've got to forget her. She's getting married. You might as well hook up in the bathroom. It's not like you have a reason to be faithful.*

I hit the road again and drove for over an hour, trying to get okay with my new-old reality.

But the only reality that felt right was when my thoughts were silent and the engine filled my ears.

∾

The next morning, I met Ben and Celeste at the gym. "How are you?" Celeste asked right away, her hand on my arm, gaze critically assessing.

"Fine, thanks. What's new?" I gave her a quick hug.

She knitted her brows. "Not much. Are you sure you're fine?"

"Can we work out?" The sympathy vibe was wearing thin.

She dropped her hand and flashed an apologetic smile. I twisted my lips, and she led us inside.

Celeste headed to spin class while Ben and I hit the treadmills. "How was the party?" he asked while we warmed up. "Or do you not want to—"

"It was okay. And by okay, I mean fucked-up and awkward." I upped my speed. "But it's over, and that's good. I got a call from my Uncle Brian yesterday. I filled in at his bar last night."

"Yeah? How was it?"

I laughed as I ran, thinking of how tired I'd been. "Awesome. A blast. A lot of work. I'm going to do it for a few weeks."

"That's cool. Good money?"

"Decent. Plenty of beer, too. And girls." The words came out unplanned, but I didn't clarify. Maybe if I said it, I could start to believe it and move on.

Ben didn't speak for a mile or so, but I felt the question coming before he asked it. "Back in the saddle, then?"

"Mm, you know. Whatever. Just want to get back to normal." *That, at least, is true.*

"Got you. Take care of yourself."

"I always do. Come on, let's do weights." I punched the stop button and jumped off the belt, not waiting for him to follow.

Ben got the hint. The rest of our workout was spent talking like old times, trading insults and discussing whatever came up. Later, the three of us went out. Even Celeste let my little saga go. It was fun. It was normal.

It would've been perfect if only I could've stopped thinking of Mel with every fucking breath I took.

# 26

# MELODY

The future Mrs. Storms didn't wear jeans and t-shirts. She wore stylish pants and tops that made her look traditional and classy. The future Mrs. Storms had black hair *all* the time, except for the few hours every morning when she and her darling fiancé worked out with a trainer, when she wore a scarf instead.

I learned all this as soon as I moved in on Monday. Jesse found me sulking over a sandwich. Leaving Dad this time had been tougher than all the others, and I'd only moved about half an hour away. Jesse grabbed a seltzer and gave me a kiss. "Red?" he greeted.

I touched my ponytail. "I don't usually wear the black at home." The apology in my voice irritated me.

"Uh-huh, but you never know who'll drop by. It's best if you stick to the image, okay babe? Also, when you're settled in, you can change clothes. Use the ones Fern picked. You'll look great."

*Because I don't look great the way I am?* I glanced at my beloved concert tee and nodded silently.

I got used to my clothes and hair fast. The two looks *had*

saved my ass with Seth in New York, so complaining made no sense. The more difficult adjustment was with how slowly time moved when I was stuck in Jesse's house. I had social media to work on of course, but with the article edited and waiting for press and most of the wedding plans in place, there wasn't much to do.

Morning workouts became my favorite part of the day. The burn satisfied, and it was nice to have time with Jesse the man, not the celebrity. If it weren't for that, I don't know if I would've survived. With every day that passed trapped in the house and this new, rigid role, Jesse Storms the pop star was turning into a monster in my mind.

A monster I had agreed to marry. A monster who held the keys to my writing dreams. A monster who had boxed me into a life I'd never asked for. It was hard to say who I hated more, him, or me.

The week crawled. We flew to Houston on Friday for two shows over the weekend. Peter set me up for an interview with *Today's Hollywood*, a weekly celeb magazine—the one I'd written for once upon a time, actually.

I sat in the hotel suite, dressed in a crisp white blouse and khakis, and tried to relax and play this role. The journalist smiled sweetly at me while a mini team of photographers snapped us from all angles. Her questions were all about Jesse. How did we meet? How did I react when he won *Pop*? How blindingly giddy had I been at his proposal? She asked me about his trip to Europe, and I gave her the response Peter and I had crafted: "We worked past it. It helped us see what really mattered, how much we love each other."

"Lovely," she murmured. "But tell me, Melody. What were you doing while Jesse was gone?" Her eyes narrowed in faux sympathy, lips pursed in a secretive frown.

I paused as a barrage of memories bubbled in my chest. *Falling in love and ruining lives, mine included.* "I was writing my story," I said softly. "Taking time for myself."

After that, we got into wedding details. I "confessed" my colors were gold and navy and dropped vendor names of my baker and my dressmaker. Yes, the wedding would be in the Downtown Presbyterian Church in Nashville on September 7th and, yes, I had a workout routine and a strict diet.

We continued the charade with a shared laugh when I whined about how hard the trainer liked to push me. I threw up in my mouth when she used the term bikini-body.

The second she thanked me and shook my hand, we both exhaled loudly. Our expressions slipped, and we traded closed-lipped smiles. *Of course you love this as much as I do. We're both enthralled, right?*

The door opened, and Jesse strode in. Instantly, he captured everyone's attention, especially the journalist's. "How'd she do?" he asked her.

I watched her rapid blinks and the hint of blush that crept to her cheeks. She nodded, but I wouldn't have been surprised had she ripped her blouse open for him instead. "We, ah, got what we needed, Mr. Storms. Enough for the article."

Jesse kissed my cheek. "You're so quiet for a girl who's so good with words."

I didn't bother to reply, because *exactly* was the only thing I could think to say. He put his arm around my shoulder and looked down at his phone, clearly forgetting everyone else in the room. The journalist deflated as she turned to gather her bag.

He looked at me again once the room was clearing out. "Maybe we won't do too many more interviews. It's okay if you have an air of mystery. You don't have to be a diva, just as long as you give them something."

"Sure thing, Jess."

"Awesome. Want to come nap with me before the show?"

I shifted, and he dropped his arm. "Actually, I think I might swim. I feel restless."

"You got it. I'll see you later in the lobby." He touched my nose and leaned close to my ear. "Put on a swim cap."

*Thanks for that,* sweetheart. *Like I needed reminding again. Gah, why did I change my look in the first place?* In the bathroom, I tucked my hair into a rubber cap and scowled at the mirror.

The hotel pool was empty. My toes curled over the edge while I stared into the placid blue water, suddenly and immensely alone. "My story," I murmured. "My leap."

I thought about standing on the ledge of that house. Was it really only a few weeks ago, not years? I thought about Nick's hand squeezing mine. I thought about my hair stuffed into this damn cap. *Like fucking Rudolph.* I thought of the Christmas cartoon and laughed at the absurdity.

I stood frozen on the edge of the pool a long time; then, abruptly, I threw myself into the deep end. The water closed around me, and I sank like a stone to the bottom. Kneeling on the tiles, eyes pinched tight, I stayed there until I couldn't stand the burn in my lungs anymore. Only then did I push to the surface, gasping for air.

As I floated on my back, it occurred to me that gasping for air was the perfect metaphor for everything lately.

# 27

# NICK

"My turn to pick." I dipped my hand into the jar of requests and pulled a slip of paper. "'Let's Talk About Sex.'" I laughed as I read, and then turned to Colin with a serious expression. "Is this a subject you're familiar with?"

The crowd roared.

Colin winked at the front tables. "Got my PhD in it. How about you, Nicky?"

"I gave a TED Talk about it. Let's go." I pounded the opening notes, and Colin and I began to sing again. We were well into our set for the second Saturday in a row. I was a little drunk and having a blast, sweating and belting out songs.

My throat was dust by 10pm, but we had one more request to do. The final strip I pulled left my stomach somewhere around my knees when I read the scrawled words. "'Would You Mind.'"

*Stay in character.* I bit my cheek and gave Colin a skeptical frown.

"What is that?" he asked. "I don't know that song."

"It's Jesse Storms's new song!" a female voice called.

"Oh, okay, yeah—*nope*." Colin shook his head, and I tossed the slip over my shoulder. I could've played that damn song with my eyes closed of course, but "Sweet Caroline" closed the show so much better.

I was so drained that I almost fell over when we bowed goodnight, but I caught my third wind seeing Ben and Celeste seated at the corner of the bar. They clapped and whooped for me while I chugged a glass of water.

"You didn't have anything better to do tonight?" I laughed.

Celeste rolled her eyes. "Are you kidding? I *had* to see this."

"It was a good show, buddy," Ben agreed. "Let's get you a proper drink."

Colin appeared and slapped a stack of bills on the bar beside me. "Another good haul, man."

Ben eyed the bills. "Who's buying that whiskey again?"

"Fine, shut up, this round's on me. Colin, meet my friends. They'll be boring you with talk of china patterns and wedding bullshit before I return." I spun toward the restroom—and stumbled over my feet when Ben shoved me hard in the back. Laughing and throwing up a middle finger, I jogged away.

There was a line about five deep for the pair of unisex facilities. I had just reached for a doorknob when red-manicured fingers covered my hand.

"Me first." The brunette's lipstick matched her nails as she flashed me a sexy smile. "Unless you'd like to join me?"

*Two weeks in a row, really? Maybe this is a sign. Go with it. Move on.*

"Nah, you go ahead. I was just going to wash my hands anyway." I cringed at the rasp in my voice. It was from singing, but really just made me sound nervous as hell.

She laughed. "Funny, I don't need to go anymore. Buy me a drink?"

I shrugged, so she followed me back to the bar. Halfway across the room, I gave myself a mental slap. *Keep your shit together. Be cool.*

"Hey, guys, this is, uh—"

"Jana." The girl held out her hand while Colin and Ben smirked. Celeste's eyes went round.

I curled the side of my lip and glanced at the guys. To Celeste, I said, "So, you liked the show?"

"Um, oh, yes. Yes, of course! It was fabulous." With every word, her dismay faded into enthusiasm that truly did make me smile.

"Thanks, cuz." I flagged the bartender for a rum and coke for my new friend and drained my whiskey. "I'm pretty beat. Y'all ready to head on?" Ben and Celeste nodded, so I turned to Jana. "Have a good night, okay sweetheart?"

She frowned. "Are you sure? I could let my friends know if you wanted me to go—"

"Nah, I've got to crash. See you around, maybe next week." I kissed her cheek, high-fived Colin, and escorted my friends outside.

The moment we were on the sidewalk, Celeste whirled to me. "I mean, I like to think I'm hip, but what the hell, Nicholas? Did you bang that girl in the bathroom?"

I sneered. "Really, Celeste, is that an appropriate question?"

"They're consenting adults, baby. It's fine." Ben couldn't keep a straight face as he put his hand on her shoulder.

She frowned deeper but nodded. "Guess so. Just seems soon."

Teasing vanished. "Soon? How long am I supposed to

wait to look at another woman while *she* plans her *wedding*? How exactly does that work?"

My cousin's big green eyes softened at the edge in my voice. She sighed and rubbed her forehead. "I want to say the right things with this whole Mel situation, but I mess up every time. I'm sorry again, Nick."

I pulled her into a hug. "You're just looking out for me. I can't be mad at that, but hell. I'm don't know what I'm doing either. I just want to have some fun."

*And yet, I can't seem to stomach it.*

She squeezed me, and I let her go. Celeste brightened and slipped her arm around Ben's waist as we ambled for the cars. "Well, like I said, you were amazing up there! The show was great, and you sounded fantastic. If you weren't my cousin, *I'd* consider banging you in the bathroom after a performance like that."

"Wow," Ben drawled while I burst into a coughing/laughing fit. "I can never un-hear that."

Celeste giggled merrily. "Oh, and if I weren't with this guy, of course."

"Damn, a year ago you'd have washed out my mouth for a joke like that."

We reached the parking lot chatting like usual, making plans to meet at our friends' concert the following night. David and Kira were about to go on a mini-tour to expand their image; this show was their last before they left town, and we wanted to show our support. I promised not to be late and jumped in my car.

Cruising kept my thoughts quiet as usual, but as soon as I fell into bed, they started up again. *Let's Talk About Sex.* The song from earlier made me sneer in the darkness. *You've got to get over this, or you'll never have anything to talk about again.*

That thought didn't have the effect I'd intended. Instead

of steeling my resolve, I pictured Mel astride my lap, shouting my name so loud the neighbors could hear.

Impulsively, I fumbled in the nightstand for the head-phones I kept in the drawer and grabbed my phone from beside the lamp. I plugged in and tapped the file I knew too well, letting her breathless pleas fill my ears.

Twelve minutes, thirty-six seconds later, "Please... *Nick!*" sent me over the edge of climax.

I collapsed, gasping, and opened my eyes. *This isn't moving on, loser.*

But fuck all, it was still hot.

Thanks to Mom, my shoulders were tight again when I slid into the booth the following evening for the concert. Lunch with the parents had turned into the Spanish Inquisition about my personal life. It had been a good two months since I'd gotten the treatment. I should've seen it coming, but damn. Mom still held on to the idea that I'd settle down with a nice girl—and the odds were very, very good that she knew precisely the girl I needed. Maybe it was so-and-so's daughter, or the sweet bank clerk, or the dog's groomer.

What it always was, though, was a waste of time.

At least the familiar surroundings of Bar 40 let me settle in and enjoy Dave and Kira's show. Since last fall, they'd put a lot more into their act, and *damn* did it show. As their harmony filled the room, I wondered if they'd let me do their album. It was definitely time for them to put some-thing to press. My brain spiraled off on ideas of working for Jack and Cellar Door, building a client list that started with You & I and grew from there. No stress, no fucking pop stars,

no ghosts from my past. Just good friends and my favorite
kinds of music.

Lost in the daydream, my shoulders were loose again as
we turned our palms red with applause after their first set. I
turned to ask Celeste a question when—

"Hey, guys."

A knot of anger formed in my chest just looking at Liv,
her pink hair wound around her finger. I didn't speak while
Celeste echoed Ben's murmured greeting.

She smiled at them, and then at me. Her smile didn't
show her teeth like it usually did, and her eyes wore a
guarded, guilty look. "Hello, Nick."

My teeth clenched. "Excuse me. I need a drink."

I ignored my half-full Manhattan and stalked to the bar
for a shot of bourbon. The glass was in front of me when I
caught sight of her in my periphery. "Jesus, just leave me
alone," I groaned.

"No can do, I'm afraid. I miss my friend, and I need to
apologize." Her tone was firm but gentle—extremely un-Liv.

I glanced at her. She was beautiful as always, but something was different. Her sassy edge had eased into a streak of
confidence that looked very, very good on her.

The bourbon stayed on the bar while I exhaled and
turned to face her. "I do, too."

"Me first. I shouldn't have been so rude to your girl that
night. It just threw me, after we'd been, uh, hanging out.
Which I knew was stupid to begin with, but then you
vanished, and it just felt like a slap in the face on levels. To
be fair, the girl handled my shade like a champ." She
grinned.

*Of course she did.* I rubbed my eyes. "I did vanish, and it
was a dick move. We definitely didn't need to let... hanging
out... go any further than it already had because we're

*friends.* And as a friend, it was shit of me to disappear without a word. Rest assured that karma has kicked me in the balls for it on your behalf."

Liv grabbed my hand and squeezed. "I never wanted that, Nick. Never. I love you, buddy. You know this."

"I know this. Same." I returned the squeeze and found half a smile as thanks for her words. Liv had never seemed so sure of herself. I was glad for her and glad to keep my friend, but something about our chat poked all the wrong bruises.

"Give me a hug, boy." We embraced, but when Liv stepped back, her brows were knitted. "Nick? Are you alright? Need to talk?"

Realizing I'd nearly collapsed into her arms, I twisted my lips and reached for the bourbon again, tossing it back with a wink. "Nah, I'm fine. Don't worry about me."

"I'm here if you need, but, ah, I really should get back." Her attention wandered across the room to where Megan sat with two guys I'd never seen before. One had his arm around Meg; the other watched us intently.

"Is that your new fella?" I teased her.

Liv glanced back at me, her cheeks flushed. "Maybe. I'll see you, Nicky."

I watched her hurry away and raised my empty glass in salute.

Celeste and Ben both wore questions in their eyes when I returned to the booth. I shrugged. "We're cool." The words let me find my smile again.

It still took two hours of cruising along the interstates before I wanted to go home.

～

Down, up, down. Since when was my life a fucking roller coaster? Scratch that, because the answer was obvious. Better to say that I'd long ago passed the hang-on-and-enjoy-the-thrill feeling. I was deep in the I've-already-puked-once-just-get-me-off zone when I caught sight of Mel's "Exclusive Interview!!" with *Hollywood Today*:

"The Soon-to-be-Mrs. Storms Speaks! Exclusive details of the Big Day, her wedding diet, and what Jesse Storms is REALLY like behind the scenes!"

The headline greeted me in the lobby at work midweek. My stomach hit my knees again, but I swiped the damn thing and stalked to the conference room to hide out and torture myself.

First, I paced around, throwing nasty glares at the glossy cover. The proposal photo that had put me on Ben's bathroom floor dominated the page, with side-panel images of her ringed hand and the happy couple staring into each other's eyes.

I dropped hard into a chair and tapped the cover. *Don't read this bullshit. It's all fake anyway.*

I read every single word.

Actually, I read the part where she talked about Jesse's time in Europe four times. "Writing my story; taking time for myself."

*Wild idea, wasn't it, Mel?*

I slapped the pages closed and leaned back with an exhale so hard it nearly made the ceiling tiles shake.

# 28

# MELODY

The week after Houston was more of the same: tweets, wedding details, exercise, and sitting on my hands around the house. By Friday, Fern and I had created table assignments for the reception, confirmed the band, catering, cake, and flowers, and visited the dressmaker for a final fitting. Jesse was busy all week with business and promoting the album. He and Peter met with the record label to confirm the tour would begin almost immediately after we returned from our honeymoon in Italy. Plugging in concert dates on my calendar took up a whole morning, mostly because I dragged it out just to have something to do.

I started a journal. Even though the entries were dull, I kept at it every day as exercise for my brain. No telling how long I'd have to wait after the wedding before I could get another assignment. *Now Playing* hadn't contacted me since the article was put to bed. There was no reason to think they needed my services again, but I refused to be discouraged.

Well, I tried not to be.

Saturday morning I lay in bed until the sun scorched the grass. *In a week's time, I'll be married.* I ran through my mental thesaurus for an emotion to apply to that fact, but nothing fit. Finally I gave up and rolled out of the sheets. No training session today, so I dressed in linen shorts, a sleeveless top, and black hair. The future Mrs. Storms was ready for another day.

Peter's voice floated up to my ears as I descended the staircase. "Everything looks good, Jess. Album's buzzing hard, the U.S. tour's on lock, and your wedding is a week away. We're walking high, man."

"No doubt," Jesse agreed, but then exhaled hard. "Wedding. Jesus, I'm getting *married*."

"Fern says it's in order, all the details and whatever shit."

"Mm-hmm. I just wish Melody seemed more excited about it."

I stopped three steps from the foyer and held my breath.

"She's excited. She's *definitely* thrilled," Peter insisted.

But Jesse hummed. "You don't know her like I do. Melody is a different kind of girl. I'm concerned this isn't right for her. Her interview was... thin. She's been quieter than usual lately. Hell, she even asked why I proposed. I just hope this is right."

"Jesse, listen. What did I tell you?" Peter's voice hardened to the tone he used when he wanted Jesse to agree with him. I wondered if Jesse noticed the change, if he realized how persuasive his manager could be.

"Yeah, I know."

"No. What did I *tell* you?"

Jesse sighed. "You said I should lock it down with her after the clinic."

"Why?" he persisted.

My lungs began to burn.

Another sigh. "Because she was slipping away from me. Because she's good for my image, she's good for my press, and she was slipping away. You said I should move quick."

"Right."

"Do you think she was with someone else? Or was she just happier on her own?"

"Jesse, when I saw her in New York, she had the look of someone who had been getting laid for a week straight."

I wished desperately I could see Jesse's reaction—or maybe I didn't. It was hard to know.

After an eternal, heavy silence, my fiancé cleared his throat. "Who the hell would she—"

"Nick."

*Oh, god, I'm going to pass out.*

"Nick?" Jesse echoed.

"They went to high school together. I checked it out. It's the only person who would make sense."

Silence.

"Maybe she'd be happier with him," Jesse mumbled, and my heart twisted.

"Not your problem. You need her. You two make a good team."

"Yeah... guess so."

"She'll be fine. She'll love being your wife. Just give her time."

My heart untwisted. Ice settled in my veins.

Fucking Peter.

I ninjaed up the stairs and locked my door, careful to keep it from making a sound despite the fact that my hands were shaking. I paced on the carpet for a few turns while a scream bubbled deep in my gut. Grabbing a pillow, I dove into the closet and threw myself to the floor. Amid all my fancy new shoes, I broke into wailing, uncontrollable sobs. The pillow made it hard to breathe, but at least it muffled my noisy frustration and pain.

Damn Peter to hell, he was the one who had done this. He was looking out for his client, but in the process, he'd fucked my life royally. *You were a* fool *to ever think you controlled this story.* I sobbed in anger for being such a pawn, for being so naïve, for everything I lost when Jesse opened that velvet box. He wanted to give me my cut and keep me close, but in doing so, he robbed me of my story and replaced it with his own.

And I had let him do it because I thought I knew all the angles.

The pillow took my tears and punches like a champ until, spent and exhausted, I sat up slowly and looked around the closet. The carpet was white. The girl in the mirror was a wreck. Blood-red cheeks, watery eyes, and crooked hair equaled a ghastly sight. I closed my eyes and pictured pink carpet and a much younger me, but the image only made more tears fall. With a sigh, I yanked off the wig and stumbled back to bed. In seconds, I fell into a deep, dead sleep.

Jesse's knock an hour later jolted me awake. "Baby girl? Are you sick?" he called through the door.

I bolted upright, disoriented, and cleared my throat twice before speaking. "Had a headache this morning, Jess. I'll shower and be right down."

"Do you need anything?"

I cracked the door open and hoped my thick voice sounded more sleepy than sad. "No thanks. But, um, would it be okay if I went to Dad's house tonight?" *Did I really just ask permission to see my own father?*

"Sure thing. Well, but there's a party in Memphis we got word of this morning. Would you rather come to that?"

I peeked out and confirmed the false invite by his expression, exactly as I expected. I smiled at his half-smile. "Silly boy. You go have fun. Bachelor party, right?"

He grinned and caressed my face. "That was kind of the idea. You look shredded, Melody. Take care of yourself today, okay?"

"I will."

Once Jesse left for Memphis, I settled out on the terrace and gazed blankly at the lawn. The landscapers were out, and the mower's drone and the scent of cut grass soothed me.

While I sat, wheels began to turn in my mind that had been at a standstill since that moment on the bridge. But my thoughts were still muddled, unsure what the next step should be. I had no intention of going to my father's house; neither did I wish to stay at the mansion. Having zero friends thanks to a life on the move suddenly became a real problem.

I fished my phone from my pocket and stared at the home screen, hoping for inspiration. Tweets and Facebook posts came in. I idly liked a few things, but then closed the apps and kept staring. *Come on, what's the plan?*

The idea that came to me was so inappropriate I might as well have called Nick himself. The longer I sat there, though, the more compelling the thought became. Finally, with a quick breath, I touched my contacts. The phone rang... and rang... and rang.

Just before I disconnected: "Hello?"

"Is this Celeste?"

"Yes? Who is this?"

My nerve evaporated. "Melody Thomas," I squeaked out. "Uh, Mel."

Facing Olivia in that bar was nothing compared to Celeste's phone silence. Each passing second made me shrink with guilt that I knew I deserved and, in a way, wanted to be held accountable to.

She exhaled after an eternity. "Wow."

That one syllable broke the bubble of tension. Celeste seemed to shift, maybe sit down, and then her voice came through louder and definitely not unfriendly. "Hey, Mel. What's up?"

Guilt morphed into adrenaline and butterflies in my stomach. My nails cut into the palm of my free hand as I closed my eyes. "I'm sorry to bother you. This isn't your business, I know. God, do I know, but I'm freaked out, and I didn't have anyone. See, I overheard—no, forget that, you don't care—I guess I just—shouldn't have called you." My babbling broke off when tears welled up.

"But you did," she said gently. "So, tell me what you need."

With a deep breath, I tried to keep my voice level. "I feel trapped. I need to get out of this house for a while, and I couldn't think of anyone to call. You said—I know that was before, when Nick—"

"I said to call if you needed a friend. And you called."

"Uh-huh." I sniveled like a baby.

Celeste waited for more, but I couldn't speak. She tried again. "So, do you want to go out tonight, or what?"

Tears blurred my vision; I bit my lip hard. "Uh-huh," I repeated.

She laughed. "Sounds good to me. Why don't we meet at Virago at seven for dinner? Do you know where that is?"

"I'll figure it out. Seven. Thank you." I hung up. My cheeks were wet, but a smile crept in, too.

This was a new angle. This was my story again.

*Mel* walked out of the house right on time that night. I wore my favorite Grecian sandals, an emerald scoop-neck tank, and white linen capris. *My* hair was scrunched into beach waves and back in a low ponytail. I even had my favorite shade of red lipstick from Sephora on. Too noticeable for "Coming Storms," the red popped perfectly with my coloring.

Those simple details eased the anxiety in my gut as I swung my car into the restaurant's parking lot. Celeste was already out front in a black beaded halter dress and a sleek high pony of her own. She caught sight of me and waved. "Adorable outfit," she said in greeting.

"Love your dress."

My reply was reflexive. Night after night of parties and clubs, of trending and buzz, had trained me well in flattery. Her compliment, however, threw me much more than a simple hello would've. *When were you last out with friends? Six months? More?*

We headed inside and followed the hostess to a table. Once seated, we each ordered an elaborate cocktail and eyed each other. I pushed away awkward thoughts about my pathetic social life and broke the silence. "Thanks, Celeste."

She waved dismissively. "Everyone gets a bachelorette party, right?"

I smiled a little. "Yeah, guess so. Speaking of, have you and Ben set a date?"

"Uh-huh, April fourteenth, but I'm barely thinking about it yet."

She wasn't as excited to talk about her wedding as I'd anticipated. *Stop looking for angles, freak, and talk to the woman.*

Our cocktails arrived, serving as a well-timed distraction. I'd gotten a Miyagi Mule, and she'd gone for a wasabi martini. We both took a drink before she dropped the small talk. "Sorry, Mel, I'm just not sure what the rules are for this situation. I have to be loyal to Nick, but, then again, I told you to call me."

I was nodding before she finished. "That's totally fair. I wouldn't ask you to tell me anything... about... him. Or, um, anything weird like that." *Eloquent. Bravo, Mel.*

Celeste tilted her head. "Let's talk about you, then. Are you okay?"

I gulped the drink. "No. No, I'm not okay. I'm... stuck."

Her beautiful eyes narrowed. "I'm listening."

*She has to be loyal to him. Tread lightly.* I sighed. "Maybe you're the wrong person to unload on."

"Almost certainly," she agreed with a shrug. "But we're here, so say whatever you want."

I considered my next line, told myself not to trust her, then dropped my shoulders and gave up the script. "I've screwed up so bad. I just want a redo on the last month."

She breathed a laughed. "Boy, do I know that feeling. I was there, Mel. I've been there for *real*."

I looked up from the crab sushi roll that certainly defied my wedding diet. I didn't give a damn about calorie counting, but I had to hear her story. "What did you do about it?"

"Well," she drawled, "first I got really, really drunk and insulted a few people. Then I threw up in my mom's flowers."

I laughed despite the situation, and she twisted her lips and lifted her gaze to the ceiling.

"Classy, right? Anyway, after that, I faced the fact that I had made some serious misjudgments, both about myself and my situation. I dealt with it. I got okay with the fact I was wrong, and I apologized. I quit trying to pretend like I had the answers and let life take me where it would. And I was okay with that, too."

"And?" I whispered. Chills ran down my neck at the coincidence. I knew from those few sentences that calling her had absolutely been the right thing.

Celeste's eyes lit up with the look I'd expected from my first question. That glowing softness I'd marveled at when Megan asked about her ring returned. She twisted the gold band and smiled. "And it worked out perfectly."

"Wait. That was about Ben?"

"It was about me. But it led me back to him. Which," she laughed again, "was exactly where I wanted to be." Her gaze sharpened and flicked over me, but her tone was soft. "I think I'm really glad you called me. Like, *really* glad."

I smiled faintly. "Me, too."

Dinner was lovely. We kept up light conversation about music and work through the delicious meal. When the bill came, she shooed me away and plucked her credit card. "What should we do now? It's your bachelorette party, even if it is the world's smallest one. What would you like?"

"Maybe we could grab another drink? Or shoot pool, if you're into that?" I cringed at my awkward syntax, but I'd expected her to be done with me as soon as the check was signed.

Celeste steepled her fingers in front of her mouth. "We could go see Nick."

I fell back against the booth, all the air rushing out of my body. "No way. He doesn't want to see me, and I have nothing to say."

She put her elbows on the table, lips twitching. "No, I meant *see* him, not 'see' him."

I arched a brow at this coy suggestion, but I think she knew she hooked my curiosity.

She checked her phone and looked back at me, a gleam in her eyes. "He performs at a bar not far away. He wouldn't even know we were there, and it is a lot of fun. No pressure, of course, if you think it'd be wrong."

We stared at each other, silently agreeing it would be terribly, terribly wrong. Finally, my lips tugged up, and she grinned broadly. "Wow, this is a bad idea," she laughed.

"So bad," I agreed.

"We can take my car."

"Perfect."

It was a short drive. I paid for parking, and we walked arm-in-arm like old friends through the downtown crowds made worse by the holiday weekend. We showed ID to the bouncer and had our hands stamped. Celeste led me inside to a metal staircase. Muffled music drifted from above, but I paused on the bottom step, gripped with sudden panic.

"Celeste, this is insane."

She pursed her lips and looked down from two stairs higher. "I know. Nick would kill me if he knew."

"He *can't* know." I shook my head so hard my ponytail bounced.

"Totally agree. So, what should we do? Your wedding is in a week, but you said you were stuck. Do we turn around and go home? Or..." She let the thought finish itself.

I pictured the lake and the balcony and planted my foot on the next step. "Let's go."

The hostess pushed open a heavy black door for us on

the second floor, and we floated into a steamy room and an ocean of applause. My eyes adjusted to the dim light, but all I could see was the bar and a roomful of packed tables.

What I heard, though, was a whole different story.

"Oh, y'all feeling a little romantic tonight, huh? Okay, we can do romantic if you want."

Nick's voice came through the speakers, hit my ears, and shivered straight down to my toes. Women screeched and fell silent as the piano began. Celeste touched my elbow to guide me to a pair of empty seats on the back wall, but my feet tangled to a stop when I saw him.

He sat at a piano, the cuffs of his white button-down shirt rolled up while he caressed the keys. "Your Song," originally by Elton John but probably requested thanks to Lady Gaga's cover for the biopic, poured from his lips into the microphone. His sweat-spiked hair licked his forehead; his glasses slipped down his nose.

My heart sobbed.

The ultra-romantic song burst out of him with a raw energy that took my breath away and ignited my body from knees to throat. His lips almost grazed the mic, and I nearly swooned as I covered my mouth, tears yet again in my eyes.

Celeste pulled on my elbow and dragged me to a barstool. Climbing onto it with such wobbly knees was possibly the least graceful thing I've ever done, but I couldn't care. I couldn't do *anything* but watch him. Hot chills whispered along my clenched muscles while I propped my arm on the table and kept my hand at my mouth. "Holy god," I swore against my palm, eyes flicking over every detail I could soak in.

A black vest and tie with the white shirt made him look very sleek but fitted dress jeans kept him casual. His partner was a hip-looking guy with ankle-length trousers and a designer t-shirt. Their harmony was tight.

It was... He was...

The song died away. Nick lifted his hands from the keys, and the audience's attentive silence gave way to delirious applause again. The women in front of us squealed and turned to each other: "My god, Shawna, he is sinful!"

Shawna screeched and nodded. "I told you!"

Celeste and I both heard them; we caught eyes and began to laugh. "Glad we came?" she asked.

I nodded, but *glad* was definitely not the right term.

"Dude," Nick's partner said into the mic, "you just put Elton to shame. Am I right, ladies?"

The noise skyrocketed again. Nick ducked his head and tried to play it off with a look patented to elicit more shrieks. His theatrics made me laugh and shake my head while they started a new song, this time with Nick on backup.

Celeste sang along with the rest of the audience, but all I wanted to do was watch. This was the most voyeuristic I'd ever gotten to be with him. At the studio, I couldn't do more than catch glances on the sly. When we were together, the dynamic was different. Here, I could absorb the easy confidence of his posture and the cool sexiness he exuded, turned on full blast for the performance but still a natural part of him. The light in his eyes enhanced the grin he flashed so freely.

*These women might think he's handsome, but nobody knows like I do how perfect he is.* A smug smile curled my lips at the thought.

Celeste nudged me. "You're staring."

"He is *everything*. Oh, god, I love him so much."

The words flew out before I could stop them. My

stomach bottomed out to say aloud the secret I'd held so close to my heart.

Celeste's eyes widened, but, unlike my dismay, her face broke into a radiant smile. "I know you do. I just can't believe you said it."

"You know?" I wheezed.

"Of course." She squeezed my arm, then bit down on her lips to smother a delighted giggle. "You can say it again if you want to."

"I love him." I groaned, hiding my face. "I love him *so much*. Oh, god, I'm *screwed*."

Her joy died. "What are you—oh, we have to go. This is their last song. Come on."

We downed our whiskeys and took off at power walk all the way to the garage. Sweat plastered my shirt to my back and soaked the underwire of my bra; my hair frizzed around my temples. Celeste blasted the AC on the silent drive to my car.

Before I got out, I turned to her. "Thank you so much for this," I said from the bottom of my conflicted heart. "Tonight was perfect. Well, maybe not perfect, but—"

"I understand."

I knew she did. I smiled. "What did you tell Ben when you left tonight, by the way?"

Celeste returned my smile. "I told him I was out with a friend."

"I haven't had a friend in ages. Pathetic, I know."

"I understand." She said it so quickly that, again, I knew she did. Celeste bit her lip. "What are you going to do, Mel? Sorry, I shouldn't ask, but—"

I closed my eyes and let the air try to cool all the heated, muddled emotions in my chest. Nothing seemed like a plausible storyline. "I really don't know."

"Well... good luck."

The concern in her green eyes made me twist my mouth. "If only it were that simple. Goodnight, Celeste." She nodded, and I was gone.

My footsteps echoed on the marble foyer when I stepped into the empty mansion. I tossed my bag on the stairs and wandered into the living room. Impulsively, I powered on the stereo and called up the original version of "Your Song." Volume on max and my arms outstretched, I danced around, belting the lyrics, and then put it on repeat and lowered the sound to a decent level. A little nervous energy had burned off thanks to that performance, so I tumbled onto the couch and kicked off my shoes, my feet on the cushion.

Visions of Nick filled my head. With a sigh, I closed my eyes and lifted my hips to shove my pants down, skimming my body with feathery touches that made me shiver. This had been coming since I heard his voice. I relaxed and let my thoughts run wild.

His lips against that microphone became his lips against my body and between my legs. Those hazel eyes glassy with lust while he—

"Sucked... kissed... loved me." Words tumbled out and made me smile as I pushed my underwear aside and soaked my fingers. My back arched off the cushion, but I didn't let up; I fucked myself with strong, rhythmic pulses. Gentleness wouldn't satisfy this kind of fire.

The song made me glow as I pictured lying on my back in the bed we shared.

*Nick over me, the covers hiding us from the world. His glasses bumping my cheek. His stubble scratching my neck. His fingers on my ribs—no, no, it tickles, but—* "Nick, Nick, please, I love you."

Like the memories that flowed through my head, my orgasm hit me in waves. Once it started, it was all I knew, all I needed to know, and all that mattered.

Just like being with him.

I hitched up my pants and hurried upstairs to my bedroom to fall facedown in the pillows. When I woke, mental wheels were turning again.

*"I stopped pretending I had all the answers and let life take me where it would. And I was okay with that, too."* Celeste's words echoed in my ears.

Could I ever be like that? Would I ever be able to accept an unknown story?

# 29

# NICK

It had been a weird weekend. I had performed Friday and Saturday because the bar had been short-staffed, so by the last number Saturday I could barely see straight. On top of that, I was antsy about the impending album release and wedding, anxious and dreading it all at once. That I hadn't received an invitation was a surprise, but it was also a relief to know my role in Jesse's crew was over. Rick had given me another project to produce, but I still got his death glare anytime Jesse was mentioned. In a week's time, maybe we could all just move fucking on from this disaster.

But that show ended like every other, and I was too beat to bother thinking about all that mess as I chugged water at the bar.

"You know you're getting a reputation, right?" Colin asked when he found me. He emptied the tip jar and gave me a *tsk*.

"Excuse me?"

He dropped a request slip, "accidentally" missing the counter and thus making me bend to swipe it from the floor. "Thanks, asshole," I muttered while he laughed.

*One more request, Nick? Make me sing in your shower
tonight. xoxo, Amy*

My lips twitched. "Creative."

Colin laughed. "She was as red as her hair when she
gave me that. Said to find her by the restrooms in ten
minutes." I pocketed the slip and reached for my half of the
money, and he eyed me. "Well? You're going to go for it,
right?"

"I'd be a fool not to." I clapped his back and made
toward the restroom.

Halfway across the bar, I spotted a redhead giggling with
her friend and stopped dead. A glance over my shoulder
confirmed Colin was chatting with the bartender, so I wove
through the crowded tables and hit the exit before anyone
spotted me.

*No redheads ever again.*

Well. Except the one in my headphones once I was
in bed.

When I rolled up to the family Labor Day party the next
day, it struck me hard how much older I felt than when I
was there two months ago. Even enduring the third degree
from Ben on that afternoon seemed so innocent now.

But some things never change, and there was comfort in
routine. Same as last time, I revolved my way through hugs
and hellos in the house, promised my aunts that all was
great, and escaped with a burger to find Celeste and Ben on
the patio.

"No beer today?" Ben asked when I dropped into an
empty chair.

I saluted with my water. "Nah, I thought I should take a

break." My body had been screaming for water recently, what with the shows and lack of decent sleep, so I was happy to lay off the booze a bit.

I bit into my food and caught eyes with Celeste. "What's that look?" I asked with my mouth full.

Her gaze dropped to her cup. "What look?"

"That swallowed-the-canary look you just gave me. What's up?" She took a drink, so I glanced at Ben. "Any idea what's going on?"

Ben narrowed his eyes at his fiancée. "I'm curious, too. What *was* that look for?"

"I didn't give a look!"

"Yes, you did," we said in unison, and I added, "You're giving it again."

She held up both middle fingers, then flipped her hair and changed the subject. "How was your show last night?"

"Good, thanks. Would've loved to see you again, but I know y'all have 'stuff' to do." I put air quotes around stuff and grinned. "And by *stuff*, I mean fu—"

"Language!"

We all jumped. Aunt Elle stood behind me, a pitcher of lemonade in hand and a curve to her lips that she tried to hide. "Watch yourself, Nicholas Alexander," she scolded while her daughter turned pink.

I ducked my head and grumbled, "Yes, ma'am," but her obvious amusement made me want to see how far I could push before she laughed. It was the first time in ages I'd been in the mood to joke. Aunt Elle gave me a playful glare and disappeared inside before I could try it.

The three of us traded a wasn't-that-fun look before Ben returned to the point. "Actually, Celeste abandoned me last night. I should've come out."

Another guilty look flashed on her face.

"There." I pointed at her and snapped my fingers. "There's that look again. What's going on?"

Celeste swatted my hand away. "Nothing! I didn't!"

"You didn't what? Abandon Ben or give a look?" I pressed, curious at this unusual caginess from someone who was normally very direct. Another middle finger was my reply.

Ben spoke slowly, his eyes on Celeste, who studied her food. "Well, not really abandoned. She was out with a friend, so I stayed home and watched TV."

"Girls' night?" This question, at least, got me a nod. "You should've brought her to the show. I always like an audience."

"I did, actually," she blurted. "But we didn't stay to the end."

I threw my hands up and almost dropped the plate in the process. "Why the hell didn't you just say?"

Celeste shrugged. "I thought you'd be mad I didn't stay to talk."

"When have I ever been *mad* about something so minor?" Another shrug was my answer, so I tried teasing her. "Was she single and cute? Because in that case I might be mad."

"You didn't tell me you went to his show, either," Ben interjected in a thoughtful murmur.

Uh-oh. Celeste's chin lifted high. Her eyes flashed in a way that told everyone in the vicinity that she was *over it*. "Well, I did," she snapped, icing us both with her glare. "Excuse me, I need to see if Mom needs help." With an added stomp of her foot, she disappeared inside.

Ben and I looked at each other. "Super shady, right?" I asked.

"Most definitely."

"Got a guess why?"

"Not a clue, but I'll try to find out."

"Good luck with that," I chuckled. My cousin could be stubborn as hell, and we both knew it.

The afternoon slipped by with chat and music and all that slow Sunday stuff. Eyelids drooped; we took turns dozing off while the others kept the conversation going. When the shadows got long, we roused ourselves from the food/sun/family cocoon and shuffled out to our cars.

While Celeste was inside getting loaded down with leftovers, Ben turned to me. "You know we're friends for life, right?"

"Sentimental suddenly?"

"Nah. Well, maybe. I was thinking about how, less than a year ago, I stood in this driveway trying to figure out how to tell Celeste I loved her. I only got to do that because you helped me out."

I waved a hand in a slow circle. "Your point?"

Ben shrugged. "I know you don't want to talk about it, but I'm there for you. This'll be a hell of a week, so call if you need."

One side of my mouth curled up. "Thanks, man." It was the first time I didn't blow off someone's attempt at support through this mess, maybe because I knew that I had *no* idea how the week would be. "I'll text you, okay?"

"Anytime."

I punched his shoulder, but we both rushed to help Celeste as she staggered out of the house with enough Tupperware to stock small village. Half were for me, so I put them in the trunk and kissed my aunts once more, then waved at my friends and went to get a good night's sleep for once. Something told me I was going to need it to make it to next Sunday.

# 30

# MELODY

Jesse texted to say that he was in Memphis until Monday, so I went to Dad's house Sunday morning. We spent the day on various household projects—our favorite pastime—but a growing sense of restlessness and desire for action kept building in my chest.

*Maybe Dad and I could hit the open road. He's owned this house for years and never spends a penny. We could buy an RV. I could earn cash by writing 2-minute stories at fairs, maybe self-publish a book...*

*A book about what, exactly? The freewheeling lifestyle? Yeah, that's not been done before.*

"What's with you?" Dad's question jolted me out of my head while we finished our ice cream on the porch that night. "You've looked ready to climb out of your skin all day."

"Sorry, just got a lot on my mind."

"Wedding?" I shrugged, so Dad tried again. "Can't believe you're getting married next weekend. Seems like you've been engaged about five minutes."

"It was a whirlwind for sure. I can't really believe it, either."

"Uh-huh," he grunted, still holding me with a gaze as sharp and blue as my own. "But the question was what's got you so jittery, so spill it."

I sighed and set my bowl on the little table between us, tucking my feet on the chair to face him. "Dad, last month you said you worried you trained me to be too independent." He nodded. "But I'm *good* at being independent. What's wrong with that? Shouldn't I have my own goals and plans? Why would I want to cling to someone else to get by?"

Dad held up a hand. "You misunderstood. Maybe I spoke wrong. I'd never encourage you to be more *dependent*. You're brilliant and talented and absolutely should be true to yourself. There's nothing wrong with that in the least. I just meant... Gosh, what did I mean?" He chuckled and took a bite of ice cream. "Maybe I meant that sometimes I worry you're too focused on *controlling* your future. So much so that you don't make room for surprises life might have in store."

I swallowed hard. "Have in store? Like what?"

"Love."

One blunt word, spoken with no hesitation. It knocked the breath out of me.

Dad continued. "You can't plan for love or schedule it in. When it happens, everything goes upside down, and you just gotta jump in and hang on. Or, walk away knowing you let something important go."

I tried to keep the rattle out of my inhale. "Some chances don't come at the right time."

My father cupped my chin in his hand and forced me to meet his eyes. "And some chances come *twice*, Melody

Emily Thomas. How many times can you deny an opportunity before it disappears forever?"

I recoiled. "Dad! You—"

"Know exactly who's got you perplexed? You think I'm that big of a dummy, kiddo? Give me some credit." He shook his head and paused, clearly to let me recover before he asked the question of the weekend: "What are you going to do?"

"Nothing. I don't know. Hate myself forever," I grumbled, picking at my toenail polish.

"Bullshit," he chuckled. "That's not your style. Pull yourself together and light that fire back up. Deal with the mess you're in."

I glanced up and tried a tiny smile.

Dad touched my cheek again. "For now, how about a movie? I think it's my turn to pick, and I haven't seen *Ghostbusters* in ages. Sound good?"

"Perfect," I whispered.

Curled into the corner at the head of my bed, I closed my eyes even though the lights were off. The ringtone trilled.

"Hello? Scott?"

I opened my mouth, but it took a second to push the words out. "Hello? Um, no. This is Melody."

My mother paused. When she spoke again, I could hear the smile in her voice. "Melody, sweetheart, what a surprise. How are you?"

I looked around the dark room. *Why are you hiding?*

When the movie ended, Dad had thrown me another curve by tossing me the land line. "Call your mother. She's two on speed dial," was all he said as he kissed me goodnight.

I couldn't remember the last time I'd held a phone that was just a phone. I also couldn't remember the last time I'd spoken to my mother. I hadn't even told her about the wedding, and I didn't intend to mention it.

My pulse was illogically high as I clutched the bulky plastic and accidentally hit a rubber button. The beep made me jump, but it unstuck my tongue, too. "I'm fine."

"It's been, what? A year? Two? Surely you can do better than *fine*."

"Do you have a minute to talk?"

"Of course. Hold on." She spoke off speaker, and then the background noise was gone. "Okay, go."

I palmed my eyes and realized that tact had no place in this conversation. "When you left us, you said it was too much work. What was so damn hard about being my mom? His wife?"

Dead silence.

*Hang up on me, I don't care.* But the phone creaked from how tightly I clung to it.

Eons passed before she cleared her throat. "Um, wow. Definitely wasn't expecting this call tonight." She laughed, but her voice was thin. "No, Melody. Scott always did right by me, and it was *never* too hard being your mother. You were—are— a joy, even with that stubborn streak as wide as my own."

I pictured her curly copper hair, much lighter than mine, twined around her fingers, and silently agreed with her. "Then what made you quit?"

"Quit... I guess that's fair, huh?" She paused again and sighed loudly. "I didn't quit, Melody. I began my own life. I don't expect you to understand. You're a grown woman who made her own way. I was twenty-one and pregnant, and I didn't know what I wanted to do with myself. Scott was just starting out, too. We'd known each other less than a year, and suddenly found ourselves in this new, fused identity of a family. There wasn't room for discovery anymore. Eventually, I knew I had to find out who I really was. I love you to the ends of the earth—and I love your father that much, too —but I had to figure out how to love myself."

"Did you?" I whispered.

"It's not very impressive, but yes."

Tears wept freely down my face. Talking to my mother lifted something heavy from my soul. "I should go," I said. "But thank you for this."

"Oh, Melody, you can call me anytime. You're my daughter, darling. I know you never forgave me for leaving, but—" Her voice cracked.

"I think I just did."

She sobbed; so did I.

"Maybe I could call you again soon?" I sniveled. She agreed, and I smiled. "Okay, well. Goodnight... Mom."

*"I just can't handle it." You didn't mean being my mom; you meant not being you. I always thought you were so selfish, but, god, do I understand now. Who am I? Who have I become? And how the hell do I get back to Mel's story when I'm so far gone as ComingStorms?*

I wiped my eyes and swallowed hard. Still no solutions to this mess appeared, but a weight was lifted from my soul. For the moment, that was good enough.

And, oh boy, did I need a little dose of good to get me through this week.

≈

The next morning found me tweeting and teasing the fans. I sipped coffee, and Dad read the paper across the table.

"How was your talk with Angela?" he asked without looking up.

"Very good."

Dad didn't press for more, but he did chuckle at me as I whisper-edited the posts I created to get the album on the front of everyone's mind. "Don't they have promotional departments at the record label?"

I nodded. "Of course. But social media is real-time. People will see posters, hear and see ads for the album on the radio, so this is like a reminder in their ear."

"Genius," he marveled. "I cannot imagine."

"I know." I flashed a smile.

He returned it. "You look more like my Mel this morning."

"Taking one thing at a time," I admitted. "First step: tomorrow's album drop."

I eagerly anticipated the day of heavy work that stoking nonstop buzz would bring. I even looked forward to being back with the crew again in a way. What I didn't let myself look too closely at was the fact that we would track sales from InSight Studios.

Jesse and I woke before dawn for our training session. By the time we pulled up to the brick building I knew too well, sales were already starting, and my nerves had to take a backseat.

The studio head, Rick Alvin, greeted the crew in the lobby and escorted us to a large conference room. I spied my edition of *Hollywood Today*, which only added to the buzz of adrenaline that made everything surreal. Mercifully, the minute we were in the room, all focus went to the album. Peter projected his laptop on a screen so we could all see the numbers, and even Seth and Steve worked hard. Seth was on the couch, a furious glare pinned on his computer. Now and then, he'd jump up and bark directions into his phone. Steve—*Why don't we call him Eli if that's his name?*—was neck-deep in negotiations for product sponsorships, but I couldn't follow his calls with all the tweets lighting up my phone.

By midday, we were trending so strong, CNBC reported on the album. That got a cheer from all of us and let everyone but Seth take a deep breath. He was in the corner, snarling something that seemed to equal a huge purchase of shares. I sat back in my chair and marveled at both of those guys. *Maybe they do know how to do more than party.*

*Maybe, if sales continue over the week and the guys are busy making stacks of money, I can talk to Jesse. He's not ready to settle down, and he knows it. Maybe we can have a fake wedding, not sign a license, and quietly agree to give each other space. Then, in six months, we can announce an annulment, get a little extra tabloid buzz before the world tour begins—*

"How's it going?"

Every hair on my head prickled at his voice from the door behind me. I didn't move, didn't turn, just sat and stared at my computer. Jesse bellowed a hello and leapt across the room with a huge grin. "Nick, buddy, are you seeing this wildfire? You fucking genius, this thing is insane."

They slapped high-five as Nick chuckled. "I've been at the boards all day, but Rick said it was going well. Congrats, Jesse. You deserve it."

I bit back a giggle to think of all the swagger he'd thrown at the audience Saturday night, and how different he was today. *I'm not the only one who knows how to hide.*

"Bullshit. Take the credit you deserve," Jesse insisted.

"We couldn't have done it without you. Don't you agree, Melody?"

So much for staying hidden.

I blinked up from my screen and smiled sweetly at Jess. "Hmm? Sorry, what? I wasn't listening." Lies.

"I said that Nick should take credit for his work on the album."

"Oh, yeah. Definitely." I kept a keen watch on Jess between glances at the computer.

Jesse leaned his elbows on a high-backed chair across the table from me and gestured toward the door. "Baby girl, I just realized how long it's been since you were here. Nick was so deep in our crew, and you've not seen him in weeks. Tell the man hello."

Ice cubes froze in my stomach. I stared, understood that I was being tested, but didn't move for a breath too long. Jesse's gaze flicked to Peter, who suddenly appeared in my periphery. My fiancé looked back at me and cocked his head, waiting.

I slapped both palms to my cheeks and shook my head so hard my hair danced. "Oh, sorry, baby!" My airy laugh was a bit rusty, but I forced it out anyway. "I'm so out of it from staring at this screen, I totally blanked. Where are my manners?"

*Don't let your knees shake.* I stood and spun around.

Nick's hands were shoved into his jeans. His gray tee and oxblood plaid button-down hugged his shoulders, which were at his ears. Even with the tension in his posture, *god*, why did everything he wore have to be so damn sexy? I swept my gaze over him twice before our eyes locked—

And then, there was no one else in the room. Everything was silent except the rattle of my breath.

He smirked. "I saw that, kid. You just eye-fucked me."

"Maybe I did," I whispered.

In a flash, my back hit the table, legs wrapped around his hips. "Screw this shit," he growled and sent my laptop skittering to the floor before he ripped my shirt straight down the center line. I moaned and reached for his flexed biceps while Nick dropped his head to suck hard on my neck. His hands slid up my body. My skin was cool from the air conditioning all morning, but warmed fast to his perfect touch. I panted his name, squirming until my lips found his—

Nope. None of that even sort of happened beyond the blink that let me imagine it. That one-second fantasy was enough to have me warm and damp between the legs, though, and I felt it acutely as I forced a smile and said, "Fantastic work, Nick."

"Thank you so much, *Melody*." The subtle emphasis on my name and the spark in his eyes tightened my throat, but Nick barely blinked, and his voice didn't waver. "Congratulations on your feature. I bought a copy on my way in this morning. Look forward to reading it this weekend."

*This weekend while you're getting married.* Maybe it should've startled me how much I could read between his words. It didn't.

"I'm sure you have better things to do." I cast my gaze to the carpet while Jess strolled over.

"Sure I don't."

"Melody's article? Thanks for the support, man." Jesse slung his arm around my shoulders. "She's pretty quiet, but that's a front. The girl's a word wizard. She can spin *anything* and make it awesome."

"No doubt," Nick agreed.

Jesse squeezed my shoulders. "Get some lunch, Nicky. Stay awhile."

He chatted with the crew for about half an hour but didn't look my way again. No matter; the damage was done. I tingled around the edges of my body and ached in my core, and all I could do about it was stare at the screens and memorize the sensations for when I was alone later.

When Nick went back to work, Jesse roamed around the room and announced, "I think I should work with him again. He was great, right?"

Seth was off the phone and sprawled on a sofa. He tilted his head back and nodded. "Definitely. Super skilled, and a great addition to the crew." Steve and Peter agreed, and Seth laughed. "That guy gets so much ass. In New York alone, I know he had a girl at the party, and by the next night, he'd hooked up with a—"

"Seth." Fern's sharp rebuke saved me by a syllable. "I don't want to hear about that."

Seth grinned sheepishly. "Sorry, Fern. Sorry, Melody."

I grunted an acceptance, but we weren't done yet.

"What do you think, baby girl? Should I work with Nick again?" Jess asked as he stole some carrots from the plate by my keyboard.

*Ugh, this is getting old.* I sighed and looked up again, hoping to make the point that I was working. "What? Should you work with Nick again? Sure, Jess, why not? Make him your one and only producer as you develop a signature sound. Seems perfect to me."

If I didn't pass the first test, I passed this one. My curt tone and offering of an angle clearly satisfied Jesse. All of the guys nodded, even Peter, and that put the kibosh on the topic of Nick.

Money poured in all day. By late afternoon, we'd taken our feet off the gas, happy to watch the numbers tick. Fern had vanished, the guys were chatting, and the TV blared more good news. I was sprawled out on the couch when Jan called. The room was noisy, so I slipped out to the hallway.

"Melody, bravo," she began. "Have you followed the buzz?"

I bit my lip, but the grin still tugged. "Some. I've been working the album hard, but."

But, yes, I had followed *Now Playing*'s media all day. Yes, I'd seen the tweets about the article from everyone from fans to veteran, *famous*, reporters.

"Well, to put it mildly, we've had a landslide day. Several stores reported they sold out of the edition; people are talking, my dear. The criticism is wildly positive. People love your voice, your approach to the whole reality-TV world. It's," she laughed, "everything I thought it might be when I hired you."

I jumped up and down, pumping my fist. "Jan, that's fantastic," I said when I'd had my moment. "Thank you so much."

"Thank me? You're the one who made us a mint. So, are you sitting down? Is your fiancé holding your hand? Because I've got a little more to discuss."

I stopped hopping and leaned on the wall. "What's up?"

"How about a book, Thomas?" Her excited question made me yelp, so she chuckled and said, "I just got out of an editorial meeting. *Now Playing* wants to publish your book. In the meantime, we're requesting chapter two of a feature to promote it, probably in our early March edition."

"A book and a second feature?" I wheezed. She affirmed, and I palmed my forehead. "Uh, um, uh—about Jesse? Like, a bio, or a tour chronicle, or—"

"No," she interrupted. "Jesse got our support with this article. We'll cover him again when there's more than tabloid fodder to discuss. I want you to look inward. Critically, the best part of your story is your point of view. You have a narrative of your own, and it sparks in the feature. It's the angle of a strong woman who's watching this life unfold, and we want to know about the woman herself. I'm seeing a journalistic/memoir hybrid. How does a career woman live through the flash-bang of pop culture and a sex symbol boyfriend? What's real? What's for show? Tell it all, Melody. People will listen."

"Tell my story?"

"Tell your story."

When I was silent too long, Jan laughed. "Well, is that a yes, or isn't it?"

I came back to life. "Oh, god, yes! Sorry, absolutely yes. I'm just so—wow."

"Go have a fairytale weekend and enjoy every minute of it. We'll talk when you're back from honeymoon, but definitely before his tour."

I promised we would before we said goodbye.

*A book deal. A fake wedding and a scheduled annulment. Jesse's going to be all in on this plan. We've got a perfect angle for both of us now.*

"Melody? Is everything okay?" Jesse popped out of the conference room.

I looked up and grinned broadly. "Jess, guess what."

As I told him all my news, Jesse leaned on the wall opposite me and crossed his arms to listen. He did *not* smile. His brows furrowed when I finished. "Your story?"

I nodded. "What it's like to report and live in this world."

"And what is it like?" He seemed genuinely curious.

"Hectic. Unreal. Fascinating. That's what they want me to tell."

The frown was back. "But we're about to be married. Then it's *our* story all the way. Won't it be weird if my bride is suddenly doing a tell-all when we just tied the knot? That doesn't sound like good spin."

From a spin perspective, Jesse was absolutely right. It didn't stop my jaw from clenching, though. "Jess, this is my dream. A book and another feature? I couldn't have—"

"Babe, I've got you taken care of, don't I? The prenup is more than generous, and you have my media to manage. Things change, Melody. Readjust."

"Are you... forbidding me?"

He shook his head. "Of course not. I just think you need to sleep on it and figure out the right angle to play. Hey, baby girl." Jesse's voice turned to velvet as he hooked my waist and pulled me into a hug, my wrists propped on his shoulders. He nuzzled my neck. "You're the best. One story at a time, yeah?"

Tears threatened as my clever plan went down the drain. I wanted to knee him in the balls for this little show of affection, but that gasping for air sensation rendered me paralyzed. He pulled back and laced our fingers together to lead me back into the conference room.

Just before I stepped inside, intuition whispered in my ear. I looked left and caught eyes with Nick at the end of the hallway. His jaw clenched as he turned away, but my soul still reached out for him as Jesse tugged me along.

"Everyone who's anyone from here to New York is ready to host us tonight. Club, house party, hotel—we're there. We've got so many invitations, I don't know where to begin. All of us will be drowning in Cristal and X and all the blowjobs we can—oh."

Peter's smug voice snapped my attention back to the moment. Beside me, Jesse cringed while the other three men lost their grins fast.

My teeth ground together. "I thought the honeymoon started next week." Disgust laced my words.

Seth and Steve both barked a laugh before Peter glared them to silence. I appreciated the unorthodox support.

Jesse growled. "Nice work, dickhead. She's about to be my wife."

"Aw, come on." Seth straddled the arm of the couch. "Melody knew the score, and she bought in anyway. What's the big deal?"

"Chill," Steve muttered with a quick glance at me. "Melody's cool."

Seth snorted. "Then be cool," he challenged.

Jesse turned his back to the guys and bent to my ear. "It's fine, just take a breath. If you want me to stay in tonight, I will. You know we—"

"Hush," I hissed, eyes still locked with Seth across the room.

"What's it gonna be, Melody?" he called. "Can Jesse come out and play?"

*Someday, Seth Peters, you will feel my wrath.*

It took all my restraint not to hurl my phone at his smirking face. Flushed with rage, I bit my lips and gave a single nod. He grinned and winked like it was all a game. I turned to take my leave, whispering to Jess that I wanted the limo to take me home.

"He made a fortune today, and she'll cash in on it. She could be a little more grateful."

Peter's soft grumble, clearly directed at the guys, hit my ears when my hand was on the doorknob. Vision as red as my hidden hair, I whirled before I knew what I was doing. My phone hit him square between the shoulder blades, hard enough that he stumbled forward with a yell. Seth and Steve whooped in surprise, their twin stunned expressions on me while Jesse shouted my name. Peter's shirt ripped—my phone *broke* from the impact—and he whirled, cursing a blue streak.

"Your gratitude, right there Peter Lawson," I snarled. "Anyone else have something to say?"

Jesse, Seth, and Steve cut their eyes down like a trio of little boys. Peter muttered that he might be bleeding, but then he shut the hell up, too. I iced them with another glare and slammed the door behind me.

Nick was in the lobby, on his way out. He turned at my stomps. His mouth opened to ask a question but closed quick when my glare hit him, too. I shoved past and didn't stop till I was in the car.

*I had to find out who I really was... The best part of the story is your POV... You don't get to write it; you have to* live *it. And when you do...*

I stared out the tinted window as all those words rattled around in my head.

"Things change, Melody." I echoed Jesse from the hall-way, and suddenly it was true. Hands balled into fists, I closed my eyes and let the angle I'd been too scared to look at before take shape.

"Readjust."

# 31

# NICK

"Drunk gaming?"

"Nope, got something better for us to do," I said into the Bluetooth while I navigated traffic after work on Friday. "Brian called an hour ago, says he's got no one tonight. I told him I'd see what I could do."

"You and me?" Ben was clearly surprised. "What's the deal, we play piano for a couple hours?"

"Basically."

"That's it?"

I parked and rubbed my eyes. "Well," I grumbled, "truth is, I'm feeling this tomorrow shit already."

"I figured."

"Yeah."

What an understatement. Every hour was a weight stacked on my shoulders, and this had gone on all week. Ever since I'd bolted from the bar the week before, images of Mel and Jesse had plagued my mind. Why was I acting like the dork of the century in the face of her upcoming marriage? She'd freely admitted that their relationship was built on something real in the beginning. Okay, so it felt like she'd eye-fucked the hell out of me when we saw each other on Tuesday, but maybe that was my imagination. I had to move on. I *had* to. Anything else was a fool's errand, and I'd been running it too long already.

I took a deep breath and continued with my request. *It's what you need. Go with it.*

"What I'd really like to do is play a few tunes, drink way too much alcohol, and make some bad decisions with a woman whose name I have no intention of remembering in the morning. Think you can wingman for me? Also, maybe make sure I don't die of alcohol poisoning."

I was in the elevator before he spoke again. "Dude, I'm—"

"Basically married. Like I don't know," I spoke over him. "But, fuck, man. Can't you just pretend for a little bit? You don't have to actually act on anything. I just need you to have my back. You said you'd be there, and I know you'll look out for me, but if you can't or won't or whatever, I understand. It's cool."

Ben groaned. "I'll pick you up at 7:30."

"What am I getting into with this show?" he asked as he drove us downtown. I explained the setup, and Ben glared at the road and nodded. "That should be easy, especially with you."

I grinned broadly. Part of my slightly manic buzz was definitely fueled by how much fun doing this with Ben promised to be. We'd played together for so long, it took no warm-up to get us in sync.

"Did you tell Celeste? She's not coming, is she?" I asked.

"Yes, I did, and no, she isn't for exactly that reason."

"So you told her the *whole* plan."

"Of course."

"What did she say?"

He shook his head. "She hates it. I'm sure you can infer why. She also hates that she has to stay home and miss our show." He flashed a sly smile. "My girl likes to watch me play."

I answered with gagging noises.

It was the first night where the curtain of summer humidity pulled back, and a breeze wafted in from open windows while the crowd filled in. I was excited, and, as we took the stage, even Ben perked up. I took the lead and said hello, amazed by how natural this had all become in just a few weeks' time. When I introduced Ben, a ripple of feminine sighs ran through the room. He glanced at me and laughed, and, just like that, we were ready.

We kicked off with "Wrecking Ball" and kept it rolling from there. Ben isn't the chattiest of guys, but it didn't matter. We developed a natural routine that kept the shrieks of approval coming as I did the talking and he played the quiet man. As good as Colin and I were at our gig, playing with Ben was next-level awesome.

Both of us were sweat-soaked and perma-grinning by the time I grabbed the request jar for the final number. "Okay, guys, y'all took us all over the map tonight, from Miley Cyrus to John Denver, but we've done our best. What do think, did we do alright?"

"Woo!" howled the room.

"Thank you so much. We've got time for one more. Benjamin, I feel it's only right for you pick your first finale." I tossed him the jar to loud cheers.

"Too much pressure," he rumbled into the mic as he unscrewed the lid. "I have to find the perfect song."

"Aw, stop trying to read the tea leaves and pull one. I'm falling asleep waiting on you. Just kidding, ladies. I'm *far* from sleepy." My wink got precisely the response I wanted. Man, I was on a roll.

Ben closed his eyes and pulled a strip. He set the jar on the ground and read the paper. I watched his brow crease before he looked up at me with wide eyes. "Holy shit," he mouthed.

I cocked my head while the audience quieted. "What's the song?"

"Well, hmm." He looked at the paper again.

"Remember the rule: you don't know it, toss it." My theatrical voice faded as I tried to guess what he held.

Ben shook his head. "Nope, I know it. It's, uh, 'Jessie's Girl.'"

I almost dropped my beer. Rick Fucking Springfield had written me a theme song. How had that never occurred to me? Ben and I gave each other a *what-the-fuck* look while the crowed clapped.

I tapped the keys and pushed my glasses higher on my nose. With a dry laugh, I nodded. "Let's do it. I'll take the lead."

Ben gave me an encouraging smile, and the cheers increased.

I went all in, gave the lyrics a heavy treatment of sarcasm that actually made it sound pretty cool, and wrung out my vocal cords in the process. By the time we faded out with a chorus of the title, I had to laugh at the absurdity. We pounded out the last bars, and I shouted over the roar, "Let's dedicate that number to Jesse Storms, who's getting married right here in downtown Nashville tomorrow. I'm Nick, this is Ben, and *this* is the tip jar. Goodnight, guys!" We took another bow, slung our arms around each other's shoulders, and went straight for the bar.

A woman leapt off the nearest barstool, and Ben stumbled to a stop. I groaned, recognizing Celeste's auburn hair. She faced us, flushed and glitter-eyed.

"I know, I know, I'm leaving. I just couldn't miss the show," she said sheepishly, already grabbing her purse.

Ben's arm vacated my shoulder. He strode forward, threaded his hands into her hair, and pulled her straight into one of the hottest kisses I'd ever seen. For all the hell I've given them with innuendo jokes, I'd never seen them like this. Celeste melted into him, her jaw making it obvious that plenty of tongue was involved in their exchange.

Meanwhile, the lyrics to that damn song echoed in my brain and made me think of *her*. Her big blue eyes, her body, loving someone else... I gritted my teeth and cleared my throat.

They pulled apart. Celeste stepped back, looking even more dazzled than before. "I'm going," she repeated.

"Good." Ben's pitch was dark, but his smile made her take three steps backward, gaze on him, before she turned and jogged to the exit.

"Jesus, man," I grumbled. Ben just chuckled and pushed his sweaty hair off his forehead.

We made more money in tips than I had yet, so we cheersed with a shot of Jameson Black Label before Ben stood up. "Go find us a table. I'll get a round and meet you."

What a friend. I'd barely staked a back booth when he strolled up with an armful of beers and two ladies in tow who smiled shyly down at me. I gave him a grateful look and waved them to sit, but that stupid song was still in my head.

"You guys were awesome," my girl gushed, her hand on my thigh. "I mean, wow. How do you know all those songs?"

I shrugged. "Just do. Not too hard."

"Oh, it seems like it would be. You're very talented."

I swallowed a drink and put my lips near her ear. "I've got lots of talents, honey," I whispered, already fingering the strap of her metallic camisole.

"Want to show me some?" She batted her eyelashes and took a slow sip through her straw.

"Love to."

A glance at Ben made it clear he was tense as his girl inched closer and closer. Every move she made was countered by an inch backward on his part, but he caught my eyes and quirked his lips before feigning interest in the conversation again.

Within half an hour, I was pressed against the bench with a hard buzz in my brain and my girl's tongue down my throat. I knew I owed Ben huge for this night, but it numbed me exactly like I needed. A pleasant floating sensation replaced the weights of the week, and even the song had gone silent.

"Nick." Ben's voice cut through my fog. I pulled away from the girl and attempted to focus on him. "We should leave. Do you want to go to your place?"

Through my stupor, I thought of Heaven, the girl from the house party on July 4th. She was beautiful and sweet enough, but when she pulled on my arm, I knew for damn sure that her invitation to go upstairs was the last thing I wanted.

Just like I knew now that fifteen minutes of sloppy kisses in a booth was one thing, but I sure as hell didn't want this girl in my bed. I couldn't imagine *any* girl in my bed besides—

"Nick?" Ben repeated patiently.

My warm, floating feeling fell out from beneath me. I

crashed down hard into reality and the undeniable fact that I was choking on anguish. The blood drained from my face; the dim lights burned my eyes. I looked to my friend and begged him to understand without making me say it.

He sized me up with a single glance and nodded once. "Ladies, thanks for joining us. Glad you liked the show, hope you've enjoyed the drinks. Get home safe, okay? Nick, let's hit the road."

The girls protested loudly, but Ben had me on my feet and to the door in no time. I stumbled downstairs, less from the alcohol and more from the devastation. Outside, Ben moved toward the car, but I stopped him. "Walk, please. Let's just walk," I mumbled.

We strolled through the crowds down to the riverfront. The cool breeze on the water cleared my head tremendously. I stood at the guardrail overlooking the river and sucked in deep breaths while Ben leaned silently beside me. Finally I turned to him, adjusted my glasses, and found my voice. "You are the greatest. I may never admit it again, but know that I know."

"Nah, it's nothing." Ben looked out at the water, then back at me. "What... I mean, what do you—forget it." He sighed. "There's nothing to say."

Suddenly, I gripped the railing and bent in half with a loud groan. "I can't deal with this," I said through gritted teeth. "God, this *hurts*." I groaned again, just because it felt good. "I am so fucked. I have loved this girl since I was seventeen years old."

"Really?"

"Yes, really. I didn't know it, didn't realize that she was why I never wanted to date anybody for very long, but she *is*. She is everything, and she always was. I got so close and now, fuck, it's over. There will never be another person who I—*dammit*, Benjamin, what am I going to do?"

He twitched a brow. "Stop the wedding?" His tone was light, clearly a joke, but he shook his head. "I don't know, man. I can't believe I'm saying this, but maybe what you've been doing—just trying to move on—is the best thing. What else can you do?"

Anguish and everything else bled out of me while I stared out at the lights on the water. When I spoke, my tone was flat and dead, even to my own ears. "Nothing. Maybe I just moved too fast tonight."

"Maybe." He paused, then said, "I never thought I'd see you like this. Never in a million. But it kind of makes sense now, how you never really stuck with anyone."

"Yeah, it kind of does." I rubbed my eyes.

Ben chuckled to himself. "'Jessie's Girl.' That was fucked up."

"Completely." I smiled in spite of everything, and then began to laugh. "Your face when you pulled that strip." We were both laughing by then, shaking our heads.

"You sang the shit out of it. Pretty awesome."

"Thanks. What else could I do?"

Ben stood up and clapped his hand on my shoulder. "That's why you'll be okay."

"Why?" I twisted my mouth.

He rolled his eyes. "Because you can laugh about it. Because there's nothing else *to* do."

My smile faded, but I agreed. "Yeah. Guess so. Thanks, Ben."

"Sure thing. Want to sleep on my couch tonight?"

"Not ready for me in your bed yet?"

"Well you can, but you'll have to be the bottom spoon to Celeste."

I laughed again. "Hmm, it's tempting after y'alls show at the bar, but I think I'll go home. I'll be fine. Promise," I added at the look he gave me. "You should go give your woman multiple orgasms for being so cool about our plans."

"There's an idea," he muttered, but the gleam in his eye told me that was already his plan for the night.

At home, I scrubbed the bar and the girl off me, and then lay on my bed and stared at the ceiling. Tomorrow would be a trial, no matter how I approached it. I was tired and wished for the unconsciousness sleep would bring, but peace was a long way off.

I lay there for hours, thinking of nothing but my beautiful fire girl, my Mel. I thought of her red hair against the pink carpet so long ago. I thought of her wide eyes under those black bangs in the studio. I thought of her radiant smile in New York. I thought of how weird Tuesday had been and wondered again what the hell had made her storm out so angry.

Well, angry and hella sexy, if I'm honest.

Thinking of her poked all my bruises, but I kept it up until the moment sleep finally claimed me.

# 32

# MELODY

This is the story of my story. How it ended, how it began, however you want to look at it. Pay attention to me now.

I had an angle. I had a plan. My nerve was the only element in question. Well, that and about a thousand other variables. Nevertheless, I began to write like crazy Wednesday morning, three different documents open on my laptop and a scratch notebook at my elbow.

Jesse left me alone. Rephrase that: Jesse was busy quietly celebrating his album. As part of our "hometown sweethearts" image, we'd decided to forgo lavish photo shoots and pre-wedding galas, and instead saved all the pomp for the actual day. I had no idea where he was every night, but I didn't care.

We held a "rehearsal" on Friday which was really a press event to get the buzz started. Jesse gave a quick interview with me tucked neatly under his arm, and then we went for a quiet dinner with the crew. As soon as plates were cleared, the guys were off again to Seth's place. I went home, reviewed all my notes, and took a dose of cough syrup to put me to sleep. There was no way I'd get a wink on my own.

When I opened my eyes again, the sun was rising, my alarm was buzzing, and it was my fucking wedding day.

"Yoo-hoo!"

I jumped so hard at Fern's greeting, my messenger bag fell to the floor. Butterflies on speed beat in my chest when she breezed into the bedroom with the hairdresser and makeup artist in tow.

"Good morning, darling. Ready to get started?" Fern tucked a strand of hair into her pale lavender bun and assessed me with her matronly-but-super-chic gaze.

I nodded and set the bag that ostensibly held my overnight gear back on the bed. Jesse and I were booked at a hotel downtown for the night before we left for Italy tomorrow.

Fern glanced at the distressed leather case and deflated. "Oh, honey, we have to get you some proper luggage. Your things will be in Louis Vuitton trunks before you leave tomorrow, trust me."

"Thanks, Fern." *But don't bother.*

While the other women set up to transform me, Fern ran through all the details I already knew, such as how Jesse had a radio interview in an hour and would meet me at the church. After I nodded at all her reminders, she began to pace in and out. Every few minutes she was on the phone confirming something for the day, but I was immune. My nerves settled to a quiet simmer. The florist and caterer were nothing to me. All I had to do was play a doll for a few hours. There was relief in sitting back and letting the tale unfold.

Hair came first, and even then I didn't have much to do.

The stylist had a glossy black mane, longer than I typically wore, and she chatted with me and the makeup artist while she styled it with big, sexy curls and a side-sweep of bangs instead of my usual straight cut.

"This red, though. It's so lovely." She stroked the half of my head I hadn't braided yet, and I smiled. Smiles were easy when nothing mattered. "Could I braid it for you, sweetie?" Her soft Southern drawl soothed me, so I plopped into a chair and let her undo my previous work. Soon, two braids were expertly woven around my scalp. She gave my back a little scratch. "Perfect."

I thanked her as the makeup artist unpacked her case. "I'm going to do a heavy paint," she warned. "A dress like that needs glamour."

"Whatever you think is best." I turned my cheek up to her like a good little bride.

When layers of makeup caked my face, Fern reappeared with two assistants in tow, their arms straining under the huge garment bag containing my gown. Fern pointed to the bed, and they deposited their burden with an audible grunt.

As Jesse's personal stylist, Fern had been in charge of all the wedding details. Of course she picked this dress, and of course it went perfectly with the elegant concept she created for today. The bodice was corseted in the back, with a sweetheart neckline and ruched front. A crystal belt divided that from the huge, heavy swirl of tulle and organza that fanned into a chapel-length train. Snowy white, elegant, ornate, and heavy, it was a Cinderella dress if ever there was one, and perfect for the bride of a star like Jesse Storms.

Once I'd been assisted into the gown and laced up, Fern set my veil and led me to the mirror. A stranger stared back at me, a Hollywood siren with golden skin, dark hair, and deep red lips. Even my eyelashes and eyebrows were dark.

Fluttery panic turned peaceful the longer I gazed at my reflection. The girl in the mirror was a charlatan. Money, security, and opportunity were not deserving of someone so clearly fake.

And I was okay with all of it.

"It's time to go, Melody," Fern said with a hand on my shoulder. "Are you nervous?"

I smiled, careful not to crack my makeup. "I'm fine. Thanks for looking after me, Fern." I almost hugged her, but resisted the impulse, knowing it would be weird.

She helped me downstairs to my private limo. Alone in the expansive backseat, I triple-checked the contents of my bag and mentally rehearsed what I needed to say. And then, I sat back, eyes closed, and thought about everything Jesse and I had done together.

*I don't regret a thing.*

# 33

# NICK

I considered lying in bed all day, my own personal bed-in, but that got boring quick. My apartment was too small for all my restless energy, so I skipped breakfast, grabbed my keys, and went to the gym for two hours. There, I kicked my own ass hard with weights so heavy they rivaled the invisible ones on my shoulders.

Ben texted on my way home, but I didn't reply. I had an informal vow of silence going that I wanted to maintain, in and out of my head. Anytime thoughts beyond the moment tried to form, I sent them packing.

The workout didn't satisfy as much as I'd hoped. After I showered and lapped the living room again, I was back in the Camaro, cruising around for a long while. Finally, I headed north to the salon where Kira worked. She and David had done well on their little tour and had another coming up, but she still kept her hairdresser day job on the side.

She smiled when I walked in, but my expression had her frowning fast. "What's up, Nick?"

I sat down and let her fasten the cape around my neck. "Cut it." I gestured to my head, throat dry from disuse.

"Short?"

"Whatever you think. Maybe a shave, too."

My friend eyed me in the mirror as she finger-combed my shaggy hair. She nodded once and got to work, and those were the only nine words I had to say until I thanked her and paid.

"See you later, Nick." Kira still wore a worried frown when I twisted my mouth and nodded. Before I could turn for the door, she wrapped her arms around my waist and gave me a strong squeeze. I breathed a laughed and hugged her back, unable to resist her sweetness. She looked up at me, smiled guiltily, and stepped away.

"See you, Kirz." *Twelve words. Not bad.*

But that moment of warmth didn't linger. I returned home, blood sugar low from the workout. I forced down a sandwich before I stretched out on the couch and checked the time—only 2:15. *Damn.* Local TV coverage of the wedding began at four. The ceremony was at 4:30, but no way in hell would I watch it. Instead, I dropped my phone on the floor and stared at the blank TV. *As good a way as any to ride out this day, I guess.*

After this day, life would go on. The sun would rise, Nashville would still be home, and everyone would complain about the traffic and the weather. My dream job might've turned my life into a nightmare, but it was still my career. I'd still cruise in my Camaro, drink beer, and endure Mom's lame attempts to set me up. My friends would always be my friends. In time, they'd forget about "that redhead I was hanging out with in August."

But would I? While all these things continued as normal,

would I still be Nick? Or had I gone too far down this dark path to ever really come back? Would I distance myself, fade away from the world I knew? Would I still want the job? "I quit" had been on the tip of my tongue all week. Hanging out with friends sounded more of a burden than a chore. Would I ever be Nick, casual and living free, again? It didn't seem likely.

So fucking maudlin.

# 34

# MELODY

On the backside of the church, the car turned into a gate which closed once we were through. Good thing, too, because flashbulbs had begun to pop already, making everything uncomfortably real and immediate. Fern, my style team, and the photographer were there to greet me. They ushered me into the bridal room where I was inspected, adjusted, and touched-up once more.

The photographer spoke to me. "Okay Melody, we'll start in the chapel with some shots of you, then bring Jesse in for the first look."

This was it. Pictures were imminent. They wanted me to pose, to smile and blush—and lie.

My knees locked while someone fussed with my veil. The photographer's useless instructions to act naturally became background noise. The scene in front of me fell away, and I was on that balcony over the lake again. Like a movie in my mind, I could hear: *Holy fuck, I'm afraid... Breathe, Mel. Once you say jump, you have to jump.*

And he said it wasn't a metaphor.

"Okay, Miss Melody, let's go." Fern touched my elbow,

and I opened my eyes. The team began to propel me from the room.

"Stop."

We stopped. All eyes were on me, clearly awaiting instruction. I took a quick breath. "I... I need to speak to Jesse. Now." The heavy ball skirt swished as I perched on the loveseat.

Glances were traded, murmurs exchanged, but I waited, frozen and blank. Finally Fern slipped from the room, followed by the others. Moments dragged past before only Fern returned, Jesse right behind. I smiled up at my groom, so handsome in his white tuxedo and black bowtie. Under the wild partying, under the whirlwind of a young man who suddenly had the world at his feet, Jesse Storms was a good guy. I'd hated him more than once in the past month, but that was over now.

Well, almost.

*He deserves everything I'm about to give him.*

"Baby girl, what's going on?" When he spoke, my heartbeat drummed in my ears and made the world sound underwater.

I cleared my throat. My hearing cleared, and I stood. "Leave us please, Fern," I said softly.

When we were alone, I took his hand and noticed how cold mine was in contrast. "Jesse," I said in the same calm voice. "Look at what we've built together. We've come a long way, haven't we?"

His eyes narrowed, but he nodded. "You know it. We're a great team. You're the best, Melody."

"Thank you. And I'm so proud of you." I squeezed his hand. "More than that, I'm so thankful for all that you're offering me with this marriage." Another nod, but he didn't speak. I took a breath that was only a little shaky before I went on, trying to remember what I wanted to say. "I've spun you good, right?"

"The best, Melody. The best." He squeezed my numb fingers.

A small smile took immense effort. "Good, because I want you to understand that great spin is exactly what I'm about to give you." His brow creased. "I'm... not going to marry you, Jess." Tears pooled in my eyes. "I'm going to give you one hell of a headline and play the ungrateful, cheating fiancée. You'll get so much heartbreak press, your album will go triple platinum in a week."

His puzzlement cleared, mouth open. With a sigh, he crashed onto the loveseat, so I settled next to him and waited out an endless silence. At last, he coughed. "Wow."

We had to keep moving with time so short. "I know this'll ruin our professional relationship. I wish it didn't have to be that way, but I can't be your wife—or your girlfriend—anymore." My voice was surprisingly controlled. "I wrote a statement for you to give to the press, and I'll handle the web while the story stays hot. After that I'll... I'll step back."

"Don't look too far ahead," he murmured. "Who knows what comes next?"

"We'll see what happens. I've got a book to write, too."

He pushed a hand through his carefully styled hair and looked over. "I wanted to marry you, Melody."

I swallowed hard, and more tears stung. "I know, and in a different reality, I might've wanted it, too. But I'm just not this person. I can't do it, Jess."

He nodded. "I know. I *knew* it. I shouldn't have proposed. I thought—"

I kissed his cheek. "I know, baby boy. I know."

"Are you in love?" he asked suddenly.

I tasted lipstick when I bit down. "Yeah."

"Is it Nick?"

I squeezed his hand again. "Yeah."

"Hmm."

We sat quietly and faced the end of our relationships with a mutual sadness. I would miss him terribly, but I wasn't sorry.

Finally, Jesse jumped to his feet and began to stride around. "Holy shit, I wish I was wasted already." He gripped his hair. "Okay, it's almost three, so we need to move fast. An at-the-altar breakup is nasty, right? Definitely. You have to leave. Where's that statement you wrote?"

I grabbed my bag and pulled out the printed sheet, glad we were back in motion. Jesse skimmed it and nodded. "I need Peter. He should speak for me today. Better if I wait and talk tomorrow, right?"

"Yeah, that would be smart."

"Fine. I'll get with Pete. You just—you have to go." He stopped pacing and turned to me with a frown. "God, that hurts to say. I'm going to miss you, baby girl."

Tears threatened again as I nodded. "I'll miss you too, Jess. Really."

Jesse twisted his lips and sighed. His shoulders slumped a little, the paper dangling from his fingertips. I wanted to hug him, but I knew it wasn't what either of us needed. Instead, I drew in a deep breath. "Okay, let me change clothes and I'll slip out the back to the limo."

He glanced up, his frown turning confused. "Is that what we're doing? Where will it take you?"

"Well, I texted Dad not to leave his house. I thought I'd go hide there, but." I twisted my hands together as I read the doubt in his eyes.

When he opened his mouth, I already knew what he was going to say. "Is that the angle?"

It wasn't. It was the plan I'd made because it was safe, because it meant that I could ghost the scene and let the splinters fall where they would. But it also opened the door for wild speculation and nasty tabloid fodder. Anything from Jesse paying me off so he could secretly marry his illicit lover—and fill in that character profile with any type of personality imaginable—to Jesse killing me would be open for discussion. Abuse, addictions, depravity—there would be no end to the headlines, and these would *not* be the kind of buzz he could escape with his image intact. I'd played the journalism game long enough to know a vanishing act could topple his career. Here on the brink of his world tour, the stakes were too high.

*He wanted you to have your cut. He followed that dirtbag Peter's suggestions like a putz, but he didn't mean for you to be miserable. You got yourself into this mess. You can get yourself out the right way.*

ComingStorms had one more angle to play.

"No," I whispered. "No, if I disappear..." I threw my shoulders back and twisted my lips in a wry smile. "Run-away bride. We have to sell it right."

Jesse still frowned. "I don't want you to be hurt, Melody. You've done so much for me already. That crowd's going to go mad when you open that door."

I imagined the hordes of reporters all salivating to snap the early shots of our wedding. My hands went cold with terror. "Yeah, I expect they will."

"Let Seth escort you—"

"No, Jess." My voice was low but firm. "It has to be done right. And I... I can handle it."

*Yes, girl, you damn well can.*

He pulled me into his arms and kissed me on the forehead. "You're incredible, and I know you can do it. I'll be in touch after the tour, okay? We'll discuss if we want to do business then. Take care of yourself, Melody."

"Jesse." I gripped his lapels.

"Nope, none of that. You're ready. Take five minutes, then hit that door. You've got it. Time to jump, Melody."

*Time to jump.*

I swallowed hard and nodded. Jesse gave me one more kiss and a wink, and I knew that, as much as it might hurt now, he absolutely would be okay without me. Sooner rather than later.

The door latched behind him and unstuck me from my spot. I looked at the bride in the mirror again and tried to hide behind her face. She was the one running; I just had to make her legs move. I could do that, right?

I grabbed my bag and checked its contents one more time. Except for the statement, everything was still there, the essentials I planned to take when I was Mel and had my angle. In this supremely bizarre moment, the sensation of being two different people struck me hard. I fished out my phone to text my father.

Me: Plan's gone to hell. Will be in touch ASAP.

Five minutes were up. Time to go.

A Cinderella gown and a messenger bag look very weird together, but I had no choice. I slung the strap across my body and threw the door open. My shoes struck a heavy, slow rhythm on the tile of the church corridor. I wondered vaguely where everyone had gone, but knew, too, that it wasn't my business anymore.

The hall ended, and I faced the church's heavy wooden

doors with the iron knobs. In the silence of the space, I heard all the people on the sidewalk outside and pictured them as an obstacle course. Where would I go? No car awaited me. How could I get away?

I scrambled for my phone and nearly dropped it on the stone floor. My trembling thumbs clumsily summoned an Uber, but it was a slow time of day. Estimated arrival: seven minutes.

*They might devour me before then.*

But I had no time to wait in hiding. This story was going to blow open any minute when the doors opened and guests began to be seated, and, as Jesse said, an at-the-altar breakup was just gross.

My phone buzzed with an update. Estimated arrival: four minutes.

"I can handle it." I wrapped my fingers around the ornate doorknob. "One." I breathed deep and squeezed the cold metal. "Two." Another breath. "Three!"

Hundreds of heads turned when I swung the door open and squinted into the bright afternoon sunlight. A single moment of silent confusion gave my eyes time to adjust before a wall of voices hit me.

"Melody? Melody what's going on?"

"Where is Jesse? Is everything—"

"Melody! Why are you—"

*Move. Move. Don't listen, don't stop.* I jumped down the stairs, and the crowd swarmed. Head ducked, one arm in front of me to part the sea, I pushed forward. Bodies jostled, bumping each other and me. Everyone shouted, some questions of what and why, some just, "Melody! Melody! Melody!" over and over. Flashbulbs popped incessantly, creating a surreal, slow-motion effect. I couldn't stop it, couldn't change the focal point or distract with a different story. All I could do was put one foot in front of the other for the longest walk of my life.

The crowd froze for a moment when I got to the corner, a hushed silence punctuated by patient camera clicks while everyone—including me—anticipated my next move. Drowning on dry pavement, I strained my gaze left and right and prayed.

I swear, a halo of light glowed above the taxi that turned at the end of the block and rolled toward the church. I pushed around two photographers who'd knelt in front of me, twisted my ankle when my heel stuck in the storm drain, but stepped into the street and waved frantically.

Angels sang; the taxi stopped. I tumbled inside and barely kept my skirts from catching in the door as the mob descended.

"What on Earth?" the cabbie exclaimed. "Miss, are you okay? I'm supposed to pick up a Melody—"

"That's me, yes. I'm okay, I'm okay," I panted, unable to catch my breath. "Please drive. Please, I know there are a lot of people but *please, sir.*" My voice shrilled with panic.

He looked at me in the mirror and hit the gas. "Where do you want me to go, honey?" he asked softly.

I offered up the most fervent prayer of thanks I'd ever said in my life for this man and his car. "Can you just drive around for a while? We need to get away from here; we need to get away from that crowd. They're going to follow us— they might be already—so could you just, I don't know, hit the interstate and make some loops?"

He nodded and made a sudden turn, and I said another thankful prayer.

We definitely had a tail. I could see cameras pointed out the windows of at least four cars behind us while I clamored around in the backseat, too full of nervous energy to sit still.

"Miss, put on your seatbelt, please. It's not safe for you to climb around like that. We've got several cars behind us, but we're about to get on I-40. Just buckle up and take a deep breath."

I obeyed and slumped low on the seat while my driver took the ramp. He merged and maneuvered like a pro. I stopped paying attention to the route and the tail. The wind from the cracked windows gusted my face. My brain was overloaded, unable to process everything that had happened. Whenever I blinked, my Mac's spinning beach ball appeared behind my eyes.

We must've done a thorough tour of Nashville's inner loop given the smooth arcs the car took whenever the road forked. At last we made our way north on I-65, and the city disappeared behind us.

*This is the way to Dad's house... Oh, god. Oh, god, I did it. I jumped.*

I shot up straight and sucked in lungsful of fresh air as reality hit me. The driver's concerned glance in the rearview reminded me to do my best not to appear a step away from full psychosis.

"Thank you, sir. Thank you so much," I said over the roaring wind. "You have no idea how grateful I am."

He chuckled. "*You* have no idea how baffled *I* am, but I'm glad I could help out."

"Have we lost the cars?"

"Yes. Lost them on the four-forty loop, but I thought I'd head this way to be extra sure. Where can I take you?"

We were so far north of downtown by then that we were nearly to Dad's. The plan had been to sneak up there and hide out till the whirlwind died down. Then, I'd pick up the pieces of my life and start over.

But the plan, the script I'd drafted of how this day would

go, had been stupidly flawed to begin with. Too much stress and panic at being trapped had rendered me sloppy. How could I have thought I'd vanish and all would be well?

How could I think I could wait another day to say what I needed to say?

I looked down at the wedding dress pooled around me and let the last shreds of the plan flutter out the window. "We need to go south. If you give me your phone, I'll put in the address."

He nodded and swung us onto the next exit to turn around. I texted Dad:

Me: Third chance time. Wish me luck.

En route, I did what I could to look like myself without stripping naked in the back of a cab. I rummaged in my bag for makeup remover wipes and turned three golden with foundation before a pass came up clean. Then, I dabbed on a little moisturizer and lip gloss and added a drop of rose oil on my heart for luck. It was the most basic primping, but the car was already rolling through Berry Hill by the time I stashed the bottle. Quickly, I slipped my fingers up to my scalp and pulled off the black mane and veil all at once.

"What in the heck?" the cabbie exclaimed. "I swear, I've seen it all now."

I caught his gaze in the mirror again and laughed. "Yeah, I guess you'll have quite a story to tell, won't you?" With my braids out, the strands of red on my shoulders helped me breathe a little easier.

"Reckon I sure will," he chuckled as he pulled to a stop at the curb. "We're here, Miss. You sure you'll be okay?"

I stared up at the building for a moment. "Yes, sir. I'll be fine," I murmured. "I think."

He tried to stammer a refusal when I tipped him more than the cost of the fare, but I just smiled and pushed the door open. With a little salute, my guardian angel cabbie pulled away, and I was alone on the sidewalk.

The placid sounds of birds and traffic on nearby streets filled my ears. My ankle was killing me. The four-inch heels didn't help, so I kicked off the shoes and scooped them into my arms to limp toward the final leg of this epic journey. A trashcan sat just outside the sliding glass doors. I tossed the shoes and hair in without a second glance.

There were only a few people in the lobby, but every single one of them stopped what they were doing to stare at me. I glanced around, and then quickly ducked my head, hurrying to the elevators.

Whispers began behind me while I watched the lights scroll down from the third floor. The bell dinged at the moment someone said, "Ma'am, can we help you?"

"No thanks!" I called, yanked my skirt into the lift, and stabbed the "door closed" button. A wave of tremors hit my hands and knees on the slow crawl up. The Talking Heads song, "Once in a Lifetime," began to play in my mind.

My god. What, indeed, had I done?

# 35

# MELODY

My last barrier stood shut in front of me. All I had to do was control my trembling enough to knock. Well, knock and hope he was home. Well, knock, hope he was home, *and* hope he didn't slam the door in my face the second he saw me.

I stood on my right foot, sweat pricking my back, and touched my knuckles to the dark wood, *knock, knock, knock.*

Nothing.

Another fist, another three raps. This time I heard movement inside, so I rapped again. "Minute," came the mumbled reply, and I shook from head to toe.

Intuition told me when he peered through the peephole. Still no reply. The silence was as loud as the mob had been back at the church. Thirty seconds or thirty minutes passed, I'm not sure, but finally, *finally,* the lock snapped back, the knob turned, and the door opened. That deafening silence roared as I turned my gaze up to his face.

"There's been a mistake," Nick said quietly, one hand braced against the doorframe. "I definitely ordered the French maid girl, not the bride."

He smirked, but my jaw slacked. I was completely unprepared to laugh in this moment.

Nick cleared his throat. "What are you doing here?"

I'd gone mute. All the thoughts in my head, all the ways to start this sentence, died on my tongue. My story, unfolding in front of me, and I had no words to put to it.

"Mel? I asked what you're—"

"Oh, shut up. Just *shut up*," I blurted when my tongue finally remembered its function. "You know why I'm here."

His brows arched over the black rims of his glasses. "Hell no, I do not."

We frowned at each other. Even though my script for the day had shredded to bits, I'd assumed when I got to Nick, things would just work like they always had. Yet another error in my foolish plan. I shifted my stance, and my ankle throbbed.

Nick startled at my wince. "What's wrong? Are you hurt?"

"A little. I twisted my ankle when I ran to the cab."

"The cab," he echoed.

"From the church."

He eyed me, still leaning in the doorway. "You knocked on my door in a wedding dress, with a twisted ankle that you got running from the church—*the* church, as in the one you were going to be married in—and, I have to assume, also running from a bunch of journalists and guests, and I'm supposed to know what this is? Are you kidding me? These things don't happen in real life, Melody."

He was right, but his words also let me see the story from an outsider's perspective. *You did all that. You planned it, and you pulled it off. Bravo, girl. Bravo.*

I wiggled my toes and nodded. "Real life, right. I know the details are a bit crazy, but sometimes real life is the strangest story of all, huh? I left Jesse, Nick. All that's left is raw, unedited, *real* life. I don't know what comes next. Maybe I shouldn't have come straight here. Maybe I should've called first, or waited, but." I looked down. "But there was nowhere else I wanted to be."

I wanted him to smile when I met his gaze. I wanted his grin that was impossible not to return, wanted his arms around me, wanted the dream ending that I knew I didn't deserve.

I got pain instead.

Nick squinted, his brows drawn, mouth pinched. "I want so fucking badly to believe this is real, but something tells me I'd be a damn fool to be so gullible. You want to be here? Why? No, screw that. Answer this instead: if I let you in right now, how long do I get to keep you this time?"

Tears filled up and spilled before I could contain them. I bit down hard on my bottom lip, but it wobbled in my teeth. Nick watched, clearly conflicted, but he didn't budge from his stance in the doorframe.

"I've got no script, Nick. We have to find the answer to that question together."

Nick's reaction was purely physical. His pupils dilated, spine straightened, head tilted. Still no smile, no move to reach for me, though. I chewed on my lips and clenched my fists.

"That's some dress," he said at last.

I looked down and sniffled. "I know. It's a beast. Fern picked it out." Nothing made sense, so why not talk about my wardrobe?

"It's nice, but it doesn't suit you."

"I know."

Nick's stepped backward and beckoned me inside. I limped through the door, and he looked me over again, hands in pockets. My heart surged with the glint of mischief that sparked in his eyes and tugged at his lips. "It would look better on my floor."

My weepy laugh was more like a cough, but *damn* it felt good. "Nice line, Field. Very original."

"Sometimes I like the classics." He shrugged and winked, but then turned thoughtful. "I'm not processing this. I need to know—screw it. Later." And then, his fingers were in my hair, thumbs on my temples to tilt my face up.

"We can talk first if you..." I trembled and let my lips part as he bent to me. "If you need."

His nose rubbed mine, breath warm on my lips. "I need a lot, Mel. I'm out of my mind and barely believe this is happening."

I drew up the courage to tell him the truth. "I love you, Nick. But—"

His familiar, fresh scent had just started to steep in my brain when it was gone again. Nick withdrew, and I swooned and nearly toppled over in the process. He crossed his arms. "Actually, no. Even a guy like me has to have a line somewhere, and I guess this is it. I put my career and my soul on the knife block this summer like a fucking idiot for a couple weeks with you. I've got nothing left to gamble, Melody. I can't lose anymore."

He dug his fingers into his hair and winced. "I don't do complicated. Friends, family, and music. I told you in high school that was what mattered to me. It's still what matters. My life is a simple formula—except for you. You show up here, telling me you've broken your engagement and run from your wedding. You've got no script? Bullshit. Bull*shit*, Melody Thomas. You know a damn lot more than that."

"What do you want me to say?"

He ticked items off on his fingers. "What made you leave

Jesse? When did you know you were leaving? Did he know? What did he say? Did he know about us? But, more than any of that," he lowered his hand and adjusted his glasses, "what does it mean that you're here? What are the rules for this round, Mel? I need to know what you want, and I can't assume a single thing with you. Never did, but especially not this time."

My throat closed. "I'll tell you the story later, but I need you to hear me about why I'm here. I love you, Nick. But—"

His laugh scratched my ears. "Twice you've said those words, and both times they've ended in a but. You love me, but. There's always a but, isn't there?"

*Foolish girl. You thought it would be easy, that love was enough. How naïve. He'll never trust you again. He shouldn't. Third chance, yeah right. What were you thinking?*

Part of me wanted to fade into the background, like I'd grown so used to doing with Jesse. But this was Nick, this was *life*, and I couldn't slink out of there without knowing I'd done all I could. I'd showed up, but it wasn't enough. The only asset I had left was my greatest one: my words.

I just wished I knew what the hell to say.

Tears rolled down my cheeks as I opened my heart. "There—" My voice cracked, so I tried again. "There is no story to draft, no angle to consider, no lead, or spin, or hook —*nothing*—better than you and me together, Nick Field. That's the only answer I have. I know it doesn't fit, but it's all I know right now. I love you, Nicholas, but I don't deserve another chance with you. I've hurt you. I've hurt us. I don't deserve a happy ending to a story I've stetted since it began."

"Stetted?"

"Ignored. *Twice*, Nick. I ruined us twice, when both times my heart knew damn well that... that you... I love you, Nick."

His eyebrows rose above his glasses while I held back a

crying jag that threatened to flood the banks of the Cumberland River if it began. "That's the but?"

I nodded.

"Fuck, kid, I—"

I've never seen someone smile like he did then. Nick *beamed* at me. He pushed his hair away and laughed at the ceiling. The joy he radiated eased my imminent tears, but when he drew me into his arms, a few leaked out anyway.

"Aw, Mel," he murmured before his lips were on mine, commanding my jaw to relax and answer.

As soon as I did, the gates flooded. A sob escaped, and Nick laughed. I buried my face in his chest and imagined my tears watered the little seed of hope that his smile had planted in my heart.

"Shh," Nick soothed, his arms tight around me. "Why are you crying?"

"I don't—I told you, I—"

"No, *I* told you. Did you not listen? Or are you afraid to hear it because you didn't script it?"

I paused and sniffled hard. "W-what?"

Nick shifted his stance and held me closer. "I told you already how stupid I am for you. I told you while you sat on my couch that you're not like anyone else, that I will commit to anything you want. Did you think I was kidding?"

"But that was before I—"

He laughed again. "You don't deserve us, I heard you. Neither do I, I guess. Maybe you never deserve what you need most, but, hell, Mel. Even if you leave here and never look back, nothing changes. My heart is pledged to you."

Fireworks exploded behind my eyes. I gripped his arms and made my lip stop trembling enough to warble out, "I love you, Nicholas. Deep. Crazy deep." Every time I said it, the fear lessened.

Nick's throat tightened with a swallow when I peeked up at him. "I'll love you forever, Mels. I... I want to marry you, kid."

So much for self-control. I crumbled and wept hot, messy tears into his shirt. "Really?"

"Yeah. Just not in this dress."

My tears turned to laughter until I could lift my head and look at him again. I wiped my eyes. "Do, um, do you want an answer?"

"Uh, yes? I don't know, do I?"

I went up on tiptoe and kissed him. "My answer is yes— for tonight. Meaning, I think we need to get some distance from today's madness together. If you're sure after things settle down, ask again. My answer will be the same. If you decide you're not sure, then don't ask, and this will still be a perfect moment."

He wove his fingers into my hair. "That's the worst line I've ever heard," he murmured, making me giggle again before his lips were on mine.

I'm not sure that the way we devoured each other could be defined as a kiss. Our tongues tangled and lips pulled hard, hands frenzied and everywhere at once. I vaguely registered how much shorter his hair was, how the cropped sides tickled my palms until my fingers slithered into the length on top. He grunted and bent to my tug, and I went on tiptoe to get us as close as possible.

"Oh, *Christ*, roses," he groaned into my neck, then ran his tongue up to my ear. I keened from the sharp, sweet pressure of his mouth, but Nick drew back enough to meet my gaze. I blinked and caught my breath at the smear of my lip gloss on his mouth and the hooded, dangerous look in his eyes. "Again. Say it again." His voice was dark and low.

"I love you, N—"

He kissed me long and deep while I reached between us and slid my hand into his shorts.

His lips tore away and skimmed down my throat to my dress, and I had to hold on tight when my knees buckled. Nick's laugh rumbled against my cleavage. "How in the *hell* do I get you out of this thing?"

"Untie the ribbons in the back." I scrabbled for his shirt.

Nick tugged it off, but then he caught my wrist and stopped my hurry. I stared into his eyes while he lifted my palm to his lips.

"Don't you dare lick me again," I whispered.

Pursed lips turned into a brief smile. He flicked his tongue out, but before I could complain, the lick turned into a hungry kiss. That kiss pressed to my palm, moved to suck on my wrist, and continued up my arm. Another wave of heat unleashed between my legs at the fiery burn and the cool trail of moisture he left in his wake.

He reached my shoulder and slipped his free hand to my waist to gently turn me around, still holding my wrist so that my elbow bent toward my head. He sucked on my fingers, and I squirmed. He kissed my neck, and I squirmed. He laughed; I squirmed. "So anxious," he purred with that cool confidence I loved and trusted so much.

"You're a damn tease." He pressed his hips into my ass, and I laughed. "I can't even feel that in this skirt."

"Now there's motivation," he chuckled.

Nick began to work on the ribbons, and my lips curled into another grin. "I've got more motivation, if you'd hurry up."

"I don't need any more, trust me."

When the bodice was sufficiently loose, I turned and tossed my hair. "Never mind, then." But as I said it, I slipped the dress down a few inches to reveal the top of my corset and the ample cleavage it provided.

Nick leaned against the wall and wiped at his mouth, so I slipped the dress a little lower. "Who's the tease?" he muttered.

I shoved the dress to the floor to reveal my Agent Provocateur bustier, white lace panties, and gartered stockings. Nick's gaze flicked up and down my body. A flush of blood pinked his cheeks. "You look like an angel," he said finally. "A *highly* fuckable angel."

I crashed into his chest when he pulled me forward. Strong hands explored the satin bodice and made me hold on tight. Our kisses grew deeper, harder, more urgent. His lips bruised mine, and my nails dug red tracks across his back. It wasn't sensual or even romantic. It was carnal, and it was desperate, and it was equally both of us, sharing an unspoken fear that if we let go or let up, this reality might disappear.

Cool air hit me when Nick found the ribbons on my hips and pulled the panties away. He tried the garters next, fumbled a couple of times, but I couldn't wait anymore. I pushed his hand aside, shoved his shorts to the ground, and spun so my shoulders hit the door. The pain in my ankle be damned; I stepped wide and guided him between my legs.

Nick clenched his teeth and flexed his hips. "Here?"

"Right here."

He thrust inside of me, held me in place and rolled his hips while I held on tight and stared down at where we connected. I was still in the corset and garter belt, ivory lace and satin over flushed flesh and slick sex, and the sight stole my breath even more.

Nick followed my gaze. "Goddam, that's a sight."

"It's pretty, right?"

"I meant *you*."

The fire in my veins condensed to one single ache until every nerve ending from my hair to my feet hummed. I couldn't stop watching us move together. "I-I," I stuttered through clenched teeth, teetering on the edge of release. Nick understood. His touch drifted from my waist to my backside, then snuck between my legs and pressed steadily.

Detonation.

I wouldn't be surprised to know that the people in the lobby heard Nick's name, I screamed that loud. Through the tidal wave of sensation that shook my body, I heard him say, "Again, say it again," and so I did, over and over, his name the only word in the world in those ecstatic moments.

He thrust harder, not letting me come off my high before he stiffened and slapped the door. Then *my* name resounded through the room in his hoarse rumble.

In the silence that followed, I leaned against the wall and imagined myself as a phoenix, reborn, boneless, and without a single damn for what came next. Redheads have a rep for being passionate, but I had no idea I was capable of so much physical intensity.

"Wow." Nick seemed to read my mind as he carefully lowered me to my feet. He fingered my hair and traced my chin. "So much fire," he whispered against my mouth.

We pulled apart. Nick frowned at the way I stood like a flamingo, my right toes on my left calf. "I'm going to wrap your foot." Before I could respond, he scooped me into his arms and carried me straight to the bedroom.

Just like a bride should be.

Nick loaned me a t-shirt once he set me on the bed. He disappeared and returned with an ACE wrap. "Dare I ask where your shoes went?" he asked while he bound my ankle.

"Trashed them and the hair on the way inside." I yawned and flashed a proud smile. "Another crazy detail." His tender attention and the sweetly familiar scent of his sheets were a heady elixir. My eyelids grew heavy.

"This whole thing is crazy, but, *damn.* You in my bed is a beautiful sight, Melody Thomas."

My fingers danced over the gray quilt. "Mm, I like being in your bed." I opened my eyes, suddenly alert again, and crooked my finger. "Come here."

Nick crawled over me, his lips dusting against mine as he caged me with his arms. "Is this fucking real? Is this how our story wraps up, Mel? When I fall asleep tonight, will this still be real in the morning?"

I ran my fingers along his jaw and stared deep into his eyes. "I guess that's our chapter to write together."

# 36

# NICK

I woke up alone.

My sleepy eyes slowly focused on the blank stretch of mattress beside me. The sheets were cool when I reached for the emptiness. Sunlight crowded around the blinds to tell me I'd slept late, but fuck clocks; the dread that gripped my stomach was far more pressing.

Muted singing and a series of taps floated in from the living room, hit my ears, and snapped me upright so fast I almost threw my back out. I fumbled for my glasses and barely thought to pull on sweats before skidding to the door.

Melody sat at the kitchen table, singing a vaguely familiar song under her breath while she typed on her laptop. Her feet were tucked on the seat, hair glinting fire in the morning light.

I leaned against the wall and tried to contain a deep sigh of relief. I kept it mostly under control, but she turned to me anyway, eyes and smile bright.

"Good morning."

"Hey." *Stay casual. Do not throw yourself at her feet and bury your face in her lap.* "You're here."

"Where else would I be?"

"I wasn't sure for a second."

"Mm, sorry. I needed to write."

"I see." I strolled over; her lips parted for my kiss before I bent my head.

"Give me five minutes, I swear I'll stop," she promised when we pulled apart.

I put coffee on and got lost in thought. Mel glowed this morning. I'd seen her radiant before, well-rested and sexually satisfied, but this was different. Everything was different today, and the simple thought, *I need to buy Splenda,* brought it all to a point.

"What's that grin for?" she asked when I set a mug by her elbow.

"For you sitting here at my table," I drawled. She blinked rapidly, and I grinned harder.

"I, um, need a few..."

"Take your time." I dropped into a chair, happy just to watch her work.

Women have woken up in my apartment before. Mel had woken up here before. But, never once did it occur to me to buy groceries for someone else. Already I was rearranging my life for her, and it was precisely what I wanted to do.

Jesus Christ, I'd proposed. I knew it was madness even as I said it, but those were the words my overwhelmed heart had been screaming since I looked through that peephole. Too soon? For sure. A mistake? Not at all. And, in her uncanny way of getting me, Mel had given me a yes and an out all at once.

The thing was, I didn't want an out. I wanted Mel at my table every morning, preferably in the t-shirt and panties look she was currently rocking. I wanted my shoulder to be where she fell asleep and where she cried when she needed to. Everything I never planned or wanted to have, all that stuff Mom envisioned for me, I wanted with her. Only her.

Always her.

"Okay, I'll stop now." Her face appeared when she slapped the laptop shut.

"Your book?" I smiled, thrilled for her all over again.

Her eyes crinkled. "Yeah, had some ideas I wanted to outline before I forgot or got too busy."

"Busy?" I wiggled my brows.

Mel laughed, but then cut her gaze away. "Well, yes. I didn't mention this last night, but I'm technically still working for Jesse." I cocked my head, unsure what to say. "It's temporary, another week or two at most. I promised to handle the media after he gives his announcement about yesterday. He texted earlier that his press conference is at two. Is this weird?"

I considered it. As usual, the best answer was, yes, but. Yes, it was weird to spin your own broken engagement from your fiancé's point of view, but Mel loved her work and was damn good at it.

"You're here." I shrugged. "I don't think it's fair to be jealous."

"Exactly. Because if... well. Who knows what comes next?" I waited for clarification on this vague idea, but she studied her coffee and redirected. "Anyway, it'll be a firestorm this afternoon for several hours. I, um, figured I'd work at Dad's."

I set my mug down and gestured across the room. "I've got a desk I never use. You can have it. You can work here, Mel. You could stay here."

She chewed on her lip. "I'd like to stay today. I know you have work tomorrow, so of course I'll—"

"No." I cleared my throat. In the daylight, without the rush of desire, I was more nervous than I'd been to say the M-word last night. *Man up, jerkoff.* "I meant you could live here."

Blue eyes went wide. Mel stood and shuffled forward until our knees touched. I held her waist, and she finger-combed my hair. "Really? You'd like that?"

"Nah, I'd love it," I sighed, blissed by her touch and already stirring in my sweats. "You?"

Her lips curved up. "Hmm." I arched a brow, and she straddled my lap. "Hmm," she repeated while she sucked on my lip.

I stood suddenly, holding her tight. Mel squealed and wrapped her legs around me, but I laid her on the table and grabbed her ribs. "Hmm? What's 'hmm' mean?" I challenged while she thrashed and shrieked.

"Hmm means *stop it*," she gasped. "Nick, please, I—"

She finished that thought by palming my cheeks and opening her mouth against mine. Immediately I stopped tickling, my touch running up her body as I leaned closer and let her arms hug my neck.

When we were kids, Mel's words were what first made me notice her. She gave a speech in history class, and I made it a point to sit beside her every day after that. But for all her brilliance with words and stories, it was the beautiful silence of her kiss that said it all best.

# ACKNOWLEDGMENTS

I wrote one of these just a couple months ago, and yet I could still fill pages with all the people I'm grateful for.

Sara, my little one, first thank you. I'll never forget when you texted me you'd gotten to the end of this book and how much you loved it. Thank you for being an incredible little sister and a beautiful human being.

Sarah Smith, thank *you* for being such a huge cheering squad and for all the support we give each other in this writer's life! Lady, I don't know what I'd do without you.

Avery, this cover is gorgeous and you are a wizard. Lily and Eva, *Off the Record* is all it can be because of your amazing feedback.

Finally, this book is dedicated to You. Not because I had to, not because I lost a bet or anything silly like that. Because that's how it should be. Without you, my story wouldn't be nearly as fun. There's truth and beauty in that.

So thank you, all of you, from the bottom of my sparkling heart.

# ABOUT THE AUTHOR

Skye McDonald is the author of the Anti-Belle books, contemporary romance novels set in her hometown of Nashville, Tennessee. As an English teacher, a die-hard romantic, and a huge fan of Nashville's s hip new vibe, Skye's Anti-Belle series are standalone books featuring sassy GRITS (Girls Raised In the South) learning to love themselves before they can claim their happily ever after. (Spoiler: they always do!) Her first book, *Not Suitable for Work*, is out now via Amazon/Kindle.

When she isn't lost in a love scene or grading student essays, Skye can be found cheering for the University of Tennessee (go Vols!), exploring Brooklyn with her adorable Corgi, or heading off on some new adventure. She'd love for you to connect with her on social media!

## ALSO BY SKYE MCDONALD

Not Suitable for Work: Anti-Belle Book One

Nemesis: Anti-Belle Book 3 Coming soon!